Praise for *New York Times* bestselling author

BRENDA JACKSON

"Fans of her tender and forbidden love stories will fall head over heels for Jackson's newest addition to the saga…sure to tantalize readers with this unforgettable tale of secret love and the unrelenting power of friendship."
—*BookPage* on *Inseparable*

"This deliciously sensual romance ramps up the emotional stakes and the action with a bit of deception and corporate espionage. Short, sexy, and sizzling."
—*Library Journal* on *Intimate Seduction*

"Jackson does not disappoint…first-class page-turner."
—*RT Book Reviews,* 4½ stars Top Pick, on *A Silken Thread*

"Superb storytelling, an original plot and combustible chemistry between the leads will have readers flying through the chapters, desperate to see how Jackson's tale ends."
—*RT Book Reviews,* 4½ stars Top Pick, on *Bachelor Unclaimed*

"Jackson does a masterful job of drawing readers into the characters' lives and minds as she unfolds the story of their meeting, romance and happily ever after. A page-turner from start to finish."
—*RT Book Reviews,* 4½ stars Top Pick, on *Hidden Pleasures*

"Brenda Jackson has reached a new pinnacle of literary and commercial excellence."
—*RT Book Reviews,* 4½ stars Top Pick, on *One Special Moment*

New York Times Bestselling Author
BRENDA
JACKSON

A
Madaris
BRIDE FOR
CHRISTMAS

HARLEQUIN® KIMANI ARABESQUE®

ISBN-13: 978-0-373-09143-0

A MADARIS BRIDE FOR CHRISTMAS

For questions and comments about the quality of this book, please contact us at CustomerService@Harlequin.com.

Printed in U.S.A.

ACKNOWLEDGMENTS

It gives me great pleasure to present my 100th book to you. I would be amiss if I didn't take this time to thank a number of people who not only made this journey with me, but who inspired me, motivated me, supported me, and made writing each and every book such a memorable experience.

I thank God for giving me the gift to write and who makes all things possible.

To the man who is the love of my life, Gerald Jackson, Sr. My one and only. Always.

To my sons, Gerald Jr. and Brandon Jackson, who constantly make their mother proud.

To my faithful and loyal readers who motivate me to write love stories that help them escape into a world of love and romance. I thank you and I appreciate you.

To all my editors—the late Monica Harris, Karen Thomas, Glenda Howard, Monique Patterson, Mavis Allen, Evette Porter, Kelli Martin, Brenda Chin, Stacy Boyd, Valerie Gray, Krista Stroever, Melissa Jeglinski, Joan Marlow Golan and others. Your editorial expertise helped me to present the best stories to my readers.

To my agent, Pattie Steele-Perkins. Your unwavering support has always been appreciated.

To all the publishers who ever released a Brenda Jackson book. I thank you for the opportunity you gave me.

To my present publisher, Harlequin. Thank you for your undying support and for always making me feel special.

To my family and friends, whose support I will always appreciate.

To my classmates from Northwestern High School and William M. Raines, Class of 1971, who were my first readers.

Special thanks to Keisha Mennefee for your assistance in my research on chefs.

Special thanks to Angie Lee, Resident Chef and Instructor, for all your information on chefs and culinary schools.

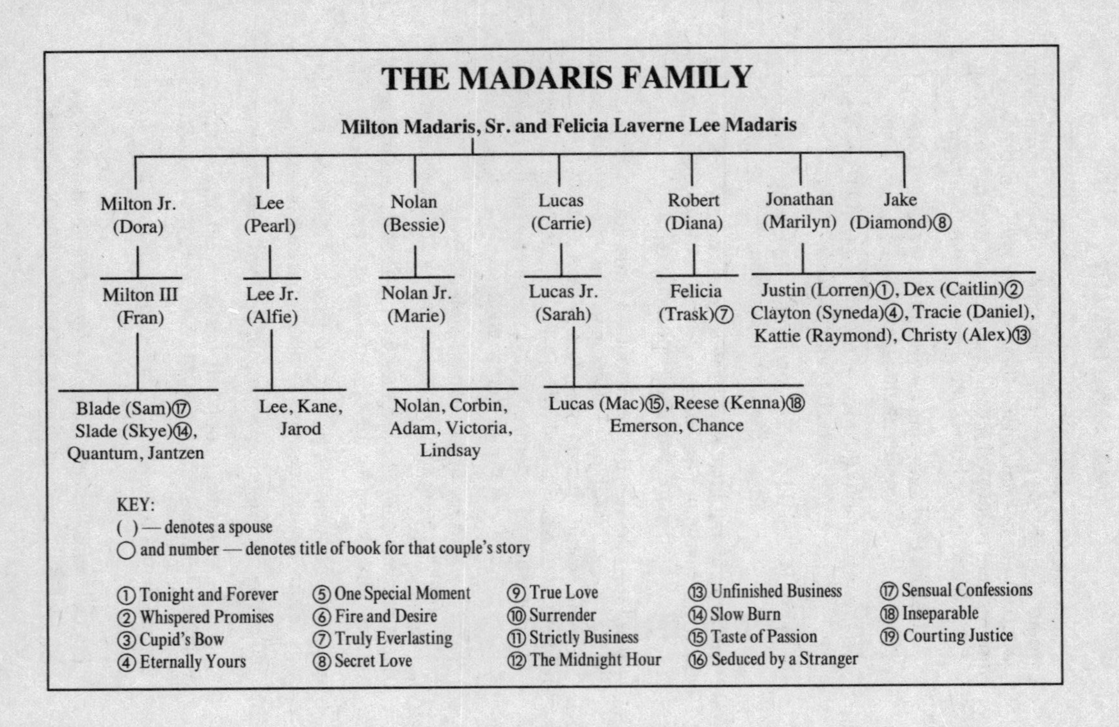
THE MADARIS FAMILY
Milton Madaris, Sr. and Felicia Laverne Lee Madaris
Milton Jr. (Dora)
Lee (Pearl)
Nolan (Bessie)
Lucas (Carrie)
Robert (Diana)
Jonathan (Marilyn)
Jake (Diamond)⑧
Milton III (Fran)
Lee Jr. (Alfie)
Nolan Jr. (Marie)
Lucas Jr. (Sarah)
Felicia (Trask)⑦
Justin (Lorren)①, Dex (Caitlin)②
Clayton (Syneda)④, Tracie (Daniel),
Kattie (Raymond), Christy (Alex)⑬
Blade (Sam)⑰
Slade (Skye)⑭,
Quantum, Jantzen
Lee, Kane,
Jarod
Nolan, Corbin,
Adam, Victoria,
Lindsay
Lucas (Mac)⑮, Reese (Kenna)⑱
Emerson, Chance
KEY:
( ) — denotes a spouse
○ and number — denotes title of book for that couple's story
① Tonight and Forever
② Whispered Promises
③ Cupid's Bow
④ Eternally Yours
⑤ One Special Moment
⑥ Fire and Desire
⑦ Truly Everlasting
⑧ Secret Love
⑨ True Love
⑩ Surrender
⑪ Strictly Business
⑫ The Midnight Hour
⑬ Unfinished Business
⑭ Slow Burn
⑮ Taste of Passion
⑯ Seduced by a Stranger
⑰ Sensual Confessions
⑱ Inseparable
⑲ Courting Justice

THE MADARIS FRIENDS

Maurice and Stella Grant

|

Trevor (Corinthians)⑥,
Regina (Mitch)⑪

Angelique Hamilton Chenault

|

Sterling Hamilton (Colby)⑤,
Nicholas Chenault (Shayla)⑨

Kyle Garwood (Kimara)③

Ashton Sinclair (Netherland)⑩

Drake Warren (Tori)⑫

Trent Jordache (Brenna)⑨

Nedwyn Lansing (Diana)⑭

Sheikh Rasheed Valdemon (Johari)⑯

DeAngelo Di Meglio (Peyton)⑲

KEY:
( ) — denotes a spouse
◯ and number — denotes title of book for that couple's story

① Tonight and Forever
② Whispered Promises
③ Cupid's Bow
④ Eternally Yours
⑤ One Special Moment
⑥ Fire and Desire
⑦ Truly Everlasting
⑧ Secret Love
⑨ True Love
⑩ Surrender
⑪ Strictly Busisness
⑫ The Midnight Hour
⑬ Unfinished Business
⑭ Slow Burn
⑮ Taste of Passion
⑯ Seduced by a Stranger
⑰ Sensual Confessions
⑱ Inseparable
⑲ Courting Justice

Dear Reader,

I never imagined when I penned my first book, *Tonight and Forever*—the love story of Justin Madaris and Lorren Jacobs—that eighteen years later I would still be writing about the Madaris family. I am proud that I began my writing career with a Madaris book and that my 100th book is based on that same family.

The Madaris Family is a special family, not just because it was my first family, but because over the years you've made them your family. I once said that the Madaris men have become your heroes because they represent those things you desire—men with looks to take your breath away, and who have the ability to make you appreciate the fact that you are a woman.

Over the past few Madaris books, we have seen the matriarch of the family, Mama Laverne, play matchmaker for those single men and women in her family. She feels that it's now Lee Madaris's time and she is determined for him to have a Madaris bride for Christmas.

I hope you enjoy reading *A Madaris Bride for Christmas,* and I hope you add this to your collection of the Madaris Family and Friends series.

All the Best,

Brenda Jackson

The Lord is my shepherd; I shall not want.

—*Psalms* 23:1

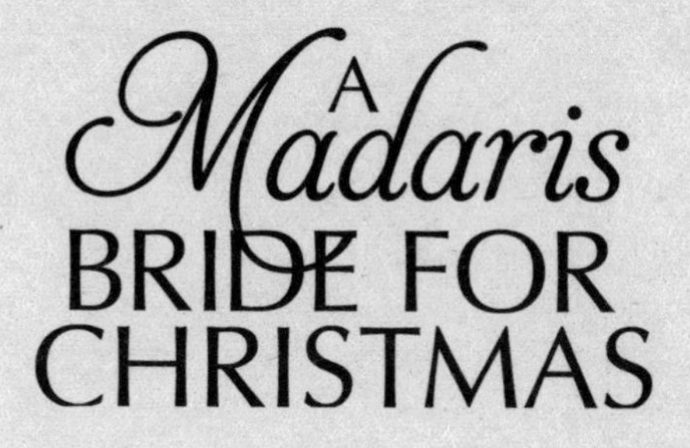
A Madaris
BRIDE FOR
CHRISTMAS

Prologue

"Are you sure you saw what you think you saw, Carly?"

Instead of answering her best friend, Carly Briggs took a sip of her drink. The liquid nearly scorched her throat going down. *Vodka?*

"Where did you get this?" she asked, drawing in a cooling breath. As far as she knew, the only alcohol she and Heather Kramer kept in their apartment was wine.

Heather shrugged. "Lori gave it to me. She cleaned house and said it was left over from the New Year's Eve party she gave three years ago."

Carly remembered that party. She and Heather had just moved to Miami and into their apartment near South Beach. Lori Cummins, a neighbor who lived in the apartment across the hall, had thrown a party that weekend and invited them.

"Now, let's not get sidetracked," Heather said, reclaiming Carly's attention. "Are you sure you saw—"

"I didn't *see* anything," Carly said, her agitation not yet helped by the alcohol. "It's what I heard—coming through a vent in the wine room. Several men were arguing in the alley outside the restaurant. They accused this guy of being a traitor. Then I heard a gunshot that seemed to be muffled with a silencer."

The conversation was something Carly would never forget. The deep, raspy, intimidating voice of one man and the terrifying sound of another man pleading for his life. It was a wonder she hadn't screamed and given her location away.

Instead, she'd frozen and then her surroundings went black. The next thing she remembered was being awakened by Chef Renaldo, who didn't want to hear anything she had to say about men and gunshots. Instead, she had been scolded about going over her break time by ten minutes and not pulling her load on a busy night.

Fearing someone was possibly bleeding to death in the alley, she'd talked one of the staff waiters into going outside with her to look around. She'd made up some excuse about hearing a kitten crying. They had checked all over the place and found nothing.

"Maybe you only thought you heard it," Heather said, looking at her with concern in her eyes. "You even admit that Chef Renaldo woke you up. Maybe you dreamed you heard it."

Instead of taking another sip of her drink, Carly placed the glass on the table. "Why would I dream such a thing?"

Heather stood and waved off her question. "How would I know? You've been working a lot of crazy hours and Chef Renaldo has been getting on your last nerve. Maybe all the stress is catching up with you."

"Maybe you're right," Carly said, although she knew Heather wasn't right.

She knew what she'd heard, which was why she'd arrived home tonight needing a strong drink, why she had called the police tip line. The tip-line operators promised to scramble callers' phone numbers so the call couldn't be traced. She was glad it was anonymous. The last thing she wanted was for anyone to think she was a loony tune.

Carly stood. "I'm going to take a bath and go to bed. The restaurant is opening early tomorrow for a baby shower and I'll be one of the chefs on duty to help prepare the desserts."

"But tomorrow is your off day," Heather reminded her.

"I know, but I can use the money."

"Now you're making me feel bad about moving out."

Carly reached out and grabbed Heather's hand. "Please don't feel bad. It's not every day a woman meets the man of her dreams. I love you, girl, but had it been me, I would have married Joel months ago. He's the best."

And she really meant it. The guy Heather had met and fallen in love with last year, Joel Garcia, was CEO of a marketing firm in Spain, where they would make their home. The wedding was planned for next month. A June wedding. And Carly was the maid of honor.

"Don't forget that you have that job interview with the hotel in Vegas next week," Heather reminded her, standing too.

Carly nodded. She had gotten a call from one of her instructors from the Parisian culinary school she had attended. He'd advised her that a newly opened hotel in Las Vegas was looking for a pastry chef and he had thought of her. He had wanted her to apply for the job and promised that he would highly recommend her for the position.

That Chef LaPierre would go out of his way to call her and offer her a recommendation was all the encouragement she'd needed. A few weeks later she'd received a letter inviting her to Vegas to be interviewed.

"After last night, I'm going to need the trip."

"And the job would be nice too," Heather said, laughing.

"Of course."

Carly had made the right decision, moving to Miami with Heather three years ago. Heather's job as program coordinator with a major cruise line had transferred her here, and Carly had just broken up with Nathaniel Knox, the minister she'd met while volunteering to feed the needy, after a serious relationship. At the time, leaving Porter, Connecticut, had been the best thing.

Although Carly liked Miami, there was really nothing to keep her here once Heather married and moved to Spain.

"Yes, the job in Vegas would be nice, but if that doesn't work out, I'll be fine here. Rumor has it that Chef Renaldo has his eye on that position opening up at a restaurant in South Beach."

"And you hope he gets it, right?"

Carly smiled. "It would definitely make my life easier. The man can be simply horrid."

"Well, I'm hoping something works out with that interview. Moving to Vegas would be good for you."

Carly chuckled. "Yeah, me and Sin City. If I do get the job, the next time I go home, Aunt Ruthie is sure to pray all over me." Ruth Briggs was the grand-aunt who'd raised her since she was a baby.

Heather threw her head back and laughed. "Yes, I can see your aunt doing that."

Carly bade Heather good-night and made her way to her bedroom. Without Heather to distract her, her thoughts shifted back to what she'd heard through the vent earlier that evening.

She had checked the alley for victims. She'd given the

police a tip. There was really nothing more she could do. First thing in the morning she would check the newspapers to see if anything was mentioned. If not, she would no longer lose sleep wondering what did or did not happen in the alley.

One week later

In the middle of the night, four men gathered in an empty warehouse near the Miami Beach marina. Even through the steel walls, the sound of waves, remnants of last week's tropical storm, beat against the sides of the boats docked outside.

"Why was this meeting called, Palmer?" The man's voice was deep, authoritarian and annoyed. "I thought we wouldn't meet again until—"

"Some woman called the tip line about Harrison. Wouldn't give a lot of information, only said she thought someone had been killed in the alley," Palmer said. "I heard the tip but couldn't trace the call."

The room quieted and all gazes turned to another of the men, Addison Bracey. "I got the word earlier today from our inside man. Luckily, he intercepted the tip. He went out himself to make sure you didn't get clumsy that night, Nash. I wish nothing had been done with Harrison until I got back from Chicago."

There was a snort and Nash's deep, raspy voice said, "Couldn't wait when we found out he was a traitor. I handled it, and I didn't get clumsy."

"With no evidence left behind, right, Nash?" the deep authoritarian voice asked.

"No evidence was left behind," Magnus Nash agreed. "Like I said, the problem was taken care of."

"And the person who called the tip line?" the authoritarian voice asked.

"No one was in the alley that night, I'd swear it. But if there's a loose end, I'll take care of it," Nash said haughtily.

The others were quiet until the man with the deep voice said, "Make sure that you do. My concentration needs to be on expanding the business, not on taking care of traitors. That's your job. This meeting is adjourned."

Chapter 1

Four months later

Lee Madaris glanced at the clock on his wall before rubbing away the tension forming in the back of his neck. Although it was nearing midnight, he was still in his office working. It was imperative that he do so.

Five potential investors would be arriving tomorrow and spending four days at the Grand MD Vegas hotel. He would be catering to them at a level that was unprecedented. The five men had enough cumulative capital to balance the national budget, if they'd chosen to do so. However, balancing the national budget wasn't Lee's goal. His objective was to get them to invest in his next hotel—the Grand MD Paris.

After the success of the Grand MD Dubai, as well as all the attention the hotel in Vegas had received since opening its doors four months ago, a number of investors were ready to provide funds for his next venture. But he didn't want just anyone; he wanted men willing to take a chance on a hotel that would be astonishingly different from its two predecessors. It would be a hotel of the future.

Both Grand MD hotels had been Madaris–Di Meglio joint ventures—highly successful and breaking sales records. But the third hotel, the one planned for Paris, France, would use state-of-the-art technology while maintaining the rich architectural design Paris was known for.

Lee's cousin and the architect in the family, Slade Madaris, had designed the first two Grand MDs and would likewise design the one proposed for Paris. Slade's design was nothing short of a masterpiece and would be unveiled at one of the meetings this week. Slade's twin brother, Blade, would be the structural engineer. No two Grand MD hotels would look the same. Each would have its own unique architecture and appeal.

Pulling in a deep breath, Lee returned his attention to the documents in front of him—bios on the five men. The name that topped the list was that of his grand-uncle Jake Madaris. Lee didn't need to read his uncle's bio.

The man was a walking genius when it came to playing the stock market, and as far back as Lee could remember, Jake had been financial adviser to the entire Madaris family. If it hadn't been for his uncle's smart move of establishing a trust fund for all his nieces and nephews when they were still in high school, Lee would not have had the money to partner with his good friend DeAngelo Di Meglio to build their first two hotels.

Jake and another family friend, Mitch Farrell, had been the hotels' financial backers. Mitch—the second man on the list—and Jake had already confirmed they were on board for the Paris hotel since the last two hotels had been a successful venture for them.

However, the price tag for a Paris hotel was higher than the price of the other two combined, and Jake had suggested bringing in other investors. All were good friends of Jake's, but his uncle had warned Lee that convincing them to invest would be Lee's responsibility.

He was ready.

The third person on the list was Kyle Garwood, a multimillionaire who made his primary home in Atlanta. Kyle was married, the father of six. Lee liked Kyle and highly respected him.

The last two men were sheikhs from the Middle East. Sheikh Rasheed Valdemon of Mowaiti had such a close relationship with the Madaris family that he had been named an honorary family member and occasionally went by the name of Monty Madaris when he did business in the United States.

Finally, there was Rasheed's brother-in-law, Sheikh Jamal Ari Yasir of Tahran. Lee had never met Sheikh Yasir but had heard he was a shrewd businessman, always looking for a good investment. He was married to an American woman, the former Delaney Westmoreland.

Lee would be wining and dining the five men in the Grand MD style. Everything was in place and would be set in motion as soon as they arrived tomorrow morning.

Their visit had been strategically planned down to the last detail. They would be given a tour of the hotel before they were served lunch. Since tomorrow was a traveling day, no meetings had been planned. However, early the following day, Lee's skilled marketing team would kick things off with several video presentations and meetings. Around three, the men and their wives would be given the chance to rest and relax before a dinner fit for royalty.

Afterward, they would enjoy the nightlife Vegas was famous for—from right inside the Grand MD. The casinos, live shows, state-of-the-art IMAX theater and the exquisite mall on the fifth floor that offered twenty-four-hour shopping all guaranteed that the Grand MD would gain a reputation as the hotel that never closed.

A winning hotel had to have a winning staff. He and Angelo had handpicked all of his executives and managers. Each had hotel experience and had come with sterling résumés and excellent recommendations. He and Angelo were pleased with every staff member, and those who didn't deliver were quickly replaced. Second-best was not an option at the Grand MD.

Lee moved away from his desk, intending to walk around and get his blood flowing, but the moment he stepped into the executive suite's lobby he stopped to stare at the huge picture hanging on the wall. It was a portrait of his great-grandmother Felicia Laverne Madaris the First, whom they fondly called Mama Laverne.

She was the matriarch of the Madaris family. Having borne seven sons, his grandfather Lee being one of them, Mama Laverne had raised her sons by herself after her husband, Milton, had died. All her sons were still alive except for Robert, who had been killed in the Vietnam War. Lee's grand-uncle Jake was Laverne's baby boy.

Mama Laverne had insisted that Lee hang this particular picture of her right there on that wall. She'd given the same directive to his other cousins. They all had the same framed photograph hanging in the offices of their various businesses. She was dressed in her Sunday best, with a huge dressy hat on her head, and she appeared to be looking directly at the viewer with those shrewd eyes and an all-knowing smile. At least she *was* smiling. A Mama Laverne frown could make him quake in his boots. She definitely liked giving orders, and she expected them to be carried out.

Lee chuckled. He wished he could say she was getting bossy in her old age, but as far back as he could remember, she'd always been bossy. Besides that, she was a notorious busybody when it came to meddling in the lives of her children, grandchildren and great-grandchildren. Even at ninetysomething, he figured she would still be around to meddle with the great-great-grands' lives as well.

He didn't want to think of a time when she would no longer be in their midst. Their love for her was the main reason why he and his still-single brothers and cousins overlooked a lot of her shenanigans, especially her determination to marry off each of them.

Closing the door behind him, he walked along the spacious lobby hallway, noting the elegance, style and sophistication that were such integral parts of his Vegas hotel. Besides being the tallest building on the Strip, with seventy-five floors, it had an amusement park on one of its lower levels, making it an ideal place to stay for both adults and families. From the carpeting on the floor to the paintings on the wall, from the furnishings to the hotel's special amenities, anyone would agree that the hotel deserved the seven-star rating reviewers were giving it.

Sliding back huge glass doors, he stepped out onto the terrace of the executive suite. Normally, he wasn't one who took the time to appreciate a lot of greenery, but with the quality of the hotel on his mind, he couldn't help doing so. Various plants had been flown in just for this terrace.

Lee inhaled deeply, breathing in the scent of the plants mixed with the September air. He looked beyond the Vegas view to study the looming desert. The rain had lessened the heat and now a sultry breeze stirred the air. The sky overhead looked dark and dreary. There didn't seem to be a single star. A part of him longed to be back in Houston, gazing up into a Texas night.

Lee shook off the longing. He had too much work to do to be melancholy. He hadn't been home since last Christmas and another one would be coming up soon, but opening the two Grand MDs had taken up all his time, personally and professionally. Now luring investors for a third hotel would make him even busier.

Just as he turned to go back inside, his gaze landed on a woman standing on the balcony a couple of levels below. His breath was snatched from his lungs. A low groan passed from his lips as a jolt of sexual energy rocked him to the bone.

She was beautiful. Sensually stunning. Picture-perfect.

She stood leaning against the balcony rail, wearing a sexy green dress and chocolate-colored stilettos, her hair blowing in the breeze. From her expression, as she stared down below, he could tell she was fascinated by the bright lights of the Strip.

Was she a guest at the hotel? He scanned the balcony connected to a tri-level observation deck. It appeared she was alone. Something about her pulled at him. She looked happy, peaceful, but lonely.

Lee didn't know the woman yet he felt as if he could read her perfectly. He stood and watched her, totally mesmerized. A slow heat flowed through him and pooled in his groin—she was arousing him in a way no other woman had. What was there about her that made every muscle in his stomach tie into knots? Made full awareness of her fill his every pore?

Granted, he hadn't dated in a while because of his stringent work schedule, but still, there was something about this particular woman that had lust rushing through his veins.

Nothing like this had ever happened to him before.

He checked his watch. It was getting late, but he had to

meet that woman and find out why he found her so captivating.

Anticipation filled him as he made his way off the terrace and toward the elevator bank.

She simply loved it here, Carly thought. Bright lights lit the Strip and each hotel seemed to compete to shine the brightest.

It was hard to believe she had gotten the job of pastry chef at the Grand MD's Peyton's Place restaurant a little more than a month ago. The hotel had been gracious enough to give her time to resign from her job in Miami and remain in Florida long enough to pack up her things and attend Heather's wedding.

Initially, she had missed South Beach and wondered if she would ever get acclimated to Vegas's dry summer heat. But she had discovered that in addition to being a fun city with its infamous Strip, Vegas was also a nice place to live.

Her house was in a residential area of town not far from shopping. Because she had everything she needed right at her fingertips she rarely came into town on her days off.

Except for today.

Today was her twenty-eighth birthday, and she had decided to celebrate with a night on the town. She had even treated herself to a night at the Grand MD. It had to be the most beautiful hotel she had ever seen. Her room on the fiftieth floor was to die for and the service was excellent.

Carly had stumbled across this particular balcony a few weeks ago while on break. She loved the view, and it had become her favorite. There had been several other couples here earlier, enjoying the view as well, but they had departed, leaving her alone. She didn't mind. It was the story of her life.

Carly forced the depressing thought from her mind.

After all, it was her birthday and she intended to have fun. So far it had been a beautiful day. Before leaving home this morning she'd gotten calls from Aunt Ruthie and Heather. They had remembered, and they were the only two people in her life that counted.

There was a party going on in one of the ballrooms upstairs. She could hear the music playing, a Marvin Gaye classic. She felt like dancing. What the heck. It was her birthday and she had every right to be silly if she wanted to.

Turning from the rail, she waltzed across the floor. She closed her eyes and pretended she was at a party, celebrating her birthday in style, dancing around a ballroom filled with tall, dark, handsome men. One would come forward, claim her hand and ask—

"May I have this dance?"

At the sound of the deep, husky voice, Carly's eyes flew open and she stared into the most gorgeous pair of dark eyes she'd ever seen. And there was a very handsome face to go along with those eyes. Where on earth had he come from? She blinked, wondering if she was still clutched in the throes of her fantasy. She had to be.

"Are you real?" she asked, making sure she hadn't conjured him up in her mind.

He smiled and the sight of the dimple in his chin nearly brought her to her knees. It definitely caused every hormone in her body to sizzle.

"Yes, I'm real. Now, how about that dance," he said, taking her hand in his. A different song was playing now, this one by Luther Vandross.

Carly nodded her consent and he pulled her into his arms. The man was a total stranger. Had it not been her birthday, she would not have allowed him to hold her. But she had already decided that it was okay for her to act silly today. And it wasn't every day that such a good-looking man asked her to dance. Not only was he handsome, but he smelled good too. And to top it off, they danced well together. The way their bodies swayed and moved against each other had her fighting a desire she hadn't felt in close to four years.

A desire that had never been this strong.

She was reminded how it felt to be held by a man, in powerful arms. Every part of her body tuned in to the solid hardness of his. It was staggering; she was mindful of his every movement, the steady sound of his breathing, the way his arms encircled her waist.

Carly looked up at him to find him staring down at her. His predatory look made her insides simmer. Swallowing deeply, she said softly, "Where did you come from?"

He smiled again and she felt a tingling sensation in the pit of her stomach. "From my terrace."

She nodded. He was a guest at the hotel.

"What about you? Are you a guest here?" he asked.

"Yes." She wasn't lying. She had checked into the hotel that day. There was no need to tell him she also worked here. "It's a beautiful hotel."

"I think so too. I'm Lee, by the way."

"I'm Carly."

His smile widened. "Nice meeting you, Carly. Is there a reason you were dancing alone?"

Her face warmed as she wondered if he thought she'd looked ridiculous. "It's my birthday and—"

"Happy birthday," he said.

She smiled up at him. "Thanks. I was having my own private party of one."

He tilted his head. "That's no fun. A beautiful woman should never party alone."

He was smooth, she thought. As smooth as he was handsome. And she'd noticed he wasn't wearing a ring. She knew some men didn't cherish the sanctity of marriage vows, but she did.

"For me that's no problem. I'm a loner anyway," she said.

"Why?"

She doubted he wanted to listen to her sob story. She had few friends and had learned early on that the only person she could truly trust was herself. "I prefer things that way. What about you?"

"A loner?" He shrugged. "I couldn't be a loner even if I wanted to. My family's too big."

"Really?" she asked. She couldn't help but envy anyone who belonged to a large family.

"Yes, really."

The Luther Vandross song ended and they slowly parted. "You're an excellent dancer," he said.

"So are you." She glanced at her watch. "It's getting late and—"

"You're calling it an early night on your birthday?"

She chuckled. "Afraid so. I'm checking out of the hotel in the morning."

"I see. Well, thanks for the dance."

"No, I should be thanking you. It was nice meeting you. I hope you continue to enjoy the Grand MD."

His smile widened. "Oh, I'm sure that I will."

Carly's gaze held his. She wasn't sure why she did what she did next. It could have been his scent surrounding her or his overpowering masculinity or his handsomeness—any of them could have been responsible for obliterating any semblance of her common sense.

Before she could talk herself out of doing so, she leaned up on her tiptoes. She only intended to plant a light kiss on his lips, but the moment their mouths touched they were caught in a barrage of desires they could no longer downplay. He pulled her into his arms. Her body pressed against his, and she felt every single inch of him. She moaned at the feel of his arousal against her.

She was surprised by how easily she was stimulated. She was usually in total control of her emotions, which was why, her ex-boyfriend had claimed, he'd sought out another woman. He'd said she was cold and passionless. If that was true, then what was happening here?

It could be the way Lee had taken control of her mouth, kissing her with a hunger she hadn't known was possible, cupping the back of her head to make sure their mouths stayed locked the way he wanted.

She knew if he kept this up she would beg him to take her to his room or she would be hauling him off to hers. Acting silly on your birthday was one thing, but going all-out loco was another.

While she still could, she broke off the kiss, drew in a deep breath, smiled and stepped back. "It was nice meeting you, Lee."

She watched him lick his lips as if he had enjoyed the taste of her. "It was nice meeting you as well, Carly."

She turned to leave and made it to the sliding glass door before he said, "It's a minute before midnight. Leave one of your shoes behind, and I bet I'll find you."

Carly threw her head back and laughed. "I'm a loner, remember?"

"And what about that kiss?"

Good question. "I was tempted, and since it was my birthday, I yielded," she said honestly.

He shoved his hands into his pockets, a sensuous smile spread across his lips. "When it comes to me, you can yield to temptation anytime."

"I'll remember that."

And before he could say anything else, she slipped through the glass door, refusing to yield to temptation by looking back.

Long moments after Carly left, Lee continued to stare at the door she had slipped through. What the hell had just happened? The woman had blown his mind with a kiss he was convinced would remain in his memory forever.

He licked his lips again. Her taste was still there. How? Why? And what had sent him flying across the terrace to catch two elevators to meet this woman who had taken his breath away from a distance?

Her name is Carly.

At least that was the name she'd given. Even without knowing her last name, he could track her down, if he took a mind to do so. But as much as he was tempted by that thought, now was not the time. He had too much on his plate to get caught up in romantic entanglements.

He was putting together the biggest deal of his life. When Carly checked out of the hotel tomorrow he would never see her again. And maybe that was for the best. She had warned him that she was a loner, although he couldn't help but be curious about why.

There had been something about her—other than her ingrained sexiness—that had touched him. A woman of her beauty should not be alone, especially not on her birthday. He was glad that he had shared a part of it with her.

When he had stepped out on the balcony and had seen her waltzing with her eyes closed, he had stood and stared. There might have been a dark, moonless sky overhead but she had looked totally enchanting beneath it. Her hair had tumbled around a beautiful cocoa-colored face. She had high cheekbones, beautifully arched brows and a mouth so sensuous his body had hardened just looking at it.

And that dress. It had clung to her hips, showing off

curves and a great pair of legs. It had also revealed enough cleavage to tantalize and enough thighs to entice. He had found himself moving toward her and asking for a dance. When she had snapped her eyes open and he gazed down at her, he'd fallen under her spell. A spell that hadn't broken, even now.

The kiss had been the sinker. He hadn't expected it, but damn, had he enjoyed it. Heat burned his insides remembering how easily his tongue had slid inside her mouth. For the first time in a long time, he had felt unrestrained passion and an unexplained connection for a woman.

As he walked toward the door, he consoled himself with the knowledge that once he finalized the financing on hotel number three he would have plenty of time to date. Maybe he'd even think about settling down, starting a family that could share the wealth he was creating.

His mind returned to the work waiting for him in his office and he pushed all thoughts of Carly aside.

Chapter 2

She had kissed a stranger.

The intensity of that bizarre action weighed heavily on Carly's mind the next day as she folded laundry. She could claim the "birthday silliness" defense all she wanted, but the bottom line was that it was so unlike her that the excuse didn't pass muster. And then there was the undeniable fact she couldn't let go of.

She had enjoyed it.

Carly would even admit that she had enjoyed it so much she hadn't thought of anything else since. Even when she'd gone back to her hotel room and dressed for bed, a part of her had wondered what would have happened had she left one of her shoes behind. Would he have tried to find her?

She frowned at her thoughts. She wasn't Cinderella and he wasn't a prince…although he had certainly been dashing. However, she didn't deal with fairy tales. This was the real world, and in the real world men like Lee whatever-his-last-name-was probably preyed on women nutty enough to act silly on their birthdays. There was no doubt in her mind that had she invited him up to her room he would have accepted the invitation. After they parted ways, he'd probably wandered around the hotel looking for another woman to pick up. With his looks, there was no doubt he would have been successful.

So why couldn't she put the kiss behind her?

She knew the answer. The reason she couldn't forget it was because it had been just that—unforgettable. Never had she been kissed that way, so intensely, so thoroughly. French-kissing a woman undoubtedly came naturally to Lee; he obviously had a lot of experience.

Last night that expert kiss had invaded her sleep. She had dreamed they hadn't stopped with the kiss, that he had followed her back to her hotel room, that he had undressed her, undressed himself and then pulled her down on the bed. She had awakened more than once from her own loud moans as she'd envisioned him taking her nipples into his mouth and sucking hard on them, envisioned his hand slipping between her legs.

Then, when he had replaced his hand with his mouth, detonating an explosion of passion through her, she had screamed out in her sleep.

Her dream had gone way too far. Really? An orgasm? She could only imagine what the people in the hotel room next to her thought.

She'd heard of women's dreams feeling so real they climaxed, but she'd never experienced such a thing for herself. Heck, nothing of that magnitude had even happened to her in real life, definitely not with Nathaniel.

Even with all of her dreams, she had quickly dressed and packed after waking up. Since her hotel bill had been prepaid, she'd skipped the checkout desk and gone straight to the parking garage, where she got into her car and drove off.

Carly was glad that she didn't have to go back to work until tomorrow night. And since she worked in the restaurant's kitchen and was never seen by patrons, she didn't have to worry about her path crossing with Lee's. In fact, she was confident she would never see him again. She fought off the disappointment of that thought, knowing it was for the best. The man tempted her to do things she wouldn't ordinarily do. That was the last thing she needed.

She wanted to concentrate on her new job and be the best pastry chef she could be. There were a lot of opportunities at the Grand MD and she figured hard work would bring her closer to her dream of one day owning her own café. Ever since she'd moved to town, she'd been eyeing a piece of land within fifteen minutes of where she lived, not far from the mall. She could definitely see a restaurant with her name on it sitting right on that spot. The price was more than she could afford with all the student loans she was still paying back. But within a year she would have saved enough for a down payment, and she was hoping the property would still be available.

Leaving the laundry room, she planned out the few chores she needed to finish before she went shopping. Her aunt and Heather had sent her gift cards with instructions to buy something nice for herself. She smiled at their thoughtfulness and brushed aside the hurt that her mother hadn't bothered to call. She never did.

Carly had long ago accepted the fact that Gail Briggs Thrasher believed Carly to be a mistake she'd made at sixteen that she wanted to forget. With Aunt Ruthie's help, Carly's mother had not only finished high school but had gone off to college as well. Only thing was, Gail eventually decided she didn't want to be a mother to her illegitimate child. Knowing she was never wanted had bothered Carly while growing up, but she had stopped letting it be the downer it once was.

Her aunt Ruthie was a very religious woman and she believed that one day Carly would get all the happiness that had ever been missing from her life. A part of Carly hoped her aunt was right.

A few hours later, Carly sat down to the computer at her desk and pulled up the online copy of the *Miami Herald.* She'd promised herself she'd forget about what she'd heard that night in the alley four months ago, but she hadn't been able to stop checking periodically for any mention of what she thought had happened. So far, Carly hadn't connected any reports of missing people to the events she'd heard. Heather was convinced Carly had dreamed the entire thing, and now a part of Carly wondered if perhaps Heather was right.

But she couldn't eradicate the memory of that man's deep, raspy voice. Even if she never saw the man she believed had pulled the trigger, she was convinced she would recognize his voice.

If she continued to check the internet for another month or so and nothing appeared in the online newspaper then maybe she could finally let it go.

Lee stepped out of his shower thinking that so far the day had gone just the way he'd planned. His five important guests had arrived and were checked into the guest suites on the seventieth floor, which had an exclusive elevator for privacy.

The sheikhs and their wives had flown into Texas, spending a few days at Jake's Whispering Pines Ranch. The women had been left behind with Jake's wife, Diamond, to fly to Los Angeles to shop. They would be joining their husbands in Vegas tomorrow. The three men had arrived this morning in Jake's private plane. Kyle and his wife, Kimara, had been the first to arrive at eight that morning, and Mitch Farrell and his wife, Gina, had arrived within an hour or so of the Garwoods.

The Garwoods and Farrells had visited the hotel before, when they'd attended the Grand MD's Vegas grand opening, but Lee could tell from the looks on their faces that they were still impressed with what they'd seen during this visit. Of course Jake had been to the hotel several times since they'd opened their doors, but it was the sheikhs' first time at the Grand MD in Vegas. Although they had visited the hotel in Dubai, they had already commented several times on how beautiful the Vegas hotel was.

Both sheikhs had attended college in the United States and had been visitors to Vegas a number of times before, staying at several of the other hotels on the Strip. Lee had overheard Sheikh Yasir whisper to Jake just how magnificent he thought the Grand MD was. The design, different from the one in Dubai, was impressive.

So much so that Lee and Angelo owned private residences on the seventy-third floor of the hotel. Both were huge and provided all the comforts of home, including their own private pools and entertainment rooms for parties. Their balconies provided a panoramic view of the city and beyond.

Although Lee would always have a deep affinity for Houston and he still got homesick at times, he would be the first to admit that Las Vegas had grown on him. He loved the Strip and enjoyed mingling with the millions of people who visited the city every year with plenty of money to spend. His job was to make sure some of that spending cash came the way of the Grand MD.

He had entertainers lined up three years in advance,

including stand-up comedians, musicians and magicians. All the shows were sold out until the middle of next year. Since the Grand MD was the new kid on the Strip and had something for everyone, the shows had helped the hotel receive record-breaking reservations.

Reservations from guests like the woman he'd met last night.

Not only had Carly been on his mind this morning but she had remained on his mind all last night…even while he slept. To think this much about a woman was unlike him. He didn't have the reputation his cousins Blade and Clayton had acquired prior to getting married, but he had dated enough women to suit him. Beautiful women. Stunning women.

None had been as unforgettable as Carly.

Memories kept invading his mind. Their dance. Their kiss. Why had he been tempted to go down to the lobby and wait for her to check out today just to see her again? Doing so would have been a mistake and he'd talked himself out of it, but it hadn't been easy. Why did the thought of their paths never crossing again bother him?

Slipping into a pair of sweats, Lee had just pulled a T-shirt over his head when the suite's doorbell rang. He pushed a button to check the video camera and saw it was Angelo. He spoke into the speaker. "Enter your code and come on in."

By the time Lee walked out of his bedroom Angelo was walking through the door.

He and DeAngelo Di Meglio had met years ago when a close Madaris friend, Colonel Ashton Sinclair, had introduced everyone to his cousin MacKenzie Standfield, an attorney living in Oklahoma. Mac, as she was often called, was partner in a law firm with two other women—Samari Di Meglio and Peyton Mahoney.

Mac had married Lee's cousin Luke a few years back; Samari, who was Angelo's sister, was married to Lee's cousin Blade, and almost two years ago Angelo had married Peyton. Half American and half Italian, Angelo and Samari came from a family dynasty of attorneys in New York.

"Looks like everyone has settled in," Angelo said, sitting down in a nearby chair. "That's good. Tomorrow is going to be one hell of a busy day."

Lee knew that to be true. Their breakfast meeting was scheduled for nine and would include an in-depth presentation and video. They would break for lunch at noon before resuming the meeting at one. Dinner would be a private gathering tomorrow night at the hotel's most elegant restaurant.

"I understand you chose Peyton's Place for our dinner party tomorrow night," Angelo said, smiling.

"I figured you'd like that," Lee said, grinning. Angelo had named the hotel's elegant restaurant after his wife. "Diamond suggested it, and I agreed it would be perfect. By the way, did Peyton come with you?"

"Yes, and so did Sam," he said of his sister. "Blade will join her here tomorrow. Sam and Peyton went shopping," he said of his sister and wife. Angelo chuckled. "Let me rephrase that. Sam went shopping and dragged Peyton along."

Lee nodded, smiling. Everyone knew how much Peyton hated going shopping, especially with Sam. He was glad to hear Blade would be making a visit to the hotel.

"Want something to drink?" he asked Angelo.

"Yes, I'll take a beer if you have one."

"I do," Lee said, heading for the kitchen that he rarely used. There was no need to cook when there were eight restaurants and six cafés in the hotel. He would be the first to admit that room service was spoiling him. To counter all those calories, he worked out at the gym every morning and, in some instances, again at night. "Here you go."

Angelo followed him and slid onto the stool at the counter that separated the kitchen from the living room. "Thanks," he said, twisting off the bottle cap at the same time as Lee twisted off his. Both men took a long drink. "Good stuff."

Lee agreed. He leaned back against his refrigerator. "I need to ask you something."

"What?"

"Have you ever met a woman you became attracted to immediately?"

Angelo smiled. "Yes. Peyton. When Sam brought her home from college for a visit. I wanted her bad."

Lee laughed. "That's too much information, man."

"You asked." Angelo took another sip of his beer. "Why do you want to know? Is there a woman you saw that you wanted?"

Had he wanted Carly or was he just intrigued by her? Lee knew the truth without really thinking about it. "Yes. I met a woman last night I was extremely attracted to. It was kind of scary, in a way."

Angelo nodded. "I understand."

Lee raised a brow. "Do you?"

"Yes, I think so. You ever heard of fate?"

Lee smiled. "Only Justin's version."

Justin Madaris was one of Lee's older cousins. After Justin's wife died, Justin believed one day he would find someone else to love—a woman who would be his fate. Miraculously, it had happened just the way Justin had predicted. He had met Lorren and the two had been married for quite a few years now.

"Well, I guess I'm like Justin and believe in such a

thing," Angelo said. "That's one of the reasons I didn't give up on Peyton when she didn't want to have anything to do with me."

Lee remembered that time. "But things did work out."

"Yes," Angelo said as a huge smile spread across his lips. "Things did work out. Like I said. Fate. Might be the same for you."

Lee shook his head. "I doubt it. The woman in question checked out of the hotel today and chances are I'll never see her again."

Saying the words made Lee realize just what a downer that was. He finished off the rest of his beer before placing the bottle on the counter. "I'm off to the gym. Want to join me?"

Angelo stood. "No. When you're married you come up with other ways to burn off calories."

Lee shook his head and grinned. "Again, man, that's too much information."

"Isn't that exciting?"

Carly smiled over at her coworker, a chef assistant by the name of Jodie Wrangler. Jodie, who'd begun working at the hotel a week before Carly, had just finished explaining that Peyton's Place would be closed tonight for a private party. It was rumored that the two owners of the hotel had invited important guests they were trying to impress. There was even a rumor that Oscar-winning actress Diamond Swain was included in the group.

She'd missed the head chef's announcement while she'd been off work for her birthday, and Carly had wondered what the flurry was about when she'd returned to work today. The kitchen seemed busier than usual and everyone was bustling about with enthusiasm.

"Yes, that's exciting," Carly said to Jodie, but in her

mind she didn't truly think it was. She had worked in restaurants where they'd closed their doors for private parties. In most cases, the kitchen staff was reduced since everyone wouldn't be needed. That meant less pay in somebody's paycheck.

"Chef Blanchard wants to see you. He's probably going to tell you about the party tonight, so act surprised."

Carly put down the cake pan to head over to Chef Blanchard's office. Chances were, since she was one of the newest chefs, she would be one of those sent home for the evening. She knocked on the closed door.

"Come in."

She entered the office that resembled a mini-kitchen with a desk in the center. Pots lined the wall, along with numerous trophies and plaques. Dr. Blanchard was a renowned chef, and she'd heard his name a number of times in culinary school both in the States and in France.

"I understand you wanted to see me, Chef Blanchard."

"Yes, yes," he said, smiling. "Come on in and have a seat."

"Thanks," she said, taking a chair in front of his desk. The man was totally different from Chef Renaldo in both looks and temperament. Chef Renaldo had been short, stocky and had a mean attitude most of the time, where Chef Blanchard was tall, thin and had a pleasing personality.

"I have good news for you, Carly."

She wondered if he thought informing her that she had another day off was good news. "And what is the good news?"

He leaned back in his chair with a huge smile on his lips. "I'm sure you've heard by now that our two owners, Mr. Madaris and Mr. Di Meglio, have important guests here at the hotel, and they have requested a private party.

That means the restaurant will be closing to anyone except the group of thirteen who will be dining here tonight."

She'd never met the two owners but had heard several whispered comments around the kitchen by the women who had. Both Mr. Madaris and Mr. Di Meglio were rumored to be eye candy of the most serious kind.

"I see."

"I'm putting you in charge of desserts."

Carly blinked, certain she had heard wrong. "You're putting me in charge of desserts?"

"Yes. That dish you made during your interview will be perfect. Two of the gentlemen are from the Middle East and I know they will love your Pi-Sky as much as I did."

Carly was speechless. Seldom did a head chef deviate from a restaurant's menu.

"Thank you, sir. For the vote of confidence," she said, beginning to feel that excitement Jodie had alluded to earlier.

"You're welcome. I believe you'll find all the ingredients in the hotel's kitchen store, including King Arthur flour."

Because of the number of restaurants and cafés in the hotel, each one used the same kitchen supplies. To keep things simple, the hotel hired a shopper whose job was to make sure any and every item the cooks needed was on the premises.

"That's great. Thanks again."

"Don't mention it. These guests are important and we all want to make a good impression."

"Yes, sir. We will." She left the chef's office smiling.

Lee glanced around Peyton's Place, the only rotating restaurant on the Strip. It was the most popular of all the hotel's restaurants and always in demand. It seemed everyone was fascinated by the slow rotation offering a breathtaking view of the Strip and the Mojave Desert.

There would be no business discussions tonight. They had done enough of that during the day. Now it was time to eat and unwind. All five men had invited their wives to join them, and Angelo had invited Peyton as well. All seemed to be in a festive mood, and Lee was glad of that. It was a good way to end such a busy day.

He couldn't help noticing that all six men were married to what he considered to be smart and beautiful women. Over dinner, he had discovered Sheikh Yasir's wife, Delaney, was the sister of motorcycle builder and racer Thorn Westmoreland and also the sister of bestselling author Rock Mason, aka Stone Westmoreland.

Johari Valdemon, who was married to Sheikh Valdemon and was Sheikh Yasir's sister, enlightened everyone over dinner with the story of how she and her husband had been promised to each other at birth and yet she hadn't set eyes on him until she was twenty-four. They'd met here in the States. While in college, Johari had intentionally gone missing, not ready to return to her country, do her duty and marry. Rasheed had gone looking for her and had found his intended bride dancing on the tables of some club in New York. That tale got a lot of rousing laughter from everyone.

Jake joked about Kyle and Kimara's six offspring and how, for years, everyone wondered if they would stop having more children. The couple did admit they enjoyed making babies, and that their fertility had something to do with a vacation cabin they owned in the North Carolina Mountains called Special K.

Because Mitch's wife, Gina, grew up with a lot of his older cousins, Lee knew her well. Her brother Trevor was best friend to one of his older cousins, Dex; and for years Trevor had been foreman at Dex's land-exploration company. Lee liked Gina, always had, and thought she was down-to-earth. It was obvious that Mitch adored his wife.

"I understand your oldest son left this month for college." Angelo broke into Lee's thoughts when he addressed a question to Kyle and Kimara Garwood.

Kimara smiled lovingly at her husband before gazing at Angelo. "Yes, and I miss Kyle VI already. He's attending Harvard."

"An excellent university," both sheikhs chimed in to say with huge smiles. Both had degrees from Harvard.

"I agree," Lee said. He was a proud Harvard alum as well.

"I take it you couldn't persuade Blade and Sam to join us," Mitch said, smiling.

Lee chuckled. "No. They drove to Los Angeles. Sam was determined to get some more shopping in." He glanced over at Peyton. "How did shopping go yesterday?"

Peyton rolled her eyes. "Don't ask."

The waiters removed their plates and everyone agreed that dinner had been absolutely delicious and they were all ready for dessert.

"Thirteen is an unlucky number, Lee. Why didn't you bring a date?" Diamond Swain Madaris asked.

Lee glanced across the dinner table and smiled at the woman who'd made his uncle a very happy man. "The reason I didn't bring a date is because there isn't a woman I'm interested in at the moment."

"Better not say that too loud," Jake said, chuckling. "Word might get back to Mom. She'll find you a bride and start planning a wedding."

Not if I find one first, Lee thought, as the waiter poured more coffee into his cup. He wasn't interested in finding a bride, and he wouldn't appreciate his great-grandmother shoving one down his throat either. She was known to try such tactics.

His mind shifted to the woman he'd met a couple of nights ago. He wondered where she was and what she was doing. Why was he still thinking about her? Why had thoughts of her infiltrated his mind all day? When he should have been concentrating on the business at hand he'd instead recalled their dance, their kiss, her scent. Why had she made such a lasting impression on him?

His thoughts were disrupted when waiters came out carrying several plates. Dessert had arrived.

"Oh, I bet your dessert is a big hit with everyone, Carly."

Carly smiled. Jodie was definitely a confidence booster, which was really refreshing. During her years at culinary schools and working in various restaurants, Carly had discovered that most chefs were competitive by nature and very few gave compliments to other chefs. In contrast, Jodie didn't mind bestowing a compliment and she was always in a good mood. That was probably one of the reasons Carly liked her.

"Thanks. We'll see."

"I saw one of the owners today when he was showing a group of men around. All the men were extremely handsome but Mr. Madaris stood out," Jodie was saying.

Carly glanced over at her. "In what way?"

"Where everybody else got an A, in my book he got an A-plus."

Carly couldn't help but chuckle. "An A-plus?"

"Yes, doubly so."

Carly shrugged, not imagining any man looking that good…except that guy she had danced with on the balcony two nights ago. She wondered if he'd checked out of the hotel by now. And that wasn't the only thing she wondered about him. What was he doing in Vegas alone? Where was he from? She had picked up on a Southern accent.

Did he have a girl back home? Now was a fine time to think about that—*after* she'd plastered a kiss on him. But then he had plastered one on her as well. He had been the one to take the kiss to another level, not her. But still…

"Your dessert is really good," Jodie said, interrupting Carly's thoughts.

Carly glanced over to where Jodie was sitting on a stool at a counter, stuffing her face with Pi-Sky. Carly smiled. "Thanks."

Chef Blanchard had put a lot of faith in her, and more than anything she didn't want to disappoint him.

"Sweet Allah, that was the best pie I've ever eaten," exclaimed Sheikh Rasheed Valdemon.

"Evidently," his wife, Johari, said, smiling. "You ate three slices. If you eat any more you'll gain too much to get on the plane."

Everyone around the table chuckled, but Lee agreed with Rasheed. Even he had asked for seconds. The entire meal had been tremendous, but what topped it off was the excellent dessert. Rasheed and Lee weren't the only ones who thought so. Others at the table were singing its praises too.

"Who is the chef for this restaurant?" Sheikh Jamal Yasir asked Lee and Angelo. "I'm tempted to sweep him or her off to my country to work in the palace."

Lee laughed. "Then maybe we need to keep Chef Blanchard under lock and key for the rest of your visit. But it's only fair for you to meet him."

He then said to a waiter standing nearby, "Please tell Chef Blanchard that my dinner party would like to meet him." The waiter nodded before quickly walking off. Lee was glad that things were going so well and that his potential investors were impressed.

Everyone looked up when the tall, lanky man wearing a huge white chef toque and chef jacket approached their table. Lee stood. "Everyone, this is Chef Blanchard, the person responsible for our very delicious meal as well as the outstanding service we received."

Compliments were bestowed upon the man who beamed at all the accolades. "Thank you all. I'm glad you enjoyed everything. I have an excellent staff whose goal tonight was to make sure your dining experience at Peyton's Place was first-class."

"It was," Rasheed said. "And that dessert…Pi-Sky it was called? It was simply superb. I've never tasted anything quite like it. It reminds me of Australia's pavlova, but the meringue and whipped cream are different, somewhat lighter, with a different taste. And the crust—my goodness. You used King Arthur flour. It's what the cooks use all the time at the palace in my country."

Chef Blanchard continued to beam. "I can't take any credit for the dessert. It was prepared by my pastry chef. It's her own secret recipe. It's quite delicious, and I asked her to prepare it just for tonight."

"Thank you for having her do that," Mitch Farrell said, grinning. Like Rasheed, he had eaten three slices. Lee figured he would have asked for a fourth if Gina hadn't slid his plate away. Most likely all the men, including him, would be hitting the gym in the morning.

"Is she still here? Your pastry chef?" Diamond asked. "We would like to thank her personally."

Chef Blanchard's smile spread even more. "Yes, yes, most certainly. I think she would like that. She has only been with us for a little over a month."

"As long as she keeps making desserts like this," Lee

said with a grin, "I can assure you that she'll be here for a very long time."

Chef Blanchard turned to one of the waiters. "Please ask Chef Briggs to step out here for a minute."

Carly was wrapping up the leftover dessert. It would be served tomorrow morning at the poolside café as a midmorning treat. Not much remained and that was a sign that Pi-Sky had been a big hit tonight.

Several of the sous chefs had joined Jodie at the counter to get a taste of the dessert that Jodie was moaning over with each bite she slid into her mouth. "Thanks to you, I'll have to get up and go walking in the morning," Jodie said.

Since she didn't sound too bothered by the prospect, Carly gave Jodie only a quick glance as she continued what she was doing. "No one is twisting your arm to eat that pie, you know."

"Yes. I know," Jodie said, inhaling deeply between each bite. "The only thing missing is a nice glass of wine. I think I will—"

"Excuse me." Mickey, one of the waiters, interrupted them. "Chef Blanchard wants you out front, Chef Briggs. Everyone loved your dessert and wants to meet you personally."

Carly noticed the kitchen got quiet. All the other chefs had stopped what they were doing to stare at her. And she knew why. Typically, when dinner guests had compliments for the cooks, thanking the executive chef would suffice since preparing a delicious meal was a collective effort. To be singled out was definitely a feather in her cap.

"Well, what are you waiting for?" Jodie said with a huge grin on her face. "Get going. And smile prettily at the owner…the one that's single. And if you can pull Diamond Swain aside, please tell her that I've seen every single movie she's made but my favorite is still *Black Butterfly.* And that I would love for her and Sterling Hamilton to make another movie together, and that I am one of her biggest fans."

Carly smiled at Jodie as she straightened the toque on her head and smoothed down her jacket, grateful there weren't any chocolate stains on it tonight. "I wouldn't know the owners from anyone else. Besides, I doubt I'll get the chance to say anything and you know it," Carly said.

She drew in a deep breath as she followed Mickey out of the kitchen. When they rounded the corner she saw that the guests were all standing around, chatting and shaking hands. She knew that meant the dinner party was ending. The women were dressed in outfits as beautiful as they were. Chef Blanchard was standing tall, but he wasn't as tall as several of the other men.

Carly recognized Diamond Swain immediately. The woman was simply gorgeous. Carly tried not to stare too hard at the handsome man standing by the movie actress's side with his arm around her waist.

Suddenly the crowd shifted and Carly's breath caught. She almost stumbled. She could only see the man's profile but she knew it was *him.* She would recognize those broad masculine shoulders anywhere.

What is Lee doing here?

Everyone must have heard her approach since they all turned around. Her gaze connected with Lee's. And when it did, her heart pounded, a tingling sensation swirled around in her stomach and a rush of intense heat swept through her.

It was all she could do to continue walking toward the group knowing his eyes were on her every step.

Chapter 3

"Chef Briggs, I asked you to come out because our dinner guests were quite taken with the dessert you made."

Lee watched the woman who'd been on his mind since he'd seen her two nights ago. She was a chef? Here? At his hotel? She hadn't mentioned anything about it that night—in fact she'd claimed to be a guest at the Grand MD. Why had she lied?

Even dressed in her chef garb she looked beautiful. After making initial eye contact, she refused to look at him. But he was definitely looking at her. Her features were exquisite.

He heard Diamond, Jake, Rasheed and others give her compliment after compliment, and somehow he could tell that she wasn't used to getting such praise. Since he knew the others expected him to say something complimentary as well, he extended his hand to her.

"I'm Lee Madaris. The dessert was delicious." He made

the introduction for the benefit of the others who had no idea of his and Carly's prior encounter. It was better if no one knew until the two of them could talk.

Following his lead, she shook his hand. Immediately a surge of warmth filled him. "Thanks, Mr. Madaris."

Had she actually placed emphasis on his name or had he just imagined it? With nothing more to be said, she returned to the kitchen. Lee watched her retreat. If she thought for one minute this was the end of things, then she was mistaken.

As far as he was concerned, Carly Briggs had a lot of explaining to do.

"Good night, Carly. See you tomorrow."

"Good night, Jodie." Carly watched as Jodie met up with her boyfriend, Jerome Mathis, who worked as a bellman for the hotel, before walking quickly to the elevator that would take her to the parking garage.

How she'd made it through the rest of the night, Carly wasn't sure. She'd concentrated on cleaning the kitchen. Going home was her top priority. She just couldn't get out of her mind the fact that the man she'd met a few nights ago was actually L. C. Madaris, one of the owners of the hotel. That meant that technically he was her boss.

And she had kissed him.

She waited for the elevator and when the door opened she barely glanced at the person getting on the elevator with her. When she did, she probably looked as thunderstruck as she felt. It was *him*...again. Where had he come from?

"We need to talk, don't you think, Carly?"

Apparently, he thought so. She stepped back against the elevator wall. In the confines of the small space she became even more aware of his captivating presence.

"What do we need to talk about?"

His chuckle sounded like a low growl in his throat. "I think you know."

Carly had a pretty good idea. He held a key card to the scanner and a new set of numbers appeared on the keypad. She watched as he punched one.

"Where are we going?" she asked.

"To my suite."

"Your suite?" Blood pounded in her temples.

"Yes, my suite."

She tightened her grip on her purse. "I'm not sure that's a good idea."

"Neither am I, but that's the only place I know where we can have absolute privacy."

She didn't want privacy. She didn't want to talk at all. Now that she knew who he was, she could make a promise that she would keep the other night to herself. Nothing like it would happen again. She liked working here. And more than anything, she needed her job.

She was about to speak when the back wall of the elevator slid open. She hadn't expected it and would have tumbled out into a beautiful living room had Lee not reached out and caught her hand.

She wished he hadn't done that. Immediately, a sensation she couldn't describe flowed through her from his touch.

"You okay?" he asked with concern in his eyes.

She nodded. "Yes, I'm fine."

She was in full control of her balance…although she was questioning her senses…. She stepped off the elevator, which had opened directly into his suite. The place was simply gorgeous. But she shouldn't be surprised. He owned one of the most elegant hotels on the Vegas Strip; anything was possible.

"Make yourself at home. Would you care for something to drink?"

She watched him remove his jacket and toss it on the back of a chair before heading toward the kitchen. "No, thank you."

"I hope you don't mind if I do. A beer sounds pretty good right now."

She watched him open the refrigerator before what he'd said sank in.

Make yourself at home.

There was no way she could do that. "You wanted to talk."

"Yes," he said, returning from the kitchen with his beer to find her still standing. "We are definitely going to talk. How about if we sit down first?"

She preferred standing, but she sat down on a plush sofa and he did too.

"That night on the balcony," he began. "Did you know who I was?"

She met his gaze, surprised by his question. "Of course not. Had I known who you were, I would not have..." She swallowed. There was no need to remind him of what she had done that night.

"Initiated a kiss between us?"

Why had he gone there and done the very thing she hadn't wanted him to do? Since he had reminded them both of what had happened, she said, "No, I would not have initiated it."

He held her gaze for a long time, slowly sipping his beer right from the bottle. "Why did you tell me you were a guest here at the hotel when you're an employee?"

Carly nervously gnawed her bottom lip. "Because that night I *was* a guest here. It was my birthday, and I wanted to do something special, so I booked a room in the hotel for one night."

"So it *was* your birthday?"

Had he doubted her? "Yes. Would you like to see my driver's license?"

He shook his head. "No, that won't be necessary."

She had a question of her own. "Why did you lead me to believe you were a businessman passing through?"

"Did I lead you to believe that?" he asked.

"Yes."

He took another sip of his beer. When had watching a man drink beer from a bottle become so sensual? And why did he have to have such beautiful eyes? They were the same eyes that had haunted her dreams two nights in a row.

"I don't recall misleading you," he said, breaking into her close perusal of him. "I answered each of your inquiries truthfully. You asked where I came from and I told you my terrace. There was no need to explain that it was the terrace on the executive floor. You also commented about this being a beautiful hotel and I agreed."

He stretched his legs out in front of him. "Now tell me, when did I mislead you?"

She shifted in her seat and noticed the way his gaze adjusted to the movement of her body. She drew in a deep breath when she saw heat in his eyes. "Okay, you didn't mislead me per se, but you weren't completely forthcoming either. You didn't tell me you owned the hotel."

He smiled. "That's something I don't share with a lot of people. Those who need to know already do."

"Okay, now I know too," she said, standing.

He stood as well and she wished her gaze hadn't been drawn to the way his pants stretched across masculine thighs when he did so. "Well, I'm glad we got that all cleared up," he said.

In a way, she was too. She hoped that was his way of letting her know she could keep her job. "I'm glad too. We can both admit it was a mistake."

He lifted a brow. "What was?"

"That night. On the balcony." *The kiss,* she thought.

"On the contrary, Carly. That night. On the balcony. Was not a mistake." He'd emphasized each statement.

And then he stunned her even more when he said, "In fact, I think we should pick up where we left off."

Lee saw the shocked look on Carly's face and wished he could kiss her. He drew in a long, deep breath. She smelled good. She looked good. Gone were the toque and chef jacket, replaced by a cute purple blouse and a pair of snug-fitting jeans. He knew just how snug they were since he'd walked behind her a minute or two without being detected when she was heading for the elevator. She had some serious curves and the best-looking backside he'd ever seen.

"We can't pick up where we left off," she said.

"I don't see why not," he countered, finishing off his beer and placing the empty bottle on the table. "I'd like to get to know you."

She actually looked stunned. "Why?"

He could give her several reasons, but he stated the one that made the most sense. "Because I'm a man and you are a woman. A very beautiful and desirable woman."

Lee fathomed from her expression that she didn't believe him. Surely she was aware of just how striking she was. High cheekbones, skin a perfect shade of brown, an exquisite pair of lips; he could go on…so he did. She had a gorgeous pair of legs that looked damn good in stilettos, and he liked the way her firm breasts pressed against her blouse, showing the tips of her nipples.

He was getting aroused just looking at her. Surely some

man, probably several, had told her how heart-stoppingly attractive she was.

"Mr. Madaris."

He lifted a brow. *Mr. Madaris?* "I'm *Lee,* remember."

She lifted her chin. "That was before I found out you were my boss."

He smiled. "Chef Blanchard is your boss. I just happen to be one of the guys who owns the hotel."

She took a deep breath and then exhaled slowly. He figured she was trying to regroup. "Lee. Remember the one thing I told you about me? The reason I was celebrating my birthday alone?"

Yes, he remembered, and he had an idea where she was going with this. But he refused to go there with her. There was a strong attraction between them, and it was just as resilient now as it had been that night. It was sexual, hot, and something he refused to put a lid on or walk away from. Maybe his cousin Justin was right about fate; there was a reason Lee's path had crossed with Carly's again.

"I remember what you told me, Carly," he said. "You're a loner."

And just as he had that night, he couldn't help wondering why. Women who looked like her usually dated often, so what was up with this "loner" story? Had some man broken her heart and she was trying to protect herself from future heartache?

"So you know what that means, right?" she asked.

He moved around the hassock to stand in front of her. "Yes, that means you were a loner because you hadn't met me."

Carly blinked. She'd met arrogant men before, but Lee Madaris's arrogance felt more like confidence. Too bad it was a wasted effort as far as she was concerned.

Her decision to be a loner had nothing to do with him being a man and her being a woman. It had everything to do with protecting herself from ever being hurt again by anyone—family, friend or boyfriend. Aunt Ruthie was all the family she needed…all the family she had; Heather was the epitome of what a best friend should be and she didn't need another. And as far as a boyfriend was concerned—been there, done that. She'd decided that having another boyfriend at this stage in her life was too much work. She could do badly all by herself.

"Excuse me for saying so, Lee, but meeting you does not make a difference."

"I believe otherwise."

"Trust me, it doesn't," she said.

"I beg to differ."

The man was too much, and he looked too damn good. He was temptation a-plenty but regardless, like she told him, whether he accepted it or not, meeting him did not make a difference.

"It won't work."

"How do you know?" he countered.

"Because I know *me,*" she said.

He took her hand in his and immediately felt a response. The same heat stirring inside of him stirred inside of her. Holding her gaze, he said, "Then let me get to know you, Carly."

"Why? We have nothing in common. You're a man of the world. You're wealthy. You dine with sheikhs and movie stars. You own the hotel I work for. You—"

Firming his grip, he gently tugged her closer. The corners of his lips curved into a challenging smile when he whispered, "I am totally and utterly attracted to you." He moved even closer. "So tell me, after this kiss, that we don't have anything in common."

And then he closed his mouth over hers.

Carly's heart pounded in her chest the moment Lee's lips touched hers. She thought of pulling back but instead let out a breathless moan. That was when he slid his tongue inside her mouth.

She instantly became lost.

He claimed her mouth with a hunger that sent sensuous chills through her body. The kiss two nights ago had shattered her relatively calm world, but this kiss was sending that same world into a tailspin.

Never had a man kissed her so thoroughly. A surge of unadulterated pleasure ripped through her. She felt inflamed everywhere his tongue touched. The way her body was plastered against him, she felt every one of his hard muscles.

Every lick of his tongue made it hard to remember her concern about getting to know him, made it hard to remember what they didn't have in common. Instead, all she felt was the burning desire and aching need he stirred within her. All she could do was savor the moment.

"I don't think I'm asking for too much, Carly," he whispered in a husky tone, while plying her lips with a series of slow, feathery kisses.

She drew in a deep breath, bringing his scent into her nostrils. She needed to think and couldn't, not while he was still kissing her. Carly knew she had to get a grip on her senses. "I need to think about this, Lee."

He touched his finger to her moist lips. "Why think about it? You want me and I want you."

She took a step back, frustrated that she'd weakened with him. "You have no idea what I want, Lee."

He stared at her with a look of determination on his face. She found the sensuality of his features unnerving;

he had the ability to weaken her defenses if she allowed him to.

He cupped her chin. "Then tell me what you want, Carly."

"There's nothing I want. I love my life just the way it is."

"Then let me tell you what I want," he said, dropping his hand from her chin. "I want to get to know you, and I want you to get to know me. How about dinner? This weekend. It will be my treat and I'll prepare it here."

She raised a brow. "You can cook?"

The smile that curved the corners of his lips sent her pulse racing. "I might not be able to throw down as well as you, but I can hold my own. My great-grandmother forced cooking lessons on all her grands and great-grands. No one was exempted. When she gives an order, we all obey."

"She sounds like quite a character."

"Trust me, she is. So how about letting me show you what I can do?"

Carly nibbled her bottom lip. She figured she was just a novelty with Lee. No doubt he'd had his share of models and actresses and now he wanted to try a chef.

She had to admit she was curious about what he could do in the kitchen, but she needed to know what his expectations would be. "I'll get dinner out of this. What do you get?"

His smile carried a sensual undertone when he said, "A chance for you to get to know me."

Carly still wasn't sure why he would want that, and she did not plan to let her curiosity weaken her resolve, but she found herself saying, "Okay, but not here. I prefer dinner at my place. I live on the outskirts of town." She felt the need to be on her own turf.

"Okay, what about tomorrow?"

She shook her head. “I work tomorrow. I’m off Wednesday and Thursday every week.”

“I’m leaving town Wednesday for a trip to Dubai. I won’t return until the following week, on Thursday morning. Will that Thursday evening work?”

“The same day you get back? Will you be up to cooking anything?”

He chuckled. “Yes, I’ll be up to it.”

“Okay, then. Thursday evening is fine.”

She hoped she was not making a mistake.

His smile widened. “Great.” He checked his watch. “It’s after midnight. If you want to leave your car here tonight, I can have my driver take you home and he can pick you up tomorrow and bring you to work.”

Carly could just imagine the kitchen gossip if that were to happen. “No, thanks, I’ll be fine. I’ve worked past midnight plenty of times.”

“Then I’m walking you down.”

She started to tell him not to bother but he’d already reached for his jacket. “Allergies to any food?” he asked her.

She watched how easily he slid his jacket over a powerful pair of shoulders. “No allergies.”

“Favorite foods?”

It was considerate of him to ask. “I like practically everything, but if I had a choice it would be pasta and seafood.”

He smiled at her. “The choices are unlimited. What’s your address?” he asked, pulling a smartphone out of his pocket.

She rattled it off to him and he coded it into the phone. “And your phone number?” he asked. “Just in case I’m detained.”

She gave her number to him as well.

“Six o’clock on that Thursday okay?” he asked.

"Yes."

He put the phone back into his jacket. "Ready to go down?"

"Yes, but you don't have to walk with me."

"The first thing you need to know about me is that I always try to be a gentleman," he said, his fingers gently pressing into the center of her back as he led her to the elevator. "I know a shortcut."

As they left the elevator and walked toward her car, she was aware of his firm strength and his determination. Did he think she would be his flavor of the week? Was she letting him think she was an easy target?

"This is my car," she said, coming to a stop. "Thanks for taking the time to walk me down here."

"No problem. I'll see you next Thursday. At six."

She nodded as she opened the car door and slid inside. He stepped back as she closed the door and buckled her seat belt. She rolled down her window. "Good night, Lee."

"Good night." He moved closer to the car. "I'm looking forward to us getting to know each other better."

Carly gasped in surprise when he leaned down and placed a kiss on her lips through the open window. He smiled at the astonished look on her face and stepped back, leaving heat searing through her body. Heat that she didn't want to feel.

She was tempted to cancel Thursday but when she looked at him something stopped her. Her insides tingled. For the first time in a long while she felt a rush of excitement for something—someone.

She broke eye contact with him, pulled out of the parking space and drove away without looking back.

Lee couldn't sleep. He should not have brought Carly to his suite. Her scent lingered everywhere, even in his bedroom and she hadn't set foot in here. He was finding it hard to sleep without dreaming about her—and the dreams had been scorching hot.

Easing out of bed, he went into the kitchen. As he passed through the living room, her scent hit him with even more force. No other woman's scent had ever impacted him this way before. But then he'd never stayed awake thinking about a kiss before either.

He pulled out a bottled water, uncapped it and tilted it to his lips. After taking a full gulp, he wiped his mouth with the back of his hand and leaned against the counter.

So, okay, he was fiercely attracted to a woman. There had to be a reason he had allowed her to get under his skin, a reason why he wanted to get to know her, a reason why he had thought about her constantly since seeing her that night on the balcony.

There was so much about her he didn't know…but the one thing he did know was that he wanted her, in his bed, and he had no problem going through the initial getting-to-know-you stage of things to get to that point. She was leery of him, he could tell. He could only assume that some man had hurt her, made her distrustful, but he wouldn't let that be a deterrent. She was the first woman whose taste he couldn't forget, whose scent seemed embedded in his nostrils, who'd inspired dreams so hot, he'd awakened aroused.

Taking another gulp of his water, he was leaving the kitchen when his cell phone rang. Glancing around, he tried to remember where he'd left his phone. Moving quickly, he pulled it from his jacket and checked caller ID. It was his cousin Nolan, who stayed up much later than was good for him and often forgot about the two-hour time difference between Texas and Vegas.

Lee and his cousins Reese, Corbin and Nolan had all been born within fifteen months of each other. They were as close as brothers and had been thick as thieves while growing up. Mama Laverne swore her goal was to marry them all off before she took her last breath. They all told her that wouldn't happen, but then the next thing they knew, Reese had married his best friend Kenna.

Lee knew his great-grandmother had pegged him as her next victim. Catching the garter at Angelo and Peyton's wedding hadn't helped matters. It had been then and there that she'd predicted he was living his last year as a single man. He'd boasted to Angelo that he was determined to beat her at her own game, but he still hadn't come up with a way to do it.

"What's up, Nolan?"

"You're up, if Mama Laverne has anything to do with it. I'm her designated driver this week."

Yes, Lee knew. The six sons had taken their mother's car away around five years ago, which meant someone had to chauffeur Mama Laverne around to church, church meetings, visits with friends, her weekly bingo games and doctor's appointments.

Half the year she lived on Whispering Pines Ranch with Jake, Diamond and their family. It seemed her baby boy knew just how to handle his mom. But it was when she had to split the other six months with her remaining sons that the grands and great-grands were pulled into the mix. Each had their week, on a rotating basis, of driving "Miss Daisy."

"Yes, what of it?" Lee asked.

"Thought I'd alert you that today was her bingo day and she and some other older lady were talking. I pretended not to be listening."

"And?"

"And they were planning your wedding."

Lee lifted a brow. "My wedding?"

"Yes, Mama Laverne told the lady your year was long overdue. Angelo and Peyton got married last year on Valentine's Day, and she'd given you until this Valentine's Day to find a bride. You haven't."

She'd given him until Valentine's Day? Lee drew in a frustrated breath. Hadn't he told her in a nice and respectful way…and more than once…that when he married it would be his decision and not because she deemed that was the way it should be?

"So let me guess. This woman that she was talking with has a single granddaughter," Lee surmised.

"Yes. So be prepared when you come home for Christmas. You might have a bride waiting on you. They claim she's a real beauty."

Lee rolled his eyes. "I don't give a damn if she's Diamond's long-lost sister, I refuse to let Mama Laverne pick out a wife for me."

"Then tell her that. In her good ear," Nolan said, laughing.

Everyone claimed Mama Laverne had a hearing problem, but Lee and his cousins knew better. She heard just what she wanted to hear. "Laugh all you want, Nolan, but remember that if she succeeds in sticking me with a wife, then you are next."

Nolan ceased laughing immediately. "I'll leave the country first," he threatened. "I won't be forced into anything."

Lee knew just how he felt. "I need to come up with a plan. Maybe I shouldn't even come home for Christmas."

"Then you know what Mama Laverne will do. She'll have Jake fly her and your intended bride to Vegas on Jake's private plane. Either way, whether you like it or not, you're going to meet this woman. Mama Laverne's mind is made up. You're it."

Lee frowned. No, he wasn't it.

"Thanks for the heads-up. If anything else develops, let me know. She might have had a hand in finding wives for Luke, Blade and Reese," he said of his other cousins, "and I even suspect she might have played matchmaker for Angelo and Peyton, but I don't need her help. I'm not planning on getting married anytime soon."

Later, long after his phone call with Nolan had ended, Lee headed back toward his bedroom. Like he'd told Nolan, he had to come up with a plan. And like he'd told Angelo when he'd thrown that damn garter at him, he intended to beat his great-grandmother at her own game.

However, he had a feeling that doing so would not be easy.

Chapter 4

"I guess it's too late to cancel now, Heather," Carly said as she tucked her phone close to her ear and watched the truck drive away.

She was shocked to get a quick call from Lee that morning from Dubai telling her to expect a delivery around noon. A truck had arrived and the deliveryman had not only unloaded the groceries but had taken the time to put them away. Before leaving he'd handed her a note that said:

> Ingredients needed for tomorrow's dinner.
> Lee

"Pretty much sounds like it, but do you really *want* to cancel?"

Carly nibbled her bottom lip as she thought about Heather's question. "I really don't know what I want. Things are happening so fast. First I kiss a guy on the hotel balcony and two days later I discover he owns the hotel. Now he wants an affair."

"Are you sure? He didn't ask for one. From what you told me, all he wants to do is get to know you better," Heather said.

Carly rolled her eyes. "For what purpose? What guy do you know that's not looking for something?"

Heather chuckled. "If you recall, I thought the same thing about Joel but he proved me wrong. Maybe this guy will prove you wrong. Hey, he's cooking dinner for you, so he can't be all bad. And you did say he was good-looking."

"Too good-looking, which makes me suspicious. Why me when he probably has a slew of others who would die for the chance to get to know him?"

"Why not you? You're beautiful. Stop putting yourself down. You have just as much to offer as anyone else, maybe more. You're not a parasite who plans to feed off Lee Madaris's wealth, and I bet he's encountered plenty of women like that and sees you as being different."

Oh, she was different all right, Carly thought. So different that she was brazen enough to kiss him the first night they met. That was probably what he remembered the most. He probably wondered what she would initiate if he had her in the privacy of her own home.

"Well, I plan to keep my guard up. Nathaniel proved that some men can't be trusted."

"At least you said *some* and not all."

Carly smiled. "Only because *your* Joel renewed my faith in *some* men." And he had. Heather's fairy-tale courtship had been special. Carly's best friend had tried resisting Joel but he had been determined to sweep Heather off her feet and had done just that.

"Well, I'll let you know how things turn out. But don't be surprised if after Thursday he decides never to bother with me again."

"What do you plan to do?"

"Be myself. Then he can decide if I'm as boring as Nathaniel claims I am."

Heather asked how Aunt Ruthie was doing and Carly let her switch the topic, asking Heather about her parents and her brother. Heather told her how beautiful the weather was in Spain, and Carly told her about the garden she had started in her backyard. Those living in Vegas had told her that if she planned to grow anything, now was the time to plant and wish herself luck.

Then Heather said, "I'm still checking the *Miami Herald* every day online and I assume you're doing the same."

"Yes," Carly said.

Although Heather had doubts about Carly's story about what she'd heard that night, her friend still checked the paper just in case.

"But so far I haven't come across anything," Carly said. "I've decided to check for a few more weeks and if nothing comes up then that's it. It's going on six months now and I can't live my life wondering if I'm sane or not."

"You're sane, but you might have been slightly confused that night. Remember, you had worked a double the day before."

Carly remembered, but still, why did the sound of that man's voice keep resurfacing in her mind? She had not dreamed that, had she?

"You did all you could," Heather said. "If the police had found anything it would have been in the papers."

Carly knew Heather was right.

"Call and let me know how tomorrow's dinner goes. I'm still working on Joel about that trip to Vegas that he promised."

After ending the call and clicking off the phone, Carly glanced around her kitchen. It seemed that Lee meant business. She couldn't help lifting her lips in a smile.

"Dinner should be interesting."

* * *

Lee looked across the table at the three men he'd flown to Dubai to meet. They were older cousins whom he thought of as older brothers. Justin, Dex and Clayton Madaris had already been out of college and working in their chosen professional fields when Lee and his close cousins had become teens. It had meant a lot to be able to ask their older cousins those questions they wouldn't dare ask their parents. Justin, the oldest, was a doctor; Dex, the middle brother, was a geologist; and Clayton, the youngest brother, was an attorney. All three were happily married with families.

"I'm surprised the three of you could plan to come to Dubai on vacation at the same time," Lee said, taking a sip of his wine.

Justin chuckled. "Syneda planned it all. That should tell you everything."

Lee smiled. It did. Syneda was Clayton's wife and was quite outspoken. She was known for the outlandish. And everyone adored her, as they did Justin's wife, Lorren, who had been Syneda's best friend since childhood, and Dex's wife, Caitlin. All three couples were known to give lavish parties. Visiting them had always been a highlight while growing up.

"You know you didn't have to come all the way to Dubai to see us," Dex said, his lips forming a smile. "Houston was closer."

"Your reluctance to visit home has nothing to do with Mama Laverne's prophecy, does it?" Clayton asked, his eyes showing amusement.

Lee shook his head. He wished he could find the situation as amusing as Justin, Dex and Clayton did. "Did she find your wives?"

"Nope," Justin said. "I think she was taking a break during our generation."

"But she did give me grief at my wedding," Clayton said, grinning.

"Get the story right, Clayton," Dex said, taking a sip of his drink. "You were the one causing grief by breaking every rule."

Lee chuckled. He'd been at the wedding that day but had been too young to know what had been going on behind the scenes. The one thing all of them had known was that Clayton was the rebel in the family, along with one of their other cousins, Felicia Laverne, who'd been named after Mama Laverne.

"To answer your question, Clayton, I'm trying to come up with my game plan before coming home for Christmas. Nolan called a few nights ago and said he heard Mama Laverne planning my wedding to her friend's granddaughter."

"Well, she did give you fair warning at Angelo and Peyton's wedding," Dex said, shaking his head. "What can you do other than avoid coming home?"

Lee wished he could answer that question. He was saved from having to come up with something when he saw Lorren, Syneda and Caitlin heading for their table. "Here come your beautiful wives."

He watched the expressions on his three cousins' faces when they stood, waiting for the ladies' arrival. It was easy to see they adored the women they'd married. It would be nice if all marriages were like that. Lee had been exposed to enough solid marriages in his family to know they could work if both people were on the same page and in love. His parents' marriage had lasted close to thirty-five years and long marriages ran in his family.

He had an MBA. He understood business, not this emotion called love. What if there was no love? Could two people marry and become life partners?

He brought his glass to his lips just as he was slammed

with a whopper of an idea. "Why didn't I think of that before?" he said aloud.

"Think of what?" Syneda asked, approaching the table.

"Nothing." He was well aware that when it came to his great-grandmother, Syneda was one of the old gal's partners in crime. Rumor had it that Syneda assisted Mama Laverne with ending Blade's bachelor days.

Syneda looked at him curiously before giving him a hug. "You sure it's nothing?"

He smiled at his cousin-in-law. "I'm positive."

He then gave Lorren and Caitlin hugs as well. He was still smiling when he sat back down.

He'd finally come up with an idea to outsmart his great-grandmother.

Carly had never been this nervous in her life, but there was no denying that she was nervous now. And all because of one man. Lee Madaris.

She played back everything in her mind, from their first kiss on the balcony to their second kiss in his suite. That kiss had thrown her into a world of confusion, conflicting emotions and primitive yearning. Before that night had ended she had agreed to have dinner with him.

She glanced at the clock on her wall. That dinner, which he would prepare, was to commence in a little less than four hours. She hadn't heard from Lee since the food was delivered. She could only assume nothing had changed and he had returned from Dubai today.

Carly hadn't been sure what to wear tonight. She had decided on a maxi dress, with spaghetti straps at the shoulders and a ribbed band at the waist. She liked the mix of mauve, beige and green, and her feet felt comfortable in beige-colored flats.

When her cell phone rang, she picked it up off her nightstand and smiled. It was Aunt Ruthie.

"Hello."

"You okay, Baby-Girl?"

She smiled. That had always been her aunt's nickname for her. "Aunt Ruthie, yes, I'm okay. What about you?"

"Fine. Did my grocery shopping today and ran into Harriet. Her husband had a heart attack last week and he's still in the hospital."

Unlike Carly, her aunt had tons of friends. "I don't recall Ms. Harriet, but is her husband okay?"

"Yes, he'll be okay. But he'll have to change his diet. And knowing Harriet, she'll make sure he does. How are things going in Vegas?"

Carly hadn't expected her aunt to be crazy about the idea of her moving to Las Vegas for work, but surprisingly Aunt Ruthie had been fine with it.

"Things are going great. The restaurant has been busy."

"But busy is good, right?" her aunt asked.

Carly chuckled. "Yes, busy is good."

A few minutes later, Carly ended her conversation with her aunt and warm emotions flowed through her. Her aunt had always been there for her, even when Carly's mother hadn't. Carly had given up on the hope that one day things would change. Her mother's husband was a big-time businessman with an image to keep and a family to protect…from her. The man saw her as a threat to his and his family's way of life, and until that changed, nothing else would.

Carly glanced at her watch. Since she had time, and wanted to get her mind off her nerves, she pulled up the *Miami Herald* to see what was in the news.

Lee was glad to be back in Vegas. He smiled as he tossed his luggage on the bed. Usually, he did not feel that way after returning from a business trip. But this time was different. In less than three hours he would be dining with a beautiful woman. A woman he hadn't been able to get off his mind even thousands of miles away.

Visiting with his cousins and their wives had been enjoyable, but he'd been ready to leave them to their own devices. The Grand MD Dubai had a lot to offer and they would be there for seven more days to take it all in.

Now Lee would shower and get dressed for tonight. He'd prepare dinner and make sure they had a pleasurable evening. Then he would unveil his plan, the one he had come up with to outsmart his grandmother. He grinned just thinking about it. Mama Laverne would think twice before planning another wedding for one of her great-grands.

But to make it work he had to bring Carly on board with his idea. They barely knew each other. She didn't love him, and he didn't love her. He wasn't even sure they had anything in common. However, what he did know was that he craved her. Her, and no other woman.

He stripped off his clothes as he moved toward the bathroom. His dreams had gotten hotter than ever. Several times while in Dubai he'd taken cold showers. He couldn't remember the last time he'd done that. He stepped into the shower now and a rush of warm water streamed over him. He was filled with excitement about the evening ahead.

Damn, it had been a week and he'd missed Carly. He had no idea why a woman he'd seen only twice would make such an impact on him. In the beginning, he hadn't liked her hold on him, but now she was the answer to his problem.

If she accepted his marriage proposal, she would need to understand that their marriage would be based on respect and on passion, not on love. That was good enough for him and he hoped it would be good enough for her.

Lee considered himself a pretty good businessman; he had done his homework. He had contacted Alex, who was married to Christy—Justin, Dex and Clayton's baby sister. Alex was a top-notch private investigator and a former FBI agent. Lee had given him Carly's name and that was all Alex had needed. Before leaving Dubai, Alex had electronically delivered a detailed report, which proved to be interesting reading on the eighteen-hour flight back to the States.

Carly's grandmother had died before she was born and her grandmother's only child, Gail, had been raised by Gail's aunt, Ruth Briggs, a widow. Gail got pregnant with Carly in her senior year of high school. Ruth agreed to take care of Carly while Gail went to college. There were a few recorded visits from Gail, but not many.

Lee shook his head as he stepped out of the shower to dry off. From what he'd read, Gail met a man from a prominent family while at college and she married him, conveniently not telling him she'd had a child out of wedlock.

According to the report, when Sidney Thrasher, a successful businessman in Los Angeles, discovered the truth, he didn't divorce his wife but he had no problem ostracizing her child. In fact, he demanded that Gail do the same if she wanted to save her marriage. It seemed the Thrashers' two kids knew Carly only as a distant cousin. Now Lee understood why she considered herself a loner.

He couldn't imagine a mother deserting her child that way, leaving her for someone else to raise and then turning her back on the child. That was unacceptable. It made him appreciate his family all the more. Even a great-grandmother who was determined to run his personal life.

One thing was for certain: if she said yes to his proposal, she'd become part of his big family. Carly would have no reason to feel like a loner ever again. He had his game plan, which was more or less a business strategy. He would give her all the pluses and strike down any minuses she tried to present one by one.

Beginning tonight, it was Operation Carly Briggs.

* * *

Carly heard a car door close and knew Lee had arrived. He was right on time. She drew in a deep breath as she looked out the window and watched him walk toward her front door. Was he taking stock of her yard, her neighborhood? He was probably wondering how she could afford to live here on her salary as a chef.

It wasn't that she lived in a huge house, but her community was a nice one. Some would even view it as one of the most prestigious residential areas in Las Vegas. He didn't have to know that the house was really owned by Heather and Joel and had been purchased as investment property.

Heather hadn't wanted Carly to live alone in an apartment. So she had talked Joel into buying this nice house with a yard as an investment that they leased to Carly.

Carly opened the door upon hearing his knock. Lee leaned in the doorway, bigger than life—definitely a man designed purely for feminine enjoyment.

"Hi, Carly."

"Lee." She tried not to take stock of how blatantly sexy he looked in jeans and a solid blue shirt with a jacket covering his broad shoulders. Not noticing, however, was a hard thing. And he smelled good, as if he'd just showered.

"Won't you come in," she said, stepping aside.

She watched him walk through the open doorway, thinking the snug jeans fit him too well. He was definitely an amazing specimen of a man.

"I'm sure you want to start cooking, so I'll take you to the kitchen," she said.

His gaze gripped hers like a tight fist. "You think that's what I want to do right off the bat?"

Her thoughts scattered. She could feel herself losing control. Her stomach stirred with lust. She'd never been this sexually drawn to a man before.

"Yes, that's what I would assume since you offered to

prepare dinner." She wished she wasn't so fully aware of him.

"If you'll recall, the reason I offered to prepare dinner was because I wanted to see you again. I wanted to get to know you and for you to get to know me," he said smoothly. "Since you're so distrustful of my motives, I suggest that you get to know me first."

"Is that important to you?"

Did he feel the same magnetic pull that she felt? It made breathing difficult and plagued her with the inability to break eye contact with him.

"Yes. There's a reason it's important," he said in a deep, husky voice.

"Is there, Lee?"

His gaze raked over her seductively before he surprised her by wrapping his arms around her waist.

"We'll talk about the reason later. You look nice today."

Heat streamed through her body the moment he touched her. "Thank you. You look nice as well. How was your trip?"

"We'll talk about my trip later too."

That was when he kissed her, taking her mouth with a hunger that she enjoyed to an extreme that couldn't be good for her. But she figured she would worry about that later. Right now all she wanted was to indulge.

Never had her mouth been devoured with such voracious need. Her mouth felt ravaged, raided with an urgency that had her moaning. He could stoke a fire within her so effortlessly. Was it because she'd gone without passion for so long? Passion with Nathaniel had never been like this, where her breasts ached and the area between her legs throbbed.

He shifted, intentionally sliding his jean-clad leg against her. She felt his heat through the material of her dress. She felt something else as well. His erection strained against his zipper, pressing into her and creating a slow burn at the juncture of her thighs.

Lee finally broke off the kiss and pressed his forehead against hers. Their breaths mingled. She closed her eyes briefly and when she reopened them he was staring at her. He kissed her lips again gently, before dropping his hands from her waist and taking a step back.

Drawing in a deep breath, he licked his lips, as if savoring her taste. Smiling at her, he said, “I needed that.”

Carly’s heart pounded deep in her chest. She hadn’t expected the kiss. It left her senses spinning. What she refused to admit was that she’d needed that as well.

He glanced around. “Nice place.”

“Thanks.”

“Now,” he said softly, his smile widening. “You can take me to your kitchen.”

Sitting at her breakfast bar, Carly watched Lee’s ease and confidence as he moved around her kitchen. Once she’d told him where everything was located, she’d left him alone. She hadn’t wanted him to feel she was scrutinizing his every move, so she had gone outside in the backyard for a while.

When she’d returned, he had invited her to keep him company. She had slid onto the barstool and he’d poured a glass of wine for her and one for himself before going back to the task of preparing dinner.

She had yet to ask what was on the menu. From the groceries delivered yesterday, she had a pretty good idea of what they’d be eating. Lee had asked her what she liked and now he was preparing it. That was thoughtful of him. She had to admit that he’d been pretty thoughtful since the first night they’d met, which made her wonder…

“If you have a question just ask me.”

Was he a mind reader? "What makes you think I have a question?"

He smiled. "The way your forehead bunches up. I noticed that about you."

Had he? "Well, there is something that has me puzzled."

"What is it?"

She took a sip of her wine. "Why isn't there a steady woman in your life? Why aren't you taken?"

His chuckle was low and throaty. "Should I be?"

Most men who look like you usually are. "I'd think so."

He paused in the midst of chopping the tails off the shrimps. "I could ask you the same thing. Why aren't *you* taken?"

She shrugged. "I have my reasons."

"Share them with me."

"I asked you first."

Lee chuckled again. "So you did."

He put the knife aside, leaned against the island and leisurely sipped his wine, as if giving a lot of thought to what she'd asked. "One of the main reasons is because I've been too busy for an involvement," he said finally.

"We were barely getting the Grand MD Dubai erected when the opportunity came to build here. It was a miracle that Mitch Farrell got that land on the Strip. And when he approached me and Angelo about building another hotel before the first one was completed, we jumped at the chance, even though we knew doing both would be tough."

She rested her hands under her chin. "So your busy schedule is just one of the reasons you aren't involved with anyone. What's another?"

He looked down into his glass of wine. When he lifted his head his expression was serious. "I've never met a woman that I wanted to spend a lot of my time with… whether I was busy or not. In other words, Carly, there has never been a woman I craved. Until you."

She wished his words didn't send a surge of desire rippling through her. "Crave?"

"Yes, crave. You know how you get a taste of something, and you aren't satisfied until you get some more? That's how it is with me when it comes to you. I taste you, and I want to taste you again. I lust after you. Yearn for you. Ache for you."

Carly stared at him, not believing he would admit such things. She said nothing as he put his wineglass aside and picked up the knife to finish the shrimp.

He moved around her kitchen, checking on the pasta and the bread baking in the oven. Her gaze traveled over him, appreciating the way the fabric clung to his masculine thighs. He had removed his jacket and rolled up his sleeves, displaying a powerful chest, great abs and wide shoulders. He radiated sensuality that drew her in like a magnet, powerless to resist.

He placed the shrimp in the colander and walked over to the sink to rinse them off. Glancing over his shoulder at her, he said, "You never said why you're unattached."

"I didn't?"

"No."

She shrugged. "Let's leave that discussion for another day, okay?"

He held her gaze, nodded and then said, "Okay. We'll table it, but there will be another day, Carly."

Carly had no reason to doubt him.

Chapter 5

"Well, what do you think?" he asked once they were at the dining room table.

Instead of answering, she closed her eyes and slowly licked her lips before moaning softly. "Mmm." She opened her eyes and smiled. "What does that tell you?"

It told him a lot. It showed him what she could do with her mouth. She thought she'd demonstrated how much she'd savored the food, but his lascivious mind had conjured up something else entirely. He could imagine her expressing that same satisfaction after she tasted him. He could even envision how it would leave him—so damn satisfied that his erection throbbed when he thought about it. He had to force air through his lungs to get past the images floating through his brain.

"Lee?"

He blinked. Had she been trying to get his attention? "Yes?"

"Tell me about your family."

He leaned back in his chair and picked up his wineglass to take a sip. With any other woman, he would have shut the subject down as soon as it came up, letting them know up front they were with him and not his family. The Madaris name was well-known in Texas, and there were some women who wanted to wear the name because they wanted to get their greedy hands on the wealth that came with it. Madaris men and women were successful. They'd worked hard for what they had and they were selective in a mate.

But Lee had no problem telling Carly about his family. If he had his way, she would be his mate. He thought the name Carly Briggs Madaris suited her.

Still, he wanted to know her thought process. "Why do you want to know?"

She shrugged shoulders that looked beautiful in her spaghetti-strap dress. He thought she looked downright sexy. At some point she had removed her shoes. He couldn't help but admire her feet, especially her painted toes. He held in high esteem women who pampered their feet. That meant they had no problem pampering other parts of themselves as well.

"I guess I'm fascinated. Like I told you, I came from a small family, so I imagine belonging to a large one can be wonderful."

He chuckled. "Yes, it can also be a pain in the ass. When you think you have a secret, you really don't. At times, everybody seems to be in your business. But the truth is, I wouldn't change a thing. There's no other family I'd want to belong to. Over the years, you learn who, and who not, to tell your secrets to."

He paused and then added, "The support of my family is fantastic. We have our moments, like all families do, but when it comes to us sticking together, we do it better than glue."

He saw the wistful look in her eyes and figured he would tell her a little more. "The Madaris family settled in Texas back in the eighteen hundreds, after acquiring a ten-thousand-acre Mexican land grant. Carlos Antonio Madaris, half Mexican and half African-American, along with his wife, Christina Marie, were shaping their future on land they named Whispering Pines, to raise cattle."

He recited the story that had been passed down through his family from generation to generation. It was heritage he, like every other Madaris family member, was proud of. "Whispering Pines is still in the family. It's my uncle Jake's ranch."

Carly nodded. "You mentioned you have a bunch of cousins. What about siblings?"

"Yes. I'm the oldest. My brother Kane is two years younger than me, and my other brother Jarod is two years younger than Kane."

"No sisters?"

"No sisters. Not too many females born into the Madaris family. In fact, males have dominated the family for generations."

Lee was tempted to ask about her family, just to see how much she would tell him. But earlier, in the kitchen, she'd avoided any discussion of why she wasn't in a relationship, so it stood to reason she would avoid talking about her family. It didn't really matter since he knew most of what he wanted to know from Alex's report.

"Your great-grandmother did a good job with your cooking classes. I'm impressed. Even the apple pie was delicious."

"I'm glad you enjoyed everything. It was my pleasure to show you just a little of what I can do."

She smiled. "There's more?"

"Most definitely."

Besides being attracted to her, he liked her. Over dinner she'd told him that she had worked in a restaurant in Miami before taking the pastry-chef job at the hotel. She'd told him about her best friend Heather's recent marriage and relocation to Spain and about attending culinary schools in both Boston and Paris. But he'd noted she stayed away from mentioning anything about her life in Alabama and Connecticut.

He stood. "Cleanup time," he said, gathering the dishes.

"Lee, there's no way I'll let you wash dishes on top of everything else. Besides, there's something I need to talk to you about."

He looked over at her. She had stood as well, and the fit of her dress, the way it emphasized her small waist and perky breasts, made his body harden again. He cleared his throat.

"Okay, let's sit down and talk." It was either that or continue to stand and run the risk of her seeing how aroused he'd become.

He sat back down and she did the same. "So what is it you want to discuss?"

She was nervous, he could tell. She had a tendency to gnaw her bottom lip whenever she was. "I think you might be incorrect about something."

"And what am I incorrect about?" he asked.

"That you and I can have a relationship of any kind. You own the hotel I work for. Because of that, I'm not sure it's even okay for us to be friends."

He stared at her, thinking he wasn't the one who was incorrect. She was.

"I thought we discussed this last week."

"Not fully."

"Then why am I here tonight?"

She gnawed her lip again as she said, "Because you have a very persuasive nature and I wasn't thinking straight that night."

"But now you are…thinking straight?"

"Yes. I enjoyed this evening, but I need to be realistic. Not that I'm putting myself down, mind you. But you can do better."

He doubted it. His eyes drank her up, and he saw beauty she evidently couldn't see. Over the years, had others somehow made her feel unworthy of their time and attention? Did she think it would be that way with everyone she met?

"How can I do better, Carly?"

She actually smiled when she responded. "I'm glad you asked. Before you got here I had time to spare, so I went online and checked out some of the young executives working for you. I read their bios. Several women are single."

"And?"

"I've seen a number of them out and about at the hotel. They even come into the restaurant all dressed up on occasion. They look like models, starlets, women you'd want on your arm."

Lee was tempted to tell her that he had seen her all dressed up, on her birthday, when she'd worn that pretty green dress and those killer stilettos. She had looked better than any damn model or starlet ever could. Furthermore, she would look better on his arm than any other woman ever would. He would find it amusing that she was trying to brush him off on someone else if he didn't know why she was doing it.

He held her gaze. "Still trying to play the *loner* card, are you?"

Her brows rose a little. "What do you mean?"

"I know what you're doing, trying to brush me off."

"Brush you off?" She shook her head negatively. "No, that's not it. You don't understand."

"Then explain it to me."

She shook her head again. "No, I can't. It's too complicated."

Lee inhaled deeply. She didn't know complicated. At least not yet, she didn't. He stood and saw how she watched him with wary eyes as he rounded the table toward her. "Stand up a second," he said.

She hesitated before getting out of her chair. "What?"

He came to a stop in front of her. "You want to know what's really complicated? For starters, this."

He placed his hands on the shoulders he'd been tempted to touch all evening. They were soft and smooth. In response to his touch she trembled. He trembled inside as well.

"Now, that's complicated. To know touching you can arouse me in a way I've never been aroused. You stimulate every cell in my body. To know that your reaction to my touch is not fake, not a show to impress. You, Carly Briggs, have exactly what I need."

Lee saw confusion in her features. "What is that?" she asked.

He leaned in closer to her. "Passion."

She looked stunned. "Passion?"

"Yes. It's in your taste and your scent. And it's genuine. You have more passion in your little finger than most women have in their entire bodies."

Her shoulders tensed beneath his hands. "I think you have me mixed up with someone else, Lee."

"No, I don't. You're the one. I don't want to marry for love, but I can definitely marry for passion."

She tilted her head to the side and stared at him. "What are you talking about?"

"Me. You. Getting married."

"Wha…? Married! Are you crazy?" she asked, removing his hands from her shoulders.

He shook his head. "No, you're the woman I want to marry."

Carly stared at Lee, convinced he had lost his mind. Was it the wine? Jet lag? Whatever it was, it had messed with his brain pretty bad. They'd met only a couple of weeks ago and he was contemplating marrying her?

"I can explain."

She doubted that he could.

"I know what you're thinking."

She doubted that he did.

"Will you please hear me out, Carly?"

She knew she shouldn't, but for the life of her she had to hear what he would say. "Okay, I'll hear you out."

"Let's sit in your living room," he suggested.

She sat on the sofa and he slid onto the chair across from her. "I know this all sounds crazy, but you have to know my great-grandmother," he said.

She lifted a brow. "Your great-grandmother?"

"Yes, the same one who gave me those cooking lessons. Felicia Laverne Madaris, who we call Mama Laverne, the matriarch of our family. She's ninetysomething, the oldest living Madaris. She claims she stopped aging when she turned eighty."

"Oh." Carly tried not to smile. Her aunt had said the same thing when she'd turned sixty. "She sounds feisty."

"Trust me, she is…among other things. She also likes playing matchmaker and has quite a record of success. Of her seven sons, she picked the wives for five of them,

Carly had heard enough. She stood, fury nearly choking her. "You should leave now."

He stood as well, and she could tell by his expression he was surprised by her anger. "Leave?"

"Yes. Leave. How dare you invade my privacy that way?" she said in breathless rage. "How dare you!"

"Carly, I'm sorry. I thought—"

"I don't care what you thought," she said, fighting back tears. "Leave and lock the door behind you."

Then, without saying anything else, she turned and walked quickly up the stairs.

After hearing Carly's bedroom door slam shut, Lee dropped back down in the chair.

Damn. What had he done?

He hadn't meant to hurt her. He believed honesty was the best policy, in business and in his personal life. She had a right to know he'd ordered an investigative report on her.

He wanted to go upstairs and talk to her, apologize again for his insensitivity, but she didn't want to hear anything he had to say.

In fact, she had asked him to leave.

He stood and reached for his jacket, but when he glanced across the breakfast bar into the kitchen and remembered the dishes still sitting on her dining room table, he knew he couldn't leave her place in such a mess. Tossing his jacket back across the chair, he rolled up his sleeves and got to work.

Carly had a good cry and then berated herself for allowing any man to drive her to tears again.

Nathaniel, even though she had expected compassion from him because of his profession, had ridiculed her for her failure to be the sensuous woman he wanted her to be, and now Lee had reminded her of all the things she didn't have. So what if she didn't own anything other than her car, had bills to pay and couldn't afford the land for her dream restaurant? He had intended to use her situation to make her do what he wanted her to do…which was to marry him just to prove a point to his great-grandmother.

She was glad she'd found out what he was about before she let things go too far. If she'd known kissing a man would cause all this grief she would have kept her lips to herself.

Moments later, Carly walked into the kitchen ready to clean, and gawked. It was spotless. After she'd told Lee to leave he had hung around and cleaned up? Why?

She refused to soften. It had been a considerate gesture on his part, but she was too hurt and angry to be grateful for it.

That was when she saw the sheet of paper on the breakfast bar.

Carly
I am deeply sorry and hope you forgive me for my lack of sensitivity. I will make it up to you, I promise.
Lee

She reread the note a couple of times before crumpling it up and tossing it in the trash. She didn't want him to make anything up to her. She just wanted to be left alone.

"The big man called. He wants to know what's going on with the woman who called the tip line the night you got rid of Harrison," Bracey said, staring hard at Nash.

Nash glared back. Bracey had earned the big man's confidence, something that rattled Nash like hell. He didn't give a damn that Bracey had worked with Chicago street gangs and was the liaison between the gangs and the cartel. Anytime he looked Bracey in the eye he saw greed and power. If the big man wasn't careful, Bracey would try to take over. Nash had gotten bad vibes from the man from the first.

"I told you I would handle it, so get off my back," Nash said, his voice sounding deep and raspy to his own ears. "There was no one else in the alley that night."

"But someone made that call."

"I'm aware of that, but the tapes of the calls to the tip line that night are missing."

"Missing?"

"Yes."

"How is that possible?"

"I don't know, Bracey. Maybe there's another mole."

Nash watched the deep frown form on Bracey's features. "There's not another mole."

Nash smiled. "You sure?"

Bracey's gaze darkened. "If there is, I'd be the first to know."

"You didn't know about Harrison," Nash countered.

Bracey got in Nash's face. "Only because I never came in contact with Harrison. He was one of yours."

Nash didn't like being reminded of that. "Tell the big man not to worry. I've got everything under control."

He then left the room, slamming the door behind him.

Chapter 6

"Good afternoon, Mr. Madaris. I'm glad you're joining us tonight."

"Thanks, Richard," he said to the man who managed Peyton's Place. "I believe my personal assistant spoke with you earlier."

"Yes, sir. Your table is arranged just as you requested."

"Wonderful."

Lee followed the man to his table in one of the secluded back rooms used exclusively for private dinners. When he confronted Carly later he wanted privacy.

Almost two weeks had passed since he'd prepared dinner for her. Even after his oral and written apologies, she refused to take his calls. He'd even sent flowers to her home and still no luck. More than once he'd thought about showing up on her doorstep, but he'd decided to wait it out.

Now he couldn't wait any longer—he had to see her. He thought about Carly when he woke up in the morning and when he went to bed at night. No woman had ever taken over his mind like she had. Maybe pursuing her was a mistake, but it was a mistake he had to make.

Normally, he didn't do obsession when it came to women but he had allowed Carly to interfere with every aspect of his life. More than once he had thought about ditching the marriage idea or finding someone more amenable to the plan. But he had quickly dismissed both options.

He wanted Carly.

"Your waiter will be here momentarily, sir. Please enjoy your meal."

"Thank you. I'm sure that I will."

It wasn't long after Richard had left that a waiter appeared. "Would you like a glass of wine tonight, sir?"

Lee shook his head. "No, just coffee. And please bring me your dessert menu."

The young man nodded and quickly left. Lee knew that Carly was working tonight because he had checked her schedule earlier that day. If Chef Blanchard found the inquiry strange, he hadn't let on. Drastic times called for drastic measures and he needed Carly to forgive him. For her not to do so was simply unacceptable.

The waiter returned with his coffee and the menu and left again. Lee scanned the list of delectable desserts, all of which he knew had been prepared by Carly. He eyed one item closely and when the waiter returned he said, "I think I'll try some of your Key Lime Appacula."

"Yes, sir."

As he watched the waiter leave, closing the door behind him, Lee thought about what he would say to Carly. He'd made a seriously dumb-ass blunder that night and now he needed to fix it.

"Here you are, sir." The waiter placed the dessert in front of him. "I hope you enjoy it."

"Thank you. I'm sure I will."

He did. The moment he slid the scrumptious-looking pie into his mouth he had to close his eyes in pleasure. It was so delicious his taste buds tingled. This would definitely mean more time at the gym for him this week, but seeing Carly was worth it.

Before he could finish his coffee, the server had poured him another cup. "That was delicious," Lee said when the waiter removed his plate. "I must commend the chef."

The waiter smiled. "Certainly, Mr. Madaris. I'll let Chef Blanchard know that—"

"No. Not Chef Blanchard. I want to speak directly to your pastry chef. I believe it's Chef Briggs."

"Yes, sir. I'll let her know." The man quickly walked off and pulled the door closed behind him.

Lee's chest tightened. Glancing at his watch, he wondered how long it would take Carly to come to him.

And if she had a mind not to come, then he had no reservations about going into that kitchen and getting her.

Carly had just finished frosting a cake when Mickey approached her. "You have another compliment on the Key Lime Appacula."

She smiled. "That's good to hear."

"And he wants to tell you personally how much he liked it."

Carly's stomach tightened into knots. She gripped the spatula firmer. "He?"

"Yes, the big man himself, Mr. Madaris."

Carly placed her spatula aside. She knew Lee's summons had nothing to do with her pie. She had seen the missed calls; she had gotten the flowers. She had ignored his calls and had taken the ridiculously large floral arrangement to a nursing home she passed every day on her way to work. Hopefully someone there would appreciate them more than she did.

"You can tell Mr. Madaris I'm busy."

Mickey looked at her as if she'd grown a second head. "Are you crazy? You don't tell the owner of the hotel where you work that you're too busy to accept a compliment."

Carly drew in a deep breath. No, you didn't. But if she saw him and told him what she really thought about him, she would lose her job anyway.

"Relax, I was just joking," she said, smiling, as she removed her apron. The last thing she wanted was for any of her coworkers to become suspicious about her relationship with Lee.

"He's in one of the private dining rooms. The one with the double doors."

Carly nodded as she left the kitchen. Lee was smart to keep their conversation private.

The restaurant was crowded, but no one paid attention to her as she made her way toward the back. Without bothering to knock, she opened the door, went inside and closed the door behind her. He was not sitting at the table. Instead, he stood with his back braced against the wall of windows at the back of the room.

The moment her gaze snagged his, her anger turned into awareness. Total. Absolute. Complete.

And what frustrated her even more was that she saw the same degree of awareness reflected in the dark depths of his eyes as well.

Carly struggled not to respond to him and fought for control over the flare of sensual hunger in her stomach. They stood, staring at each other. She wanted to break eye contact with him but discovered she couldn't.

She'd known when she ignored his calls that talking to him, seeing him would make her lose her ability to think logically. That was just what she'd been trying to avoid, so she turned to leave.

"Don't go, Carly. Please. Let's talk."

Talk? How could they talk when he could emit sexual vibes so easily? She turned back around to face him.

"Why are you doing this to me?" she asked softly, backing up against the closed door.

"Why are *you* doing this to *me?*" he countered, taking a couple of steps forward.

She gasped when he stepped into the light. He was aroused. Seeing his reaction to her made the juncture of her legs throb. This was crazy.

"I'm sorry I came across as insensitive the other night, Carly. I honestly am. I handled things the wrong way, and I apologize."

He took another step forward. "But I won't apologize for acknowledging the attraction between us. I want you and if you're honest with yourself you will admit to wanting me as well."

Yes, she wanted him. She would acknowledge it to herself, but never to him. She couldn't. The last man she'd opened up to had betrayed her. Nathaniel had not been who she thought he was, and he'd had the gall to smile when he told her she'd never known the real him. So now she couldn't help but wonder—who was the real Lee Madaris?

When he moved a step closer she put out her hand. "Stop. Don't you dare come near me."

"Why? What are you afraid of, Carly? I won't hurt you."

She opened her mouth to tell him that he had already hurt her. She felt exposed, her soul bared and her inner secrets revealed. He knew too much about her. Things she hadn't even told Nathaniel. The only other person who knew the full story of her life was Heather. She'd taken a chance with her college roommate, but only after Heather had come back to the dorm and found Carly crying after Sidney Thrasher's visit.

Her mother's husband had told Carly she had no place in the lives of his wife and children. It didn't matter that his wife was Carly's mother. He had instructed his wife to forget Carly was ever born.

Carly figured that wouldn't be hard to do since Gail Briggs Thrasher had forgotten years ago. But hearing him say the words had hurt, ripping her heart to pieces. It had been Heather's understanding and friendship that had pulled her through. To this day Aunt Ruthie still didn't know about Mr. Thrasher's visit. Knowing would have hurt her aunt more than it had hurt Carly.

And now Lee knew.

"Trust me not to hurt you the way others have."

She blinked. Lee was now standing directly in front of her. When had he moved?

He reached his hand out to her. She nibbled on her bottom lip. Why wasn't she telling him just what he could do with that trust? Why wasn't she storming out of the room? Why was she allowing herself to be hypnotized by his eyes?

It would be easy to get him to stop bothering her. All she had to do was threaten him with a sexual-harassment lawsuit. That would end his fascination.

But would it end hers?

All the anger she'd felt over the past few days hadn't stopped her from thinking about him, remembering every kiss they'd shared and the heat they generated. That heat was a strange phenomenon to her. Regardless of what he thought, she was not a passionate person.

Then what was she? Even she couldn't deny there was something going on between them, something so charged, so hot that she was convinced she could hear fire crackling even now. There had to be a reason she responded to him this way and to no one else.

"Who are you?" she whispered, her mind swirling in confusion.

If he found her question strange, his expression didn't show it. "I am Lee Carlos Madaris III. The man who wants you with a passion I feel in every cell of my body."

Carly fought to control the turbulent emotions warring inside of her. She was so conflicted she couldn't speak.

But a part of her didn't want to speak; she wanted to feel. And nobody had ever made her feel like Lee.

Her feet moved one step and then, suddenly, he covered the rest of the distance and pulled her into his arms.

Using his mouth, Lee drank in everything that was Carly in a kiss so explosive he thought he felt the room shake. Never had a kiss been so overwhelming; the impact of this one sent sexual excitement through his entire body. His desire was razor-sharp, and her moans made the desire even stronger.

He pressed her back against the door and lifted her by the hips. Her legs wrapped around his waist. His arousal pressed hard into her, making him hate the material of their clothes that served as barriers to naked skin. He was tempted to take her here and now.

He knew he couldn't, so he released her mouth, eased her back down on her feet and stepped away. This was not the place. He licked his tongue across her lips as they both tried to bring their breathing under control. Then he slid his key card into her hand.

"Use this to come up to my suite when you get off later."

She looked down at what he'd given her and shook her head. "I can't."

"You can," he said with a desperation he should have

despised. But he didn't. His mind hadn't been the same since the night he'd seen her from the terrace.

He reached down and picked up the toque that had fallen and tenderly placed it on her head as he held her gaze. "Please come to me later."

"I have to go." She opened the door and left.

Lee drew in a deep breath as a tiny glow of hope blazed to life inside of him. She hadn't given the key card back to him.

"Good night, Carly. Enjoy your days off."

"Good night, Jodie. I will."

Carly drew in a deep breath as she moved toward the elevator bank. When she'd returned to the kitchen after her interlude with Lee, no one seemed to have noticed how long she'd been gone. They must have assumed she'd been on break.

Some break.

She was still caught up in emotions she didn't want to feel. What she needed was to get home, take a long bath and go to bed. She had the next two days off and she would spend them getting her mind together. She might even drive into Los Angeles. The trip might do her good.

Carly stepped into the elevator and pressed the number on the keypad for the parking garage. She tried not to think of Lee's request. His nearness always made her senses go berserk and she didn't need that again tonight—or ever.

So why did she reach into her pocket, pull out the key card and scan it?

Her heart pounded as the elevator moved quickly, bypassing floor after floor. She tried to ignore the surge of excitement racing through her. This was madness. Craziness. Pure insanity. Why was she setting herself up to be hurt all over again?

The tingling sensation in the pit of her stomach answered her just as the elevator came to a stop.

You're doing it for passion.

The elevator doors opened into the living room she had visited before. She stepped out and saw Lee in the dining room, standing by the table. He'd poured two glasses of wine. Had he known she would come when she hadn't known herself?

He must have read the question in her gaze. "I was hoping. Desperately hoping."

She didn't say anything, just watched him slowly move toward her with the wineglasses. When he handed her a glass, she accepted it. Her gaze held his over the rim as they sipped their wine.

Feeling bold, she took his glass from his hand and placed it with hers on an end table. Then she proceeded to do what she'd been driven to do since the first night they'd met.

She kissed him again.

She was killing him.

Lee had wanted this. Needed this. And now it was killing him. He wrapped his arms around Carly as her tongue commandeered his, sucking on it with a hunger that made his belly whirl.

She actually thought she wasn't passionate? Then what the hell was this? She was ravishing his mouth and sending spirals of ecstasy ripping through him.

He returned her kiss aggressively and walked her backward, toward his dining room table. Then he lifted her and sat her on it. He was so full of lust he couldn't think straight. That tongue of hers had driven him over the edge and there was no going back.

He barely realized he was tearing out of his clothes, and

he didn't notice much about stripping her out of hers, but he saw the hunger in her gaze when she took in his nakedness, leaving no part of his body unseen.

When he scanned his gaze over her body, his knees weakened.

"No woman," he rasped, "has a right to be this beautiful."

He touched her knee and felt her shiver as her legs parted, exposing her to his rapacious gaze. Using his fingertips, he trailed upward from her knee, pausing briefly at her small waist before making a trek toward her breasts.

He lifted his gaze to hers and saw her sharp intake of breath when he cupped her breasts in his hands. Her nipples were dark, hard, swollen. They beckoned his mouth to put a nipple between his lips.

She quivered. She moaned his name. Her nipple became more rigid and he sucked it with gluttonous intensity. He gave her other breast the same attention and his name erupted again from deep within her throat. She tasted so damn good, but sampling her breasts would not be enough.

He released her breasts and eased his hands between her legs, finding her hot and wet. Using his fingers, he spread her labia and then targeted her clit. He stroked her, moving his fingers through her wetness as she writhed, lifting her hips off the table to press her womanly mound against his busy hand.

His fingers inched deeper inside of her. Her inner muscles clamped him and his strokes became fiercer, faster. When she flung her head back and screamed his name, he watched as her hips gyrated against his hand.

Her scent filled the room and he felt the need to taste her. When she opened her eyes, her gaze hazy from her release, he licked each of his fingers as she watched.

But that wasn't enough. He wanted more and he intended to get it. He lifted her hips and buried his head between her legs.

He was trying to kill her.

Carly was convinced of it. His tongue bristled with a vitality that electrified her entire body and sent her over the edge again. She tried fighting against it. The impact of another orgasm would take away her last breath. She caught his head and tried pushing him away. But then he did something with his tongue and waves of ecstasy crashed down on her.

She screamed his name over and over. It was as if years of pent-up need had to escape and she was helpless to do anything but let it happen.

She released deep breaths and wondered if her heartbeat would ever return to normal. She found the strength to lift her head off the table and watch as he picked up his pants off the floor and pulled out his wallet to retrieve a condom.

There was no way she would have a third orgasm tonight, but she would make sure he enjoyed one. After giving her two, he was definitely entitled. She scooted closer to the edge of the table. There was something she wanted to do before he sheathed himself.

"It's my time to taste you," she whispered softly, reaching out to take him in her hand.

Lee shook his head and moved out of range. "I won't last long, baby. I need to get inside of you now."

She watched as he sheathed himself and quickly reached for her, using his knee to spread her legs wide. He probed the entrance of her womanhood just before he thrust inside her. The moment he did, every nerve ending in her body rejuvenated itself.

She didn't have time to ponder how it could happen.

He pounded into her with a force that rocked the table. Every part of her body responded and she couldn't do anything but moan. Without missing an incredible beat, he captured her mouth and played with her tongue using the same rhythm he was using on her sex. Her body felt ready to explode.

And when it did, he exploded with her. He let go of her mouth, threw his head back and released one long, fierce growl. Then his mouth returned to hers. She arched her hips as she felt him get hit with a second orgasm, just that quick. He filled her as deep as he could go and as thoroughly as any man ever could.

Moments later, he drew in a deep breath as he tenderly stroked her cheek with the back of his hand. Was he in awe of what had happened as much as she was?

"I didn't mean for our first time to be here," he whispered softly. "But I couldn't help myself."

She understood. If anyone had told her she was capable of having three orgasms in one night she would not have believed them. "I couldn't help myself either," she whispered back. She tried to pull up off the table. "I need to go."

"No," he said, detaining her. "Please stay. I want to wake up in the morning with you in my arms."

She had never counted on words from any man's lips doing her in, but those did it. "I don't know if that's a good idea."

"Trust me, it is."

This was the second time tonight he'd asked her to trust him, and the fact that she was here meant she did. But still…

She gnawed her bottom lip. She hadn't shared a bed with any man since Nathaniel, and under no circumstances had any man ever taken her on their dining room table before. No man had ever made her come three times in a single night, much less three times in the same hour. Lee Madaris definitely had master fingers, a merciless mouth and a shaft that should be patented.

"Carly?"

Why did he have to say her name with such gentleness? She met his gaze, and heaven help her, her breathing quickened. Her eyes widened. There was no way she was getting aroused again, was there?

Just in case, she said, "Yes, I'll stay the night."

He smiled and then swept her off the table, into his arms, and headed for his bedroom.

Chapter 7

Lee woke up and squinted against the brightness of the sun shining through his bedroom window. And then he looked down at the woman still asleep in his arms.

Once he had gotten her in his bed, the need to mate with her again had taken over his senses. His appetite for her seemed insatiable. They had ended up making love again before finally drifting off to sleep.

His gaze raked over her now. He liked the look of her naked thigh thrown over his leg and the feel of her breast pressing against his arm. And his erection, hard as a rock, poked against her backside. Damn, that felt good. She probably didn't feel a thing, but he certainly did. The primitive urge to mate was escalating through him again. But he didn't want to wake her, so he lay there and remembered last night—and got harder.

He tried to think of something else. Jamal, Rasheed and Kyle had not yet gotten back with him about their decision on the Paris hotel. Today was Nolan's sister Victoria's twenty-fifth birthday. He would call her later and wish her a happy birthday. She had been the first girl born in the Madaris family in his generation, so everyone remembered her birthday and celebrated it. There would be a party in Texas. The Madaris family liked parties.

Carly shifted and Lee's attention was drawn to her face. She was as beautiful as she was sensuous. As he studied her features, her eyes slowly opened.

A small smile touched her lips. "Good morning," she whispered.

He gave her what was meant to be a kiss to curl her toes. Evidently it did because she moaned and then pushed away from him to catch her breath.

"Wow!"

He chuckled and pulled her tighter into his arms. "Hungry?"

"Why? Are you cooking breakfast?"

"No," he said, reaching for the phone.

She sat up in bed. "What are you doing?"

"Ordering room service."

She reached for the phone, took it out of his hand and hung it up. "There's another way you can feed me, you know."

"Is there?"

"Yes."

Understanding dawned when he saw the look of lust in her gaze. But just to be sure, he asked, "And which way is that?"

She giggled softly and pushed him on his back. "This way."

Moving the covers out of the way she revealed the object of her interest. "Ahh, there we are."

She took him in her hands and stroked the length of

him. He hardened even more under her touch. Then she licked her lips and he recalled seeing her do that the night he'd prepared dinner for her—and the naughty thoughts that had flowed through his mind. But he didn't dwell on the memory for long. Her moist tongue made swirly designs on his stomach, and he released a guttural groan.

"Like that?" she lifted her head to ask him.

He forced a smile through quivering lips. "I love it."

She smiled and then moved her mouth lower. He drew in a sharp breath when her tongue stroked up and down his erection, gently nibbling at the bulbous head before sliding him between her lips.

"Mercy!"

He grabbed the edge of the bedspread as her mouth went to work on him. She was brazen and her mouth was deadly. It about killed him. When he felt close to the edge he tried to pull her away but she refused to move. She locked her mouth down tight. His release was turbulent, and when it should have ended, he felt another one coming on.

Moving quickly, he slid from under her, turned her around, tilted her hips and thrust inside her from behind. The moment her hot wetness touched him, he began pounding, loving the sound of flesh beating against flesh. When she screamed his name, he came again. He came hard. His body jerked, bucked, exploded and he felt his fiery release jutting through her.

This was the one thing he typically didn't do. Come inside a woman. But he was coming inside her. Too late to stop it, so he let it rip and enjoyed the feeling.

"Oh!" Carly exclaimed. Instead of pushing him away, she arched her back, pressing against him so he could shove deeper, giving her more.

When there was nothing left to give, together they tumbled down in the bed, breathing as though they had run a marathon. Within minutes, sleep overtook them both again.

Hours later, Carly watched Lee from across the kitchen table as they ate their breakfast from room service. They'd made love so many times over the past ten hours it was simply mind-blowing. Between them, spontaneous combustion was a real thing. All it took was a look, a touch or a smell and their hormones rocketed sky-high.

"This passion thing between us. Is it normal?" she asked.

He smiled at her. "I truly don't know many cases as intense as ours." He paused. "Except for one."

She lifted a brow and took a sip of her orange juice. "Who?"

"My cousin Clayton and his wife, Syneda. They have been married close to fourteen years now and to say the heat is still on is an understatement. They are two of the most passionate people I know. It amazes everyone in our family. They have made their marriage an adventure. I've watched them sneak off from family functions just to go somewhere and get it on. To be honest with you, it doesn't surprise us anymore. It's expected."

Carly's mouth dropped open in shock. "You're kidding."

He chuckled. "I kid you not. They send signals across the room with their eyes. The next thing you know they are missing for a while. They return later with wide, cheesy grins on their faces. Rumor has it their son Caleb was conceived in a hot tub. They haven't confirmed or denied it."

Carly smiled and then asked, "Is it just passion between them as well?"

Lee shook his head. "No. They are madly in love. In

fact, I would have to say that all the marriages in my family are based on love. Even the ones my great-grandmother had a hand in. I guess she lucked out."

"In that case, maybe you should give her a chance to find a mate for you. She might surprise you."

"She might, but I can do without her surprise. Besides, I don't have time to fall in love—that's too much work. And like I told you the other night, you're the one. A part of me knew it when I saw you on the balcony. There was an instant attraction, something I really didn't think could exist until that night. Don't get me wrong, I think love is a great foundation for a marriage, but I believe passion is just as important. Two people can become the best of friends and have a great deal of respect for each other and make a marriage work. If you throw in passion to the degree that we have, it can be just as good a marriage as any based on love."

He was putting up a pretty good argument. Other than Heather and Joel, Carly had never been around a couple that she thought was truly in love. There was no doubt about the love between her best friend and her husband. All she had to do was be in the same room with them to feel it. After Nathaniel, Carly had never dreamed of having a marriage like that for herself, but she hadn't thought of sharing one based on passion either.

Ideally, she would want both—love and passion. What woman wouldn't? But she had to be realistic. Few marriages were based on true love these days. She never knew if the emotional words coming from a man's mouth were true or not. However, passion was something that was there or it wasn't. It was harder to fake.

She glanced across the table at Lee, who was reading the morning paper. There hadn't been anything fake about the past ten hours with him. She had a sore body this morning to prove it. Even taking a shower with him had proved to be innovative. So much so that she had returned to bed and gone back to sleep. The man had a way of wearing her out.

"You really think passion is just as important as love?" she asked him.

He met her gaze. "Yes, I do. It's great if a marriage can have both, Carly, but if it can't, then I'll go with passion over love. If there's love and no passion then I suspect you're going to have two miserable people. They're going to start looking elsewhere for fulfillment and risk becoming unfaithful, or they'll be tempted to engage in an open marriage. I have a college pal who's in that type of relationship."

"An open marriage?"

"Yes. His parents picked his wife and he went along with it because of the financial enticements the union would bring. They don't love each other, and there is no passion. So they agreed to have an open marriage. He has a lover and so does she. And they are perfectly fine with that arrangement."

"Oh." Carly wouldn't want that kind of marriage for herself, and from the tone of Lee's voice, neither would he.

"So there you have it. I prefer passion. Because I enjoy making love…although before last night, I hadn't made love to anyone in over a year."

A grin spread across her face. "I can believe that."

He smiled as well. "But honestly, I don't think my abstinence was even a factor, Carly. I wanted you. Bad. I see you, and I want you. I touch you, and I want you. I inhale your scent, and I want you."

He had told her that before and she hadn't believed it. After last night, she did. He wanted her now…she could tell. But she had mentioned how sore she was, and he was being considerate enough to keep his hands to himself.

They ate in silence for a few minutes before he said softly, "We need to talk about last night when I slipped and didn't use protection. That has never happened to me before."

She nodded. "That's fine. I believe the use of protection should be shared, which is why I'm on the pill…although, I haven't slept with anyone since Nathaniel, three years ago. And I'm safe in the health department. Because I work around food I'm required to keep my health card in check. It's on file if—"

"That's not necessary, Carly. And just so you know, I'm in good health as well. I have routine physicals."

She nodded and took another sip of her orange juice. There was no way she would tell him that she liked the feel of him coming inside of her. It was the first time any man had done that and it had sent intense pleasure skittering up her spine.

"The other thing we need to talk about is what happened that night at your place."

Carly shook her head, preferring not to discuss it. "No, we don't."

"I think we should."

She drew in a deep breath and stood to lean against the counter. "Fine. Let's talk."

She saw Lee's gaze roam over her. While she'd slept, not only had he ordered breakfast from room service, but he'd also called one of the hotel's boutiques to deliver her some clothes as well. He'd given the salesperson her approximate size and Carly wasn't surprised that the dress was green since he'd said he loved that color on her. The woman had delivered a gift bag with panties, a bra and a pretty lemon-lime sundress. Everything fit her perfectly.

She had been touched by his thoughtfulness and, not caring what the salesperson might have thought about his purchase, Carly had thanked him in what she hoped was the most delicious way he'd ever known.

She saw him swallow as his gaze returned to her eyes. "Besides the passion, Carly, the other reason I want to marry you is because I admire you."

"You admire me?"

"Yes."

"Why?"

"Even with all you had to endure in your life, you proved to be a survivor. You worked your way through college, refusing to accept money from your aunt. Instead, you took out student loans that you're still paying for. Even with all that, you still have your dreams. That restaurant you want to own is one of them. Being a survivor is a strong, admirable trait, and it's one I'd love to pass on to my child…the one I hope to have one day with you."

Carly returned to her seat. It was either that or fall flat on her face. No one had ever given her that kind of compliment before. To say she was admirable was the most overwhelming thing anyone had ever said to her. For the first time in her life, her troubled spirits were soothed.

"Thank you."

Lee shook his head. "Don't thank me. I should thank *you* for proving there are some women out there with something more than class and sophistication."

She swallowed. "What's that?"

"Integrity." He paused. "You thought whatever was in that report I ordered was damaging, that it painted you in a bad light. It was quite the opposite. You didn't do anything wrong, but wrongs were done to you by your mother and stepfather. In the end, you were the bigger person. You were the better person."

"There's a lot about my relationship with them that you don't know," she said softly.

"I know all I need to. It was their choice not to include you in their lives."

She didn't say anything for a minute. "I remember the day I heard Gail make the decision that Mr. Thrasher wanted her to make. She tried explaining to Aunt Ruthie that this was her chance to live a life she'd only dreamed about. She said I would be fine. Years later, I figured she must have changed her mind. She would want to see me. I'd heard she'd had other children and just knew she would want them to know me."

She took another sip of her orange juice. "I waited until I left for college and my first year there I wrote to her. She never wrote back. Mr. Thrasher showed up one day at my school instead. He told me, in no uncertain terms, never to bother him or his family again. He said if I did, I would be sorry. I took him at his word and never did."

She nervously bit her bottom lip, remembering that day. It had taken her a long time to forget it.

"That report didn't tell you everything," she added. "It didn't tell you about Nathaniel."

"No, and if you don't want to tell me about him that's fine."

"It doesn't matter. You proved him wrong last night and this morning. He said I was unfeeling, a woman with no passion, which was why he had an affair. When I got upset about his cheating, he told me to get over it. He said I should be grateful that I had a man. Even a cheating one."

A muscle ticked angrily in Lee's jaw. "Those are strong words, especially coming from a minister. I'm glad you didn't buy into what he said. As you can see, as far as you being unfeeling and dispassionate, he didn't know what the hell he was talking about.

"My marriage proposal is still on the table, Carly. I need someone like you. I won't lie and say there will be love between us. There isn't, and there may never be. However, I do know there will be friendship, honesty and respect. And, most importantly, there will be passion. Only you can decide if that will be enough for you for the long haul."

He reached for her hand. "And keep in mind too you will belong to a family. The Madaris family. You'll never be a loner again."

He was offering her the one thing she'd always wanted: to belong.

"What I need, Carly, is a life partner. Someone who will be by my side, in my bed. But I'm being honest about not looking for love. I don't want you to enter into a relationship with me wearing rose-colored glasses. Those on the outside will see our marriage as one made in heaven. They will assume we have it all, especially the love. But we will know the truth."

Carly drew in a long and deep breath. "I'm going to have to think about what you're proposing, Lee."

"And you should. I've made up my mind. It's what I want to do. At first it was to best my grandmother, but now it's because I want you in my life. No other woman will do."

Carly tried not to get choked up over his words. He had spoken them with such meaning and conviction.

"You're off work for the next two days. What are your plans?"

She glanced at the clock on the microwave. It was past noon. "Today is laundry and cleaning day. Tomorrow I plan to drive into Los Angeles. There's a restaurant there I want to check out. I want to study the setup and layout and get some ideas of my own."

He nodded. "I'm taking some time off tomorrow. Mind if I tag along?"

She arched a brow, surprised. "You would want to?"

He chuckled. "Yes. I think it will be fun."

Carly smiled. She thought it would be fun too.

Alex Maxwell stared across his desk at Preston Gause and Wilbur Woodman. Both were former colleagues of his, agents for the FBI. The three had started as agents around the same time. Alex had left the bureau years ago to form his own private investigative firm, but the other two remained. Preston was now the director for the domestic-terrorism division, and Wilbur was the director of the bureau's Unsolved Crime Cases unit. Both worked closely with Homeland Security.

He had been surprised earlier in the week when the two had called and requested a meeting with him.

Alex leaned back in his chair. "Now that all the pleasantries are out of the way and family pictures passed around," he said, "which one of you wants to tell me what this meeting is about?"

Preston smiled. "Sharp as ever I see, Maxwell."

Alex shook his head. "Sharp has nothing to do with it. When two of the bureau's top men pay me a visit, I can't help but be curious."

Wilbur nodded. He wasn't smiling as he leaned forward in his chair. "We have a serious problem, Alex."

Alex knew the "we" meant the bureau as a whole. "And what is the problem?"

"Organized crime is on the rise, and I mean to unparalleled proportions."

Alex had heard that. "Any leads as to where?"

"All over the place," Preston answered. "When we think we have a handle at one end, something new develops at another. Right now we're concentrating on illegal gambling. We believe it's headed back to Vegas."

Alex chuckled. "Did it ever leave?"

Neither man responded because they all knew the truth. Organized crime had been present in Vegas since the forties. Progress had been made and it definitely wasn't as prevalent as it used to be, but still...organized crime was organized crime.

"It's become more sophisticated," Wilbur said.

"And more ruthless," Preston added. "There's this one group, the East Coast Connection. We would like to shut them down because we also believe they are linked to street gangs."

Alex raised a brow. "Street gangs?"

"Yes. The Connection supplies funds to keep their bloody wars going."

"Why?" Alex asked.

"Their rationale is that if we have a reason to concentrate on the street gangs, that's less time we have to keep on top of what they're doing," Preston said in disgust.

Alex rubbed his chin in thought. What they were saying bothered him. In his free time, he counseled a group of teens, all of whom were former gang members. Some of the things they'd been asked to do as part of the initiation process had sent chills down his spine.

"I'm troubled by all this, but I don't see how I'm connected."

Preston opened his briefcase and placed a folder on Alex's desk. "We have reason to believe that a hotel in Vegas that's owned by your cousin-in-law, Lee Madaris, is being targeted."

Alex shrugged. "Lee's as honest as the day is long. He won't go along with them."

"We figured as much, but it won't matter. We're talking

a visit, right?" His cousins had planned to visit Vegas over Thanksgiving weekend.

"Yes, we're still coming. We all need a break from work."

Nolan was president and CEO of Madaris Electronic Corporation and he'd worked hard over the past two years to make MEC a very successful company. MEC, along with Chenault Electronics—a firm owned by family friend Nicholas Chenault—had designed and installed the majority of the computer and electronic software used at the Grand MD hotels.

After ending his call with Nolan, Lee went into his bedroom to dress for today, eager to see Carly again. She had slept in his bed for one night, yet he had found sleeping in it lonely without her last night. Housekeeping had been into his suite to tidy up the place and change the bed linens, but he was convinced he could still pick up Carly's scent in his bedcovers.

He vividly recalled how his hands had skimmed over her entire body, how many times he had kissed her, made love to her, made her moan. Each one had fired something deep within him and made him want her that much more.

Lee could only shake his head. Never had he felt such deep, all-consuming lust for anyone. In all his years since reaching puberty, he'd never imagined he would desire any woman this much. That desire, which fueled their passion, was what would keep their marriage going.

Today, during their trip to L.A., they would talk. He was determined that when he went home in December, she would accompany him as his bride.

He couldn't wait to see the look on his great-grandmother's face when he hit her with the news that he'd selected a bride without her help.

He couldn't wait.

* * *

"He asked you to marry him?"

Carly drew her legs up, placing her feet on the sofa while talking with Heather. She had told her best friend about everything, even the night she'd spent at Lee's suite. Reliving those moments had sent emotions cascading through her.

"Yes, but not for love."

"I understand."

Carly raised one eyebrow. "If you do, then explain things to me."

Heather chuckled softly. "First of all, physical attraction can be powerful. I remember the first time I saw Joel. The attraction was so strong I couldn't move. I don't think it was love at first sight for us, Carly. The attraction was physical at first."

Carly saw where Heather was going with this and decided to put on the brakes. "It's not going to turn into anything more. All Lee wants is a marriage based on passion. He's not interested in love."

"Who's to say there never will be love?" Heather asked. "Friendships can turn into love, so I see no reason why passion can't as well."

Carly saw a reason. If the two people were dead set against it, as she and Lee were. She wasn't sure about Lee, but she'd had her chance at love. She had bombed out and had no desire to try it again. If they married she knew what to expect, and so did he.

"I agree with what he said—marrying him will have its perks," Heather said. "You'll get the land for your restaurant for one and you'll belong to someone, Carly. From what you've told me about him, he doesn't sound like the type of man who'll broadcast the reason the two of you married. So it won't be anyone's business. With that much passion between the two of you, you don't have to worry about him getting into other women's panties."

Carly smiled. "I still don't know, Heather. You're talking about the rest of my life. There's still a lot about him that I don't know. What if he's not what he seems to be?"

"Then get a divorce. But personally I think it's a risk worth taking. While we were talking, I looked him up. His bio is pretty darn impressive. Harvard grad with an MBA. And he ran his family's charity, the Madaris Foundation, for a few years before resigning to partner with DeAngelo Di Meglio to build hotels.

"The first one was in Dubai, and the one in Vegas is the second. He stated in an interview with *Young Executives* magazine that he wants a total of six. I know there's a bad penny in every bunch, but still. You've known him for a few weeks now, and the two of you even dined together at your place. Have there been any red flags to make you think he's not what he seems to be?"

Carly shook her head. "No, but after Nathaniel, I don't believe I'm the best judge of anyone's character."

"Forget Nathaniel. He was a minister, for heaven's sake. Most people would have felt they could trust him. And this is different. You thought you loved Nathaniel. You don't have any illusions about this marriage to Lee."

Nathaniel had come across as a man who cared for everyone he met, a man with a belief in doing what was right.

She had been a volunteer at an agency he ran to feed and clothe the needy. She'd given her time as one of the cooks in the kitchen and enjoyed doing so. They'd met when he came through one day to thank the volunteers, and he'd invited her to lunch. They began dating exclusively not long after that and continued to do so for a full year. He had been an associate minister, with dreams of one day pastoring his own megachurch with her by his side. Then he began breaking their dates or not showing up. One night, she and Heather were supposed to have been out of town visiting Heather's family and Carly decided not to go. Instead, she had dropped by his apartment unexpectedly and found him there with another woman.

Finding out he wasn't who he'd claimed to be had hit her hard. She wasn't sure she'd fully recovered. She didn't love him anymore—she was sure of that—but his betrayal left her feeling that she couldn't trust as easily.

But it had been three years. Was she willing to let what Nathaniel had done keep her from seeking out relationships? Even those just based on passion?

"There's a lot I have to think about."

"And you should," Heather said. "I just don't want you to deny what could be a chance at real happiness. A chance to never be a loner again."

Carly nibbled her bottom lip, remembering Lee had said that very thing. He was smooth. He had known all the right things to say, as if the lovemaking hadn't been enough. She still couldn't believe all the things Lee had made her feel, all the passion he had pulled out of her. She'd had more orgasms in a single night than she'd had in all her years of having sex.

"So what are your plans for today?" Heather asked her.

"I'm going to L.A. to check out that restaurant I told you about. Lee wants to go with me."

"Um, sounds like he wants to spend quality time with you outside of the bedroom. That means he wants to get to know you more than just on a physical level. That's good."

Carly wasn't sure it was good or not, but she was willing to take things one day at a time.

Lee glanced up from his menu and met Carly's gaze. Neither said anything and neither broke eye contact. Her eyes told him everything, even things she probably didn't want him to know.

Heat flowed between them, hot and heavy. If they weren't in a public place…

The hours-long drive from Vegas to L.A. had been bad enough, but it seemed the sexual magnetism between them was stronger than ever today. He was a goner the minute she opened the door wearing jeans and a cute yellow top. The jeans highlighted a slim waist that flared into curvy hips, while her blouse displayed her femininity and her firm, high breasts, which he enjoyed touching, licking, sucking, devouring…

He shifted in his seat to relieve the pressure of his erection pressing against his zipper. They had decided to sit outside on the restaurant's patio. The day was somewhat breezy, and windblown hair fell around her shoulders. Her glazed lips looked ready to be kissed. As always, she looked stunningly beautiful.

Most couples, when they genuinely wanted to get to know each other, would take the sexual element out of their relationship so they could build one on something other than the physical. But in his and Carly's case, the physical dominated everything. It was what their relationship would be built on.

The dark pupils of the eyes staring back at him flickered with a need he read pretty well. In response, his gaze relayed a silent message of what to expect later. If she really were reading his thoughts, she knew he intended to make the other night appear insignificant in comparison. When she broke eye contact, grabbed her glass of iced tea and took a huge sip, he knew she had done a pretty good job of figuring things out.

"It's only going to get worse as time goes on," Lee said, watching her wrap her mouth around the straw and recalling exactly how that same mouth had wrapped around his jutting erection a couple of nights ago.

"There's no way it can get worse."

The smile that touched his lips held intimate promise. "I have a feeling that it will, Carly. At this very minute I want you more than I did all those other times."

She nibbled her bottom lip again. "Surely, this can't be normal."

A shiver surged through his veins as a memory took over his mind—of him fully embedded inside of her. "Evidently for us it is."

He still found it amazing that he could desire any woman this much. The longing was wickedly tantalizing. He couldn't control his desires. His urges. His cravings. Never would he look at Clayton and Syneda as strange again. Now he understood.

Deciding that conversation might help them temporarily forget their heated lust, he said, "Now tell me again why you wanted to come to this place."

A smile touched the corners of her mouth. "It's called checking out your competition. You can't convince me you didn't do it before building your hotels."

He had. He had spent the night in more hotels than he cared to count while documenting what he liked and what he didn't like about each one. "Yes. So that's what you're doing?"

"Basically. Fannie's reputation has grown from a little mom-and-pop café to a restaurant with a stellar reputation. I understand you can't come to L.A. without eating at Fannie's for at least one meal. And their desserts are rumored to be to die for."

He shrugged. "I can't imagine them being better than yours."

Her smile widened and his groin jolted from the impact. He'd been telling the truth, but now he planned to give her plenty more compliments just to see that smile.

"Thanks, Lee. You say some of the nicest things. Sometimes I wonder..."

"You wonder what, Carly?"

"Are you too good to be true?"

Her words could have only one meaning. She still didn't fully trust him or trust herself with him. "What if I told you I was wondering the same thing about you?"

Surprise flickered across her face. "You've got to be kidding."

"Why would I kid you? A serious involvement with a woman was the last thing I was looking for when I met you. I'm an extremely busy man trying to run two hotels and pushing hard to open a third. Now not only have I met a woman I desire, but one who I also enjoy being with, talking to and whose morals I admire."

"What do you think you know about my morals?"

He chuckled. "It's obvious you're not a gold digger. You're not turned off by hard work. And you don't mind giving to others. I know a couple of times a week you help out in the kitchens of various homeless shelters in Vegas, and I understand from Chef Blanchard that it was your idea to donate the hotel's leftover food to feed the needy."

Lee knew it had gone even further than that. When she'd lived in Miami she and a few others had been instrumental in establishing a clearinghouse whose purpose was to connect restaurants and caterers with the various organizations that could distribute leftover food to those who needed it. And he also knew she'd met Nathaniel Knox through her charity work.

She set her chin in a defiant line. "I didn't do it for recognition or for show."

"I didn't say you did. In fact, I believed you didn't. The more I find out about you, the more I like you. And I hope the feeling is mutual."

Carly knew she would be lying if she said it wasn't. She enjoyed being here with him. When she'd opened the door for him earlier that day she'd been speechless. She had seen him in jeans, but there was something about seeing him in a pair with a white shirt, a brass belt buckle, a Stetson on his head and boots on his feet. The words *tall, dark* and *handsome* fit perfectly. You could take the man out of Texas but you couldn't take Texas out of the man.

Even in a crowded restaurant his presence was compelling. When they'd walked in, women had strained to stare at him. Carly had seen glimpses of envy in some of their eyes. She'd wondered if he was aware of the effect he had on women. He certainly knew what effect he had on her.

Because the place was packed for lunch the waiter had suggested they sit on the patio. It was a nice day with beautiful October weather. From where they were sitting, she could see the Hollywood sign, but even that landmark didn't hold a light to Lee Madaris.

When their gazes had locked, too potent with desire to break away, she had felt totally at his mercy. She would not have deprived him of anything he'd asked for. Oh, God. How could any one man have such an impact on any woman's senses?

"Tell me about your aunt."

His request broke into her thoughts, making her smile. "Aunt Ruthie is my heart. She wanted me when no one else did."

He cast an unfathomable look at her. Immediately, she wished she hadn't said what she had. She wasn't trying to solicit pity. "I shouldn't have said that. Sorry."

"Why are you apologizing for the way you feel about something? You have nothing to be sorry for."

She knew he was right, so she continued. "My mom had me when she was a senior in high school. My aunt didn't want her to toss away her dream of going to college, so my aunt kept me while Mom…I mean Gail…was away at school, and during the summers when she came home, I was supposed to be her responsibility."

She didn't say anything for a minute. "I understand things worked out fine that first year, but the second year Gail made excuses about why she couldn't come home. She said she'd gotten a job over the summer but she never sent home any money. She did come home for Christmas, but only for a day. And then she stopped coming at all. She didn't even call to see how I was doing."

Carly took a sip of her water, wondering why she was telling him this, stuff she'd told only Heather.

"When did you see her again?" Lee asked softly.

She could remember that day distinctively. "I was five and she came home to ask Aunt Ruthie, to beg her actually, not to come to Boston for her college graduation. She explained that she had met someone and it was serious and that she didn't want him to know about me. The guy was from a well-off family and he could give her things she'd never had. I remember Gail and Aunt Ruthie arguing, and I felt sad that it was about me. My own mother was saying she didn't want me. Even at five, I understood."

Lee reached out and she felt his warm hand cover hers. "Then I truly hope that at twenty-eight you understand that I *do* want you, Carly. I want to marry you, make a beautiful home for us and give you children who will want you as well."

Carly broke eye contact with him; she had to look away or else he would see the longing and vulnerability in her gaze. What he was offering was something she had always wanted. A sense of belonging. It was a horrible feeling not to be wanted.

He felt this way now because they were intensely attracted to each other. But what if…?

She looked back at him to find him still watching her. "What if it stops, Lee?" she asked, speaking her doubts aloud. "What if the passion fizzles or goes away? What if—"

"It won't. I feel strongly about that."

"But what if it does?" she countered.

"Then we'll deal with it."

She shook her head, not satisfied with his answer. "How would you deal with no longer wanting me? Will you suggest taking a lover like your friend? Will you betray me? Ask for a divorce to marry someone else who'll have more passion than I do?"

She watched his brows draw together in an angry frown. His hand tightened firmly on hers. "You're getting worked up over things that won't happen. You're going to have to trust me."

She drew in a deep breath. There was that word again. *Trust.* More than once he'd asked her to trust him and, God help her, more than anything she wanted to.

Carly decided to let the subject go when the waiter returned with their food.

"At last. I finally met a woman who's not afraid to ride on a roller coaster," Lee said, laughing, taking Carly's hand in his as they walked along the Santa Monica Pier. "In fact, I'm beginning to wonder about you."

Carly chuckled. "Just because I don't mind taking a risk doesn't make me strange."

He released her hand and placed his arm around her shoulders. He brought her closer to his side as they walked toward his parked car. Today had truly been special. After leaving Fannie's they'd driven around L.A. and taken in the sights. This was her first visit to L.A. since moving to Vegas and he'd wanted her to see as much as she could.

He'd promised they could plan another day to drive up to Malibu. A Madaris family friend—movie actor and director Sterling Hamilton—and his wife, Colby, lived there with their two kids. Sterling was one of his uncle Jake's closest friends and the one credited with bringing Jake and Diamond together.

"There's too much to see and do here," Carly said when he opened the car door for her.

"Like I said, we'll be back." And he meant it. If nothing else, today had shown him that he needed to get out of the hotel for fun and relaxation every once in a while, especially when it meant spending time with such a pretty woman.

"Did you enjoy brunch at Fannie's? You didn't say?"

He smiled at Carly when he slid into his seat. "Didn't I? If I didn't it's because I was more into you than I was into my meal."

She laughed. "You, Lee Madaris, have more lines than any man I know."

He gave her an innocent look. "I'm serious. But since you ask, the food was good and the dessert was delicious. But I said it once and I'll say it again—it wasn't as good as yours. I'm convinced the Grand MD employs the best pastry chef anywhere. We're lucky to have you. Why did you decide to leave Miami? South Beach is a beautiful place."

Carly hesitated, wondering if she should tell him everything. She hadn't mentioned that for a long time she'd been convinced she'd heard a murder. Deciding she didn't want him to think she was someone who often gave in to weird dreams, she said, "The pay at the Grand MD was better. Besides, my best friend and roommate, the one who talked me into moving from Connecticut to Miami with her, got married and moved to Spain. I decided that I wanted a new beginning somewhere else as well."

Lee started the car and pulled out of the parking space. "Tell me about your life after high school."

She had been looking out the window at all the people enjoying the pier and the beautiful blue waters of the Pacific Ocean, but now she swung her head around to look at him. "Why? Wasn't your investigator's report detailed enough?"

It still bothered her that he'd done that. Now he knew more about her than she did about him. But he *had* apologized, so she would let it go for now. However, she intended to ask him a lot of questions later.

"I want to hear you tell me" was his reply.

She didn't say anything for a moment. "My aunt was a professional cook and I enjoyed working with her in the kitchen. I knew I wanted to be a cook as well. Since desserts were my favorite, I wanted to be the person to prepare the final dish of the evening, the dish everyone would remember, the one that would tantalize their taste buds."

She paused. "I attended college in Birmingham and lived with Heather in the dorm. I won a local cooking contest and the prize was a chance to attend one of the top cooking schools in Paris for two years. I wasn't going to go but Aunt Ruthie convinced me that I should. In the end, I'm glad I went. It was such a rewarding experience. And it helped me get a spot at a cooking school in Boston and then a good job at a restaurant in Connecticut after that."

"And that's where you met Knox?"

"Yes." She had told him enough about herself; it was his turn. "Now tell me about you."

He talked and she listened. He'd already told her about his siblings, parents and great-grandmother, but he elaborated about the close relationships he had with all of his cousins, four in particular. He told her about his three older cousins, Justin, Dex and Clayton, and what great role models they'd been. He talked about his uncle Jake and the Whispering Pines Ranch and how he'd spent his summers there.

Carly could see that the Madaris family was a big one and a very close-knit one as well. She was beginning to feel a little uneasy about coming into a family such as his.

"Your great-grandmother?"

Lee glanced over at her as he smoothly moved his

sports car down the highway as they headed back to Vegas. "What about her?"

"You said she has someone already picked out for you to marry. How will she feel about you marrying me instead?"

He chuckled. "It doesn't matter to her who I marry as long as the deed is done. So please don't think she'll be upset about our marriage. Mama Laverne intends to marry off all of us before, as she puts it, she closes her eyes and takes her last breath. We've been hearing that for over twenty years now. The old gal isn't going anywhere anytime soon. She has more than ten other great-grands to help with the marriage plunge and my cousin Nolan is next. Already he's running scared."

Carly had to hide her smile. "What she's doing is funny in a way and kind of sweet. She just wants her legacy to go on."

"And it will. To arrest what I think might be your fears, my great-grandmother, my parents, siblings and numerous cousins will like you. We're a big happy bunch and we welcome new family members with open arms."

She thought about his words and knew there were families who did do that. Heather's was one of them. Her best friend had invited her home one year during spring break. Just remembering the love they'd shown her still gave her goose bumps.

"So will you marry me?" Lee's deep-timbred voice cut into the momentary silence.

Every muscle in her body tensed when she looked at him. Traffic was at a standstill and his gaze told her that his proposal was real. But she needed more time to think about his offer and what it entailed. "I'm not ready to give you an answer yet."

He nodded. "Okay, but fair warning. I plan to wear out your resistance, and if that means seducing you into saying yes, then I have no problem doing that."

Carly didn't say anything. Instead, she leaned back against the car seat as the two of them slipped into comfortable silence. She knew Lee meant what he said, but it still seemed unreal that someone like Lee could want her. That someone like him could understand her, especially her fears.

"I've got an idea," Lee said.

She glanced over at him, almost too afraid to ask. "What?"

"Go dancing with me tonight."

"Dancing?"

"Yes. There's a club—"

"Not on the Strip."

"No, not on the Strip."

He must have heard the panic in her voice. Although he might not agree with her way of thinking, he knew she wasn't ready to be seen out in public with him yet.

"It's a place not far from here. You can rest up and I'll come pick you up around seven."

The warmth of his voice touched her. "Will you have me back home by midnight?"

"Not if I really don't have to."

She bit her lips to hold back a grin. "I do have to work tomorrow."

"But not until tomorrow night, right?"

"Yes."

"Then you can't use that as an excuse. So will you go dancing with me?"

She was discovering that Lee was a man it was hard to say no to. "Yes, I'll go dancing with you."

Chapter 9

Walking Carly to her door and not asking to join her inside was one of the hardest things Lee had ever done.

Strolling off the elevator into his suite, he thought about how much he'd enjoyed today and how much he was looking forward to tonight. He'd made the necessary calls on his way back to the hotel and the evening had been planned. He had given her fair warning. They would go dancing for the first part of the evening and then later…

Lee was jerked out of his thoughts at the sound of his phone. He pulled it out of his jacket and smiled as he clicked it on. "Alex, what's going on? I understand congratulations are in order for you and Christy *again.*"

"Yes, Christy's pregnant," Alex said, and Lee could hear the joy in his words. "The doctor says she'll deliver sometime in the spring."

"I'm happy for you two. I'm sure Uncle Jonathan and Aunt Marilyn are happy to become grandparents again."

"Yes, I'm sure they are. Look, I don't want to take up a lot of your time, but I need to fly out to Vegas and talk to you about something. And it would be good if Angelo could be there too."

Lee lifted a brow. "Sounds important."

"It is. How about I fly in two weeks from now, on a Monday? I would do it sooner but I need to finalize this case I'm working on."

Lee flipped screens on his phone to show his calendar. "Two Mondays from now is good and it just so happens that Angelo will be flying in on the Saturday before. Let me know what works best for you, morning or evening."

"Let's schedule it for that morning. That way I can fly right back to Texas after the meeting. There will be two gentlemen with me, and I think you need to hear what they have to say."

Lee lifted a brow again. "Okay. Give Christy and the kids my love."

"I will. Take care, Lee."

"You do the same."

Lee hung up. What could this meeting with Alex be about? And who were the men that would be coming with him?

After stepping out of the shower and drying off, Carly applied lotion all over her body, loving the feel of it on her skin. But not as much as she enjoyed the feel of Lee's hands on her, she thought as shivers of anticipation spread through her.

She drew in a deep breath as her mind relived the time she'd spent in his arms two nights ago. She remembered all he'd done, and everything she had done. Never in her wildest dreams had she thought she could behave in such a way with a man. She had been bold, provocative and wild. How he managed to get her to such a point was still a mystery to her.

And she knew without a doubt more of the same was in store for her tonight. She was ready. The dress she would be wearing was one she had bought on a shopping spree in New York last year. It was multiprint with a high-low hem, a flirty V-neck and ruffles at both the empire waist and hem. It was the perfect dress to go dancing in…and an easy dress to slip out of later.

She went completely still at how easily that naughty thought had entered her mind. And this from a woman who had always considered herself a prude.

Why did she crave things from him that she had never even thought about with other men? And why did she feel as if she was experiencing real lovemaking for the first time in her life when she slept with him?

She had never been this hot and ready for Nathaniel, so maybe he'd been right about her all along…at least as far as their relationship was concerned. Because of Nathaniel's profession, she'd thought a man like him wouldn't want a woman who was too loose in the bedroom. But she had a feeling that even if he'd wanted her to be loose, she would not have been. For one thing, he had never brought out her passionate side.

So if she was this passionate being that Lee painted her to be, it was because Lee had the ability to bring it out of her. Something no other man had been capable of doing.

She had just finished dabbing perfume behind her ears when her cell phone rang. She picked it up, checked caller ID and frowned. Nathaniel? Speak of the devil or, considering his profession, the pretended saint.

Why was he calling her when he hadn't done so in the three years since they had broken up?

Deciding to see what he could possibly want after all this time, she answered. "Hello."

"Carly? This is Nathaniel. I'm in Miami, and I'd love to see you."

"Why?"

"Why?" he repeated as if there was an echo.

"Yes, why? If I recall, we broke up three years ago and I haven't spoken to you since then."

"For old times' sake. I'm here for a convention."

Carly frowned. "I have no reason to see you. Besides, I'm no longer living in Miami. I live in Vegas now."

"Vegas? Not that sinful, unholy city. A place where prostitution is legal," he said in a shocked tone.

Carly's anger rose. Even her aunt, who was deeply rooted in her religion, hadn't criticized where Carly lived.

"The only sinful, unholy thing I know about, Nathaniel, is not a place but a person. You. You are nothing more than a hypocrite. You had no problem sleeping with me before marriage and promising your love to me while you were screwing someone else. You should take a look in the mirror because you definitely aren't who you claim to be. Now I suggest you delete my number from your contact list. Goodbye."

She drew in a deep breath after hanging up the phone. She refused to let Nathaniel ruin what she hoped would be a wonderful evening with Lee. In a way, she felt good about what she'd just said. Nathaniel was a part of her past. Now she wanted to get ready for the man who'd asked her to be a part of his future.

"I'm ready."

The moment Carly opened the door blood shot through Lee's veins. He was certain his heart missed a beat. He stood in her doorway, letting his gaze roam up and down her outfit several times before locking on her eyes.

"I'm ready as well."

He meant it. If the purpose of her outfit had been to spike his libido, then she had succeeded. Not that it needed much spiking around her.

She stepped out on her porch and locked the door behind her. Taking her hand in his, he immediately felt what was becoming quite common between them: a passion so arousing his knees almost buckled while leading her over to his car.

"I meant to tell you earlier today how much I like your car," she said when he opened the door for her.

"Thanks. I'm glad you do," he said of the sporty candy-apple-red Lexus two-seater.

"Got many speeding tickets?" she asked.

Lee watched how easily she'd slid into his leather interior, thinking her body was made for his ride. He met her gaze and smiled. "I'll never tell."

Going around the front of the car, he studied her through the windshield. Yes, she belonged in his car.

"Why did you do that?" she asked when he opened the driver's door and got inside, buckling his seat belt.

"What?"

"Stop and look at me."

He had no reason not to be honest with her. "I like the way you look in my car."

"Oh."

"And I like the way you look in that dress. But then you always look beautiful," he added.

"Thanks. Why are you always doing that?"

He lifted a brow as he started the ignition. "Doing what?"

"Giving me compliments."

"You deserve them."

"Thank you."

He couldn't help but wonder if Knox had been stingy with his compliments. If so, then he'd never deserved her love. But Lee had pretty much made that decision when she'd said the man betrayed her.

Lee wanted to let the car's top down to see her hair flying in the wind but decided she might not appreciate it. She had it styled perfectly around her face. When she had opened her front door, he'd thought she looked like an enchantress.

"So where are we going?"

They had come to a traffic light. He looked over at her, at her lips glazed with gloss and then her eyes. "Dancing."

She smiled. "I know that, but where?"

He returned her smile. "It's a surprise. So for now, just relax and enjoy the ride."

He would try to do the same, but he wasn't sure how relaxed he could get. Certain parts of him were begging him to turn the car around and head back to her place, and he was finding it hard not to do so. He hadn't realized just how abundant his sexual needs were until he'd met her.

He made a turn into the entrance of the airport. "Why are we here?" she asked.

He smiled over at her. "This is my surprise. I'm taking you away tonight on a short trip."

"B-but I go to work tomorrow. I didn't pack anything. I didn't—"

"It's okay," he said softly, interrupting her nervous exchange. "We'll be back later tonight. I promise. Trust me."

Carly drew in a deep, slow breath. Her gaze held his and it was then that she noticed he had brought the car to a stop in front of a beautiful silver-and-blue jetliner.

"This is my company's plane and I'm taking you dancing in Phoenix, an hour flight from here. I've made arrangements at a club there and they are expecting us."

Carly moved her gaze from Lee to look back at the jetliner. She'd never dated a man who had such a luxury. To be whisked away to another city just for a night of dancing was simply unheard of for her. "You didn't have to do all this, Lee."

The way the corners of his lips curved when he smiled at her sent sensuous shivers up her spine. "No, but I wanted to. And don't worry about dinner. We're eating on board my jet."

She blinked. "We are?"

"Yes, and I believe you will enjoy the meal that's been prepared."

If I can eat it. The thought of dining with him on his jet over ten thousand feet in the sky had her stomach turning over. She tried to downplay her excitement but was finding it hard to do. "I'm sure I will."

"Good." He got out of the car and came around to open the door for her. He reached out his hand. "Come. Let our night begin."

Lee watched Carly's expression as she stepped on board his jet. He could tell she was impressed. Most people were when they came on board. He and Angelo had specifically designed the plane for their comfort when they discovered how often they would need to fly between Dubai and Las Vegas.

"This is simply exquisite. Way too much. Absolutely beautiful," Carly said all in one breath.

He chuckled softly and walked over to her, placing his arms around her waist. "You say that only because you haven't seen the jet owned by my uncle Jake. That is one striking plane."

"I can't imagine."

He tightened his arms around her. "Then I'm going to have to ask Uncle Jake to let me borrow it one day to show you."

"Borrow it?"

"Yes, just for you. I used to be his pilot at one time."

She looked surprised. "You can fly?"

"Yes. It became mandatory for some of us in the family."

"Why?"

He smiled. "Come on. I'll tell you why as I show you around."

While leading her up a stairway he told her how his uncle Jake had taught his cousin Christy to fly. If it hadn't been for those lessons, Christy and her husband both would have died when Alex had gotten injured and passed out while flying a plane and Christy had to take over. After that incident, their uncle Jake had decided all his nieces and nephews should get their pilot licenses and most had earned their flying hours as his pilot.

He stopped talking at the sound of Carly's breath catching. Her gaze was leveled on the table set for two.

Carly could only stare. The upper level had opened into a short foyer with seats made out of rich leather. And beyond that was a table set for two, with what appeared to be lit candles on the table.

She glanced up at Lee. "B-but how?"

"They aren't real candles," Lee said. "Battery operated to make them appear real."

And they did. The lighting was low and the burning candles gave the room a romantic effect. The illusion he had created was perfect.

"Come on. Let's continue the tour."

"There's more?"

He chuckled. "Yes, there is more."

He led her past the table and to a kitchenette with maple cabinets, a small sitting bar and a wine rack. Beyond that was a spiral staircase. They walked up the stairs to a set of doors that opened once he placed his palm in front of it. "It scanned my hand for identification purposes," he explained.

Carly barely heard what he said. She was looking past him into a beautiful bedroom surrounded by windows with sliding shades. The room had a spacious bed, built-in cabinets, a flat-screen television and a sound system. Another door led to a separate bathroom fit for royalty and another to a room with a desk that he probably used as an office. All the comforts of home while flying between countries.

"So what do you think?"

She glanced up at Lee and smiled. "Impressive. I like it."

He seemed pleased with her response. "Good." He leaned close to her and brushed a kiss across her forehead. "The pilot is ready to leave, so we need to go downstairs and buckle in. Once the plane has leveled off, the waiter will serve dinner."

Lee was enjoying this, seeing the smile on Carly's face and the excitement shining in her eyes. Her expression told him she found everything on his jet fascinating.

When he had seated her at a table with beautiful china, elegant silver and the best crystal, she smiled up at him. After he'd taken his seat and the waiter carried out silver trays of food—the aroma of which was so mouth-watering he had to fight from licking his lips—he leaned back in his chair to take it all in.

To take her in.

Fierce possessiveness rammed through him. He wanted to be the only man to put that look of excitement in her eyes. That ray of hope on her face. He wanted her as *his* woman. To have. To hold. Forever. He would protect her against any further hurt. She would never have a reason to feel lonely again. He felt things for her he'd never felt for any other woman. That was a start. Some married couples didn't have that much.

"This looks so good and smells wonderful."

Her words recaptured his attention. "Then let's enjoy it," he said as the waiter poured champagne into their glasses. "But first a toast," he said, holding his glass high. "To what I know will be a beautiful night."

"Yes," she said, holding her glass up as well. "To a beautiful night."

Their glasses clinked and then they each took a sip. She smiled at him when she placed her glass back down beside her plate. "That's delicious," she said, licking her lips.

The gesture caused his groin to tighten. "Only the best for you, Carly."

And he truly meant it. He could tell she wasn't used to such extravagancies and he intended to make sure she had more of them. As his wife she would have anything she wanted.

Over dinner they talked more about his family. He told her about his twin cousins, Blade and Slade, and how their construction company had built his two hotels and would soon be building a third in Paris. When he shared the news that all the investors he needed were on board, he believed the look of happiness shining in her eyes for him was genuine.

After dinner the waiter cleared off the table and Lee

took her hand and led her to the seats. He surprised her when he sat down and pulled her onto his lap.

She tried to wiggle free. "The waiter. Your pilot."

"Both will give us privacy."

And then he kissed her, sliding his tongue into her mouth on her breathless moan. It wasn't a short kiss. It wasn't intended to be. Instead, he took her mouth at his leisure, ravishing it with all the passion he felt. All the passion she stirred within him. He was consumed with a feverish need and felt like kissing her forever.

She was kissing him back, her sensuality flowing into him. Possessing him. He released her mouth momentarily for air and then he was kissing her again.

Lee wasn't sure how long he would have continued if the pilot's voice hadn't come across the intercom, letting them know the plane would be landing in twenty minutes and asking them to fasten their seat belts.

He placed her in the seat across from him. When he reached out to fasten her seat belt he inhaled her scent. "Mercy."

"What's wrong?" she asked, and he felt her tense.

He brushed a kiss across her lips to assure her there was no need to panic, that everything was fine. "Nothing. No reason for any alarm. You just smell good."

"Oh."

Lee kissed her again before sitting back against his seat and buckling his own seat belt. She knew how this night would end. He'd given her fair warning. He couldn't wait to make love to her again, get inside of her, thrust hard, go deep.

He watched her eyes journey downward to the crotch of his pants. She could see that he was aroused. Desire warred with other emotions within him, driving him to the brink, nearly pushing him over the edge. His want for her was so thick he could almost touch it. Taste it. Swallow it.

They would dance part of the night away and make love during the rest.

He couldn't wait.

One minute Carly was strapped in the seat watching the sky during the plane's low descent into Phoenix, and the next she saw the objects below. The lit buildings and houses appeared like fireflies out of the dark.

"It won't be long now," Lee said. "If you're nervous about landing, don't be. Kevin is the best pilot there is."

She glanced over at Lee. "I'm not nervous."

Just wary, she thought. Now that she was actually here in Phoenix she was antsy, but it had nothing to do with the flight.

She glanced back out the window at the exact moment the plane made a smooth landing.

"We're here."

She looked at Lee, held his gaze and nodded. "Yes, we're here."

Chapter 10

Lee had arranged for a stretch limo to transport them from the landing strip to the club he'd selected. The moment he and Carly were tucked away in the backseat of the spacious vehicle and the chauffeur closed the door, he pulled her into his arms.

For reasons he didn't quite understand, he wanted this woman with a need that scared the hell out of him. And this kiss was just as hot as all the others had been. His tongue held possession of hers as heat surged through every part of him, sending the pit of his stomach into one hell of a tailspin. When he finally broke off the kiss to breathe, he used the tip of his tongue to trace the fullness of her lips from corner to delicious corner.

"Don't you have to tell the driver where we're going?" she whispered softly.

A smile curved his lips. "He knows." He then wrapped his arms around her and tucked her close to his side, liking the feel of her there.

"You still aren't going to tell me where we're going?"

He looked down at her and another smile teased his lips. "Have you ever been to Phoenix before?"

"No."

"Then it doesn't matter. This is new territory for you, and I regret you can't see much at night. That only means I'm going to have to fly you here again during daylight hours."

He took her hand and brought it to his lips. "And how are you doing, Carly? Specifically, how is your body doing?"

He watched the bemused frown that settled between her brows. "My body?"

"Yes. Are you still sore?"

Her face tinted in a blush and he wondered if she and Knox had never discussed such intimate subjects. As much as he wanted her tonight, the last thing he wanted was to cause her any discomfort.

"No, I'm fine."

His smile curved as he tightened his arms around her. "I'm glad."

Silence ensued between them for a few moments.

"Can I ask you something, Lee?"

"You can ask me anything. Always remember that."

She nodded, and he could tell she was choosing her words carefully. "If I agree to marry you, how and when will we go about it? It was your idea, so I'm sure you have a plan."

Yes, he had a plan. He had even been thinking about it yesterday and earlier today.

"I have a plan, but it can change. If you prefer a big wedding I don't want to deny you that."

She didn't say anything for a minute. "And if that's not what I want?"

"Then we'll go with my plan, which is to marry immediately and—"

"Immediately?" she asked, glancing up at him.

"I see no reason to wait." In fact, he didn't want to wait. The sooner he could wake up with her beside him the better. "There are numerous places in Vegas that would marry us, so that's not a problem. And then you can move into my suite with me."

"But what about my place?"

"My suite's bigger, but if you want us to live there then I have no problem doing so."

She pulled out of his arms and looked at him with a stunned expression. "You would make such a sacrifice if that's what I want? You would do that for me?"

He pressed his lips together. He'd come close to saying he would do anything for her. Why? Why was he letting this woman get under his skin just because they were fantastic in bed together? Better than fantastic. Off the charts. She was definitely the yin to his yang. Never had he allowed his emotions for any woman to get this out of control.

Instead of answering her question, he presented one of his own. "Are you a witch?"

Her brows flickered. "A witch?"

"Yes."

The beginning of a smile touched her lips. "Why would you think I was a witch?"

"Because you enchant me," he said honestly. "I've dated numerous women but none like you."

She rested her chin on her hand. "How am I different?"

He thought about her question. "I think you're a remarkable woman. Warm. Sensitive. Smart. Loving and—"

"You don't know me well enough to make those kinds of assumptions."

"No, but I am spending time with you, getting to know you and letting you get to know me. I guess you can say we're courting."

She threw her head back to laugh. She had a beautiful neck. "That's an old-fashioned word."

He chuckled. "It is, isn't it? My only defense is that I've heard my great-grandmother use it a few times."

He paused. "Now to get back to our earlier discussion and to answer your question. Yes, I would do that for you. For us. Is that what you want to do, Carly? Do you prefer living at your place?"

She glanced down and nibbled her bottom lip. "It's really not my place. I lease it from Heather and Joel. But you knew that, didn't you?"

"Yes."

"Figured you did. And as far as where we live, it doesn't matter. Either way people will find out."

"You would want to keep it a secret?"

She shrugged her shoulders lightly. "I do work for you."

"I thought we'd discussed that before."

"Okay, in your mind, I work for Chef Blanchard, but the chef works for you. You own the hotel," she pointed out. "You're considered the big man."

He smiled. "Then you'll be the big man's wife."

She rolled her eyes. "I'm serious."

"So am I. Those who are going to talk, let them. There isn't a non-fraternization policy at the hotel, so we haven't broken any rules."

"But things are happening so fast. Most people will know we just met."

He smiled again easily. "Time is not a factor when two people want each other and want to be together."

She didn't say anything for a second. "When will you tell your family?"

"I won't have to. Word will get out, but I'll make an official announcement when I take you home for Christmas. Don't be surprised if Mama Laverne insists on a more formal wedding when we get to Houston. She has this thing about being a witness to every Madaris wedding, to make it official. She figures she's important enough to demand a repeat performance no matter who it inconveniences."

Carly didn't respond, and Lee couldn't help but wonder if she was leaning toward giving him a yes.

"We've arrived, sir."

The chauffeur's words had Carly raising up out of his arms and leaning forward to look through the limo's window. She then turned back to him with a bemused expression on her face. "It's closed."

His lips eased into a smile. "Yes, to everyone but us."

"Welcome, Mr. Madaris. Everything has been arranged as you requested."

"Thanks, Lewis."

"You're welcome, sir."

Carly drew in a deep breath as she examined Club Plateau. It was simply beautiful, massive—with one dance floor above the other, the two separated by a beautiful spiral staircase. She figured the three poles were for anyone tempted to dance on them. The floors appeared to be made of glass with beams of lights shining through them. Sections of the ceiling were covered with mirrors, causing prisms to glint across the room.

Suddenly, music began playing and the lights over the dance floors dimmed. She glanced around and saw the man Lee had called Lewis leave, closing the door behind him. Before she could ask, Lee said, "There will only be the two of us here tonight. Lewis will be back when it's closing time."

"And when is closing time?" she asked. Standing beneath the lights, his features looked more striking, even more handsome.

"Whenever I call him." He paused. "The music? Do you remember?"

She listened and couldn't stop her face from creasing into a smile. "Yes. It's the same music that was playing the night we met. When I was dancing alone."

"And I cut in."

"Yes, you cut in," she said, grinning.

"Well, tonight I'll start from the beginning." He leaned slightly toward her. "May I have this dance, Carly?"

She tilted her head in a nod and said, "Yes, you may."

Lee took her into his arms. The moment he touched her, an electrical charge rushed through her. A quick glance told her he'd felt the charge too. He drew her closer and she tried to relax against him. But when she felt his solid masculine body pressed against hers, chest to chest, her stomach flip-flopped and an intense need built at the juncture of her thighs. Each time their thighs touched she was assailed with physical proof of just how aroused he was. She wouldn't have been able to relax even if her life depended on it.

So they continued to dance, wrapped in each other's arms, while trying to ignore the heat stirring between them. The music didn't help matters. Each piece was slow, drugging, arousing.

Then when one song ended, the next was upbeat, both jazzy and soulful. He twirled her around, eliciting a laugh from her as they shifted into the swing.

"Hey, you're pretty good at this." She smiled at Lee.

"So are you. Where did you learn to dance?"

"From Heather. She couldn't believe someone could actually have two left feet. When she saw I was that person she taught me dancing steps in our dorm room."

He twirled her around again. "What about you?" she asked.

"My cousin Reese is married to Kenna. Before they married she took dance classes. To keep up with her on the dance floor we had to basically teach ourselves."

"Sounds like fun."

"It was," he said, twirling her around again.

"Who's playing the music?" she asked when the next song began. She hadn't seen a DJ and he'd said they were the only two at the club.

"It's set to automatic. There's enough music recorded to dance way past midnight."

Carly knew she couldn't dance that long. When the dance ended, Lee took her hand and led her toward a table where a bottle of wine and glasses sat waiting for them.

Lee poured the wine and handed her a glass. She took a much-needed sip. "Nice."

He took a sip of his own and stared at her over the rim of his glass. His eyes held hers and she felt as if she could read his thoughts. He wanted to enjoy the taste of her the same way he was enjoying the taste of his wine.

Not able to handle the intensity of his gaze, she placed her glass down. "I need to dance again," she said, swiftly moving toward the dance floor.

When he moved to follow her, she said, "No. Sit. I want to dance for you."

"Okay," he said, pulling a chair from the table and sitting down in it.

Another song played, not too fast and not too slow. She closed her eyes. Her feet began moving to the rhythm and her body followed. The beat flowed through her hips with a sensuous wiggle, a turn around the room and another wiggle. Then she repeated the routine all over again. She loved the feel of her dress flaring wide then brushing against her legs.

When the song came to an end, so did the dance, and she opened her eyes. Lee was still sitting in the chair, but he was staring at her in a way that nearly burned her to a cinder. Her nipples pressed against her dress. As his gaze raked over her, she saw the deep hunger blazing in the dark depths of his eyes.

He stood and reached out his hand to her. She walked toward him, intentionally swaying her hips seductively with every step. When she reached him, just as she had done that night on the balcony of the Grand MD, she leaned up on tiptoes and pressed her lips to his.

Lee wanted her. Now. Right here. This very minute. It wouldn't take much to strip off her clothes, take her on the table. It was tempting, and very hard not to do when she was kissing him as if his mouth was the only one she ever wanted.

She was voracious for his lips.

And he was voracious for hers.

He deepened the kiss, wrapped his arms around her and took over. His hand came to rest on her backside, a liberty he hadn't taken during their first kiss. But he was taking it now. She eased closer to him and his erection found a soft spot against her belly.

She broke off the kiss and he watched her gasp for air. "We're leaving now," he said. "Club's closed."

"No rush getting us back to Vegas, Kevin," Lee said, carrying Carly up the steps to the jetliner. He hadn't released her since sweeping her into his arms at the club. He had even held her during the limo ride back to the airstrip.

For some reason, he hadn't wanted to let her go. And he had kissed her, practically fusing his lips to hers. His desire for her had intensified with every stroke of his tongue.

He gently placed her in the jet's leather seat, buckled her in and whispered, "Only because this part is required."

He then took his seat across from her to buckle in for takeoff. His gaze traveled over her face—the eyes staring back at him, the kiss-swollen lips, the cute button nose. Whether it was habit or naughtiness, he watched as she parted her mouth to use the tip of her tongue to lick her bottom lip. He knew it was naughtiness when she crossed her legs and began easing up the hem of her dress to reveal one gorgeous thigh.

Lee felt his stomach tighten and his arousal expand. A low growl of need rumbled deep within his throat. His hand went to the buckle of his seat belt. He was tempted to get up and go to her. To kiss her. To take her. But he held firm and when he felt the jet race down the runway he counted the minutes, the seconds.

He was out of his seat the moment the plane leveled off. His fingers trembled in his haste to undo her seat belt, and then he pulled her out of her seat and kissed her deeply, needing to mate his mouth with hers.

"Please come with me," he pleaded when he ended the kiss. He wished he could carry her, but the jet's narrow stairway wouldn't allow it.

She nodded and placed her hand in his. He led her up the staircase, pausing several times to taste her lips. A thrumming heat spread through him each time his mouth devoured hers. He couldn't seem to get enough of her.

When they reached the landing, he made quick work of scanning his palm near the door, and the moment it slid open, he pulled her over the threshold. The door automatically closed behind them.

"I need you *now,*" he said, his voice throaty and unsteady as he wasted no time whipping her dress over her head and tossing it over his shoulder.

The sight of her bare breasts, plump and budding, made his mouth water. His gaze moved down beyond her small waist and landed on the sexy scrap of black lace shielding her femininity. His libido kicked up a notch and it felt as if his erection would burst through his pants.

Crouching down in front of her, he pressed his face to the juncture of her thighs and breathed in her scent. He then eased her thong down her legs and tossed it over his shoulder as well.

"Not a bad shot," Carly said through what sounded like a trembling breath.

Lee gazed up at her. "That's not my best one. You'll get my best shot later," he said, staring at the part of her he was in eye contact with. Her femininity. Using his fingers, he stroked her between her thighs. Damn, she was wet.

He opened his mouth on her. His tongue was voracious, ravenous. He alternated between licking and sucking. He feasted on her, indulging in a way that had her moaning his name aloud, over and over again.

Lee eased her legs farther apart so his greedy tongue could go deeper while pulling her hips close. She moaned and climaxed hard. He tasted it. Savored it. Felt the way her thighs trembled against the sides of his face and loved it.

He finally released her and she slumped against him, too weak to stand. He quickly swept her into his arms and carried her to the bed.

Carly could barely move as she watched Lee remove every stitch of his clothing. Her body responded, firing to life again. How was that possible when just seconds ago she had been too weak to stand on her own?

Lee returned to the bed and placed his knee on it. The smile he gave her was so devastatingly sexy her stomach stirred with renewed need.

"I want you," he said. The tone of his voice alone sent shivers of pleasure through her.

She gasped when he placed heated kisses down the length of her body and then kissed back up again, causing her to quiver beneath his mouth. He then straddled her and their gazes locked as the tip of his engorged erection probed against her entrance.

Using his hands, he lifted her hips, and before she could draw in another breath, he entered her in one smooth, fluid thrust.

He pounded hard, mating with her in a desperation that had her calling his name and pressing her fingers into his shoulder blades. The long, hard length of him plowed deeper inside of her, sending erotic sensations everywhere. Her legs wrapped around his waist, hugging tightly to his lower back.

Carly had heard of the Mile High Club. Now she was getting one hell of an initiation. She felt overwhelmed. Consumed. Possessed. Her breaths came in short gasps as Lee used strokes that seemed endless. She felt his body jerk hard and met his gaze.

"My best shot," he said in a guttural whisper.

She knew exactly what he meant when she felt his hot, molten release shoot through her, filling her all the way to her womb. He threw his head back and let out a growl as he came inside of her, keeping her body locked with his to make sure she got it all.

She wanted it all.

A forceful climax tore into her and she cried out his name once, twice and then she stopped counting. He kissed her again in the only way he could—with a passion so deep it made another orgasm slam into her and then into him.

This was crazy. Too much. Not enough. She felt greedy yet fulfilled. Moments later, when the explosion subsided, he eased off of her and then pulled her close in a spoon position. Her body curled into him and she felt the rapid beat of his heart against her back. When he shifted to throw a thigh over hers, she closed her eyes in complete and utter contentment.

The next morning, Lee woke up in Carly's bed to the smell of breakfast cooking.

Her bedroom was beautifully decorated with curtains that matched her bedspread and framed photographs depicting beautiful scenes in Paris on almost every wall. Except for one. That wall was covered with numerous plaques, certificates and awards she'd received as a chef. And in the center of her accolades was a huge framed picture of her and an older woman he assumed was her grand-aunt Ruth Briggs.

There was something about the older woman that reminded him of his great-grandmother. Not in her features but in the strength he saw in her face. She had those sharp all-knowing eyes and a pair of those speak-whatever-is-on-your-mind lips. And he would bet any amount of money she had a pair of hear-what-I-want-to-hear ears. He couldn't help but chuckle at those assumptions.

He lay back down in the bed as memories of last night washed over him. Every single detail. Kevin had followed his orders and they hadn't landed in Vegas until after midnight. Lee had driven them from the airport to her house in record time and had stripped Carly naked the moment they'd stepped inside. At some point, he wasn't sure exactly when, they'd made it to her bedroom.

The ringing of a cell phone caught his attention. It was Carly's phone, lying beside his on the nightstand. He lifted it up and from the caller ID he saw it was a call from Nathaniel Knox. He frowned. Why would that lowlife be calling Carly?

Something he recognized as jealousy flashed through him, although he knew it was not justified. She had pretty much made it clear to him she no longer felt anything for Knox. So then why was the man calling her? Did he do it often? Was he trying for a comeback?

Not appreciating the thoughts rolling through his mind, Lee eased out of bed. She had gathered his clothes off her living room floor where he'd left them and had thrown them across a chair in her room. Sliding into his pants, he went to the bathroom.

Carly had placed a toiletry kit on her vanity counter. It included a toothbrush and paste, shampoo, conditioner and a shaver. He appreciated her thoughtfulness.

After brushing his teeth and washing his face, he proceeded to shave. Moments later, he gathered both their cell phones and headed downstairs.

He found her in the kitchen. Her hair tumbled down her back, and she was wearing the sexiest little outfit—a white lace baby-doll gown with a matching robe that hit her midthigh. She stood at her refrigerator, bending over as if looking for something, unaware she was giving him a luscious view of her backside.

Immediately, his body got hard.

"Tempting position," he stated in a husky voice.

She jerked around and gasped, throwing a hand to her upper chest. She took in a deep breath. "You scared the heck out of me. I didn't hear you come down the stairs. Good morning."

"Good morning to you." He moved around the breakfast bar and placed a kiss on her lips. "Sorry if I scared you."

He slid his phone into his pocket and then handed the other phone to her. "You missed a call."

He watched her features when she checked her phone and couldn't help but appreciate her frown when she saw whose call she'd missed. She rolled her eyes and placed the phone on the counter. "Nobody important."

Lee wasn't going to let her off that easy. "Does he call often?"

She narrowed her gaze accusingly. "You checked my phone message?"

He moved his shoulders in one of those it-doesn't-matter-to-me-if-you're-pissed-off shrugs. "No. The phone rang and I noticed it was from Knox when your caller ID flashed his name." He paused a minute. When she didn't say anything he asked, "Well?"

She crossed her arms over her chest, and he tried not to notice what the move did to her breasts. "Well what?"

"Does Knox call you often?"

"And what business is it of yours?"

Wrong answer.

If she was trying to get him riled, she was doing a damn good job of it. "Since I have a marriage proposal on the table, I would think it's definitely my business."

Carly stared at him and he stared back. Then, after an unsteady breath, she said, "Nathaniel called me yesterday, for the first time in three years. He was in Miami for a convention and assumed I still lived there. He wanted to see me for old times' sake. Let's just say the conversation didn't end to his liking."

She stepped toward Lee and placed a kiss on his irritated lips. "Don't ever worry about him, Lee. He never wanted me, but you've proven on more than one occasion that you do."

Driven with a desire to show her just how much he wanted her, how much he would always want her, he swept her off her feet and into his arms.

"Wait, Lee! What about breakfast?"

"It can wait. I need this more."

He made it only halfway up the stairs before he had her straddling him and then lifted his hips to work off his pants. Following his lead, she began stripping off her clothes as well. When they married they might as well walk around in bare skin.

Moments later, they were both naked and she straddled him again. Her twin globes were in his face and he captured a nipple in his mouth and sucked.

Carly's inner muscles tightened in anticipation. Her stomach quivered as she bore down, taking him in. Inch by glorious inch. And when she had filled herself fully, every nerve ending in her body became charged.

She rode him with all the power her thighs and back could exert. Up and down, over and over again. She bore down at the exact moment he pushed up, in perfect rhythm.

They were making love on her stair steps but that didn't matter to her. And it certainly didn't seem to matter to him. The only thing that mattered was what they were feeling, the one thing holding them hard within its grip.

Passion.

Lee had claimed it was so, and over the past few days he'd shown her what he'd said was true. Passion and not love ruled them and would continue to rule them. Who needed love when you had this? She had tried love before and she'd gotten burned. Besides, being in love had never pulled these kinds of emotions from her. So what if they were dealing with the physical instead of the emotional. When the physical was this good, did it really matter?

He grabbed her hips and plunged upward as he roared out her name. She slammed down on him when an orgasm ripped through her as well. He held tight, locking their bodies in place while his release jutted deep inside of her.

"Carly…"

Moments later, she slumped down on his chest. He gently stroked her back while he whispered her name. Their bodies were still connected and neither of them made a move to separate.

It took a while for her to lift her head and look down at him. "I think that you, Lee Madaris, are bad for me," she said in a breathless whisper.

He continued to gently stroke her back. "And I think that you, Carly Briggs, are definitely good for me."

Chapter 11

Angelo checked his watch. "And you have no idea why Alex called this meeting?"

Lee shook his head as he pushed aside the stack of papers on his desk. "None."

In all honesty, he hadn't thought about it much. That wasn't good. Anything involving the hotel should be his top priority. It annoyed him at times how Carly had completely taken over his mind. Over the past two weeks she had gotten deeper and deeper under his skin, and there was nothing he could do about it. Passion had claimed his senses. He couldn't imagine it being any other way.

Lee jerked when two fingers snapped in front of his face. Angelo was grinning down at him. "Any reason you're out there in La-La Land, Lee?"

He had one very important reason but he preferred keeping it to himself. There was no way he would confess that a woman he'd met a month ago had become so ingrained in his mind that he found it difficult to think of anything else. He'd asked Carly if she was a witch and now he was beginning to think that she was. A very beautiful and sensuous witch who had the day off. They would have dinner at her place later and then take in a movie.

Instead of coming clean with Angelo, who was sitting in a chair across from him, Lee said, "I wasn't out there in La-La Land. I was just thinking about something."

"Um, something or someone?"

It was times like this he wished Angelo wasn't so astute. Lee was sure it came in handy in Angelo's occupation as an attorney, but Lee was not on any witness stand.

"What makes you think it's a *someone?*"

"Because you have one of those you-don't-know-what-I've-been-doing grins on your face."

Lee frowned. *Do I?*

"So what have you been doing lately?"

Deciding he didn't like being under the microscope of Angelo's gaze any longer, he stood and walked over to the window. "The usual."

There was nothing usual about his activities over the past few weeks. He could say the reason he enjoyed being with Carly was because he was making up for lost time. He had gone without sex for almost a year. But deep down he knew that was no excuse. He'd been too busy to think about sex. Hell, he was still too busy to think about it. But now it seemed as if he was addicted…to Carly. Because he couldn't imagine sharing a bed with anyone else.

"Okay, who is she? And don't try handing me that 'there's no one' bullshit."

Lee turned around and couldn't help but smile. Over the years Angelo had gotten to know him well. Too well. "She's not anyone you know."

That wasn't completely true. Angelo had been introduced to Carly during their investors' dinner, when she'd come from the kitchen to be thanked for the dessert she'd prepared. But he figured Angelo had probably dismissed the entire scenario from his memory already.

"Is it the same woman you mentioned the last time?" Angelo asked.

He looked over at Angelo, trying to remember when he'd mentioned anything about Carly. Angelo picked up on his dilemma, because he then said, "Last time I was here, Lee, you asked me if I'd ever been immediately attracted to a woman and I told you, yes. Peyton. And that's when I told you that when I first saw her I wanted her bad." Angelo chuckled. "And I also recall you saying that was too much information."

Lee stared at Angelo. He would take back what he'd thought earlier. The man had a memory like an elephant.

"What else do you recall about that particular conversation?"

Angelo lightly shrugged his massive shoulders. "You shared that one night you'd met such a woman. A guest in this hotel. But you figured you would never see each other again."

Angelo paused as he held Lee's stare. "So what's going on? Did your path cross with hers? Or did you hire Alex to find her?"

"Sounds like you've been busy."

Carly was glad Heather was living miles and miles away so she couldn't see the blush that spread across her face. She'd been busy all right, having the best time of her life with Lee…both in and out of bed. Mostly in bed.

She cleared her throat. "Well, I guess."

She hadn't told Heather everything, not sure what her friend would think. She had already told Heather that Lee wanted to marry her for passion and not love, but she and Lee were taking passion to an unprecedented level. It was somewhat scary that any two people could be that compatible in the bedroom.

"You've gotten quiet on me, Carly. What's going on with you?"

Carly sat curled up on her sofa. She nibbled on her bottom lip. "My relationship with Lee is very physical. You know, all that passion."

"Yes, you told me. Is he too demanding?"

Carly blushed again. "I don't know how to answer that because I enjoy it as much as he does. Is that a bad thing?"

Heather chuckled. "No. In fact that's a good thing. Some people are sensual beings and it sounds like the two of you are." She then added with a cheerful laugh, "I think Joel and I are sensual beings as well. If we could, we would stay in bed 24/7."

"But the two of you are in love."

There was a moment of silence before Heather said softly, "You want love to go along with that passion, don't you?"

Carly drew in a sharp breath. Again, she was grateful Heather was miles away and couldn't see her. "Why on earth would you think that?"

"Because I know you. And I can hear the wistfulness in your tone. Let me guess. You think the sex is so good that love should be part of the equation as well."

Yes, that was what she thought at times. Especially when she and Lee stared into each other's eyes while caught in the throes of an orgasm. He would look at her as if she was the only woman he would ever want, and she knew her gaze reflected the same sort of emotion about him.

There were also times when he would spend the night,

and they would wake up wrapped in each other's arms. Or when she went straight to his place after leaving work, and he would be there, ready and waiting for her the moment she stepped off the elevator. They had the physical. And it was a dynamic physical. So earth-shattering she felt quivers in her stomach just thinking about it.

Was she crossing the line by wanting the emotional too? Especially when he'd told her what sort of marriage they would share? Was it so wrong to want it all, something she'd never had before?

"Carly?"

Carly nibbled her lip again. "Yes. I think about it at times. If there were both love and passion in our relationship things would be perfect."

But then, Carly thought, there had never been a time in her life when anything had been perfect. And she had grown up never expecting it to be. Was she wrong to even think about wanting it now?

"You deserve perfect, Carly, if that's what you want. And if it is, then don't sell yourself short." Heather paused. "Have you fallen in love with him?"

"I'm not sure," Carly said honestly. "I enjoy being with him, both in and out of bed. And out of bed we do have fun together." A smile touched her lips. "When he found out I'd never been to Disneyland or Disney World, he took me. We actually spent an entire day at Disneyland last week. It was awesome. And the other night when he found out that I didn't know how to play cards, he taught me. And I've taught him different things in the kitchen. When he's in there with me I don't resent sharing my space. Those are the times I wish—"

"That things could be different," Heather finished for her.

"Yes, that things could be different," Carly agreed. "But then that's the story of my life, isn't it?"

"Be careful with your heart, Carly."

She heard the concern in Heather's voice and understood. Heather had been there each time Carly's heart had been broken. First by her mother and stepfather and then by Nathaniel.

"He called a few weeks ago," Carly said.

"Who?"

"Nathaniel."

"What on earth could he possibly have wanted?"

Carly heard the scorn in Heather's tone. "He was in Miami for a convention and thought I was still living there. When I told him I had moved to Vegas he went off on a tirade, letting me know what an awful place Vegas was."

"Whatever. He has a lot of nerve."

"Tell me about it," Carly said in disgust. "Sometimes I wonder what I ever saw in him."

"He was good-looking and very persuasive."

"True," Carly agreed. "And I thought he was someone he was not. I've learned my lesson. I don't assume anything about anyone."

"Um, are we talking about Nathaniel or Lee Madaris?"

Carly stood, stretched her body and glanced at the clock on the wall. She needed to dress for work in an hour or so. "Sometimes I have to pinch myself, Heather. Even without love, I often think Lee is too good to be true."

"Don't start judging Lee Madaris by Nathaniel's past actions."

"I'm trying not to."

"Then don't. I'm hoping and praying that they made only one Nathaniel Knox," Heather said.

Carly chuckled softly. "No one is praying that prayer as often as I am."

* * *

"Yes, our paths crossed again," Lee said, leaning back in his chair.

Angelo's brows drew together in curiosity. "When?"

Lee tossed a paper clip on his desk. "When I found out that although she was a guest here that night, she's also an employee of the hotel."

"An employee?"

"Yes." Lee could see Angelo's mind at work. He wouldn't ask, but there was no way he wasn't curious. So he decided to tell him. "Her name is Carly Briggs."

He watched Angelo try to remember where he knew that name. Lee decided to come to his aid. "You probably remember her as Chef Briggs."

Angelo's eyes widened. "The pastry chef from Peyton's Place? The one who prepared that delicious dessert last month?"

"One and the same. When we met before that night, we'd only exchanged first names. I had no idea who she was and she had no idea that I was the owner of the hotel. Can you imagine our surprise when she walked out of the kitchen and we discovered the truth?"

"I can imagine."

Lee didn't say anything for a minute as he remembered that night and the shocked look in Carly's eyes. "Let's go back to the day I asked you about your attraction to Peyton," he said.

Angelo smiled. "The same day you said I was giving too much information?"

"Yes. Now I need information. None is too much. I want you to help me understand something."

"If I can."

"How can a woman you've never seen before suddenly come into your life and turn it upside down with an attraction so strong that nothing else matters?"

Angelo didn't say anything at first, then he said, "All I know is how it was for me. I saw Peyton and it was like getting hit with a cold blast of air. There was something about her that drew me in. For years I thought it was one-sided. It wasn't until just before we married that I discovered she'd been attracted to me as well and, like me, had been fighting it." He paused. "Is that what you're doing, Lee? Fighting it?"

Lee shook his head. "No. In fact I've asked her to marry me."

Angelo's lips parted in absolute surprise. "Marry you?"

"Yes. In a way it's a blessing…or it could be, that fate thing you and Justin believe in. What are the odds of me meeting a woman I'm extremely attracted to at the same time I'm desperately in need of a wife?"

"Are you desperately in need of a wife?"

"Yes. I meant what I told you at your wedding after you threw that garter at me."

Angelo laughed. "I didn't throw it at you. You caught it."

"Whatever. Anyway, Mama Laverne thinks she has my future all figured out with the woman of her choosing. But like I told you that day, I intend to beat her at her own game."

"By getting married?"

"By picking the woman I want to marry without any help from her. Nolan informed me last month that Mama Laverne and some other woman are talking, making plans to marry me off to the woman's granddaughter," Lee said.

Angelo stared at him. "You don't have to be a player in your great-grandmother's games, you know."

Lee shook his head. "We're talking about Felicia Laverne Madaris, remember. The woman who's gotten more stars in her crown for putting marriages together than anyone I know. She has three generations of them to boast about, including your own…although you might not have known it at the time."

Angelo drew his lips in thoughtfully and then he chuckled. "Forget about what I just said about not having to participate in her games."

The buzzer on Lee's desk went off. He pressed the button. "Yes, Phyllis?"

"Your ten-o'clock appointment has arrived, Mr. Madaris."

"Thanks, Phyllis. Please escort Mr. Maxwell and the men accompanying him to the executive conference room."

"Yes, sir."

Both Angelo and Lee stood. "We'll finish this conversation later," Lee said.

Angelo nodded. "I guess now we'll find out what this meeting with Alex is about."

Chapter 12

"So there you have it," FBI agent Preston Gause said. "If you think I've deliberately painted a grisly picture, trust me when I say it's justified."

Lee rubbed his hand down his face. Wasn't it just a few weeks ago that he'd been thinking about how perfectly his life was going? Now to be hit with something like this.

He'd known something was wrong the moment he and Angelo had joined the men in the executive conference room.

He had known Alex a long time, namely because Alex's oldest brother, Trask, had been best friend to his cousin Clayton while growing up. And because he knew Alex had been a federal agent before going into private practice, there had been something about the other two men's mannerisms that let him know the two were federal agents.

"Do either of you have any questions?" the other agent, named Woodman, asked.

"Yes, we have plenty," Lee said. "Are you absolutely certain the Grand MD will be their target?"

It was Agent Woodman who spoke again. "According to our informant, the answer is yes."

"But we've been here for several months," Angelo said. "Why hasn't someone approached us already?"

Agent Gause shrugged his shoulder. "Not sure. My guess is that they were trying to give you time to settle in, check things out here, see how much money your casinos are bringing in to determine if you're worth the risk. This hotel is doing very well."

Yes, Lee thought, the Grand MD was doing very well and he was proud of what he and Angelo had accomplished in such a short time. He refused to accept that a group of thugs thought they could come in and ruin things.

"I was under the impression that the state of Nevada, the Las Vegas Gaming Commission and the federal government had joined forces to keep organized crime out of Vegas," Lee said. "So will someone tell me how organized crime returned to Vegas?"

No one in the room said anything as it was obvious Lee was not in a jovial mood. When neither of the two men answered his question, Lee said, "I'm waiting on an answer."

Agents Gause and Woodman exchanged uneasy glances before Agent Woodman spoke up. "Everyone assumed things were under control. And it is, as far as Nevada is concerned. As we said earlier, the East Coast mob is spreading into new territory."

"And you're just finding this out?" Angelo asked.

"No," Agent Gause said. "But we haven't been able to get in and implement a sting before they made contact. If what we do here is successful, we can get rid of them for a long time."

Lee noted the man didn't say *forever*. As long as there

was greed, there would be crime, organized or otherwise. Lee crossed the room and looked out the window at Sin City below. He was a Madaris, and he had an ingrained natural instinct to protect what was his. This hotel was his.

He turned back around. "If we go along with what you're proposing, how can we be sure your operations will be successful, that there won't be a backlash?"

It was Agent Gause who said, "There are no guarantees. We will give you a script that needs to be followed. And we will have several of our men working here undercover. They will be put in place immediately. We will be on top of this, Mr. Madaris, I assure you. And one of us will keep you in the loop so there won't be any surprises. Our goal is simple, although it won't be easy, and that is to close the East Coast Connection down as soon as possible."

What a mess.

Lee could just imagine what his friend was thinking. He looked cool on the outside but Lee knew Angelo, like him, was fuming on the inside. This group of punks didn't know who they were messing with.

It was rumored that Angelo's great-grandfather and his brothers were widely suspected of having ties to the Mafia, especially since they were Sicilians—every last one of them. It had taken years for Angelo and his family to outlive that bit of history. Both the Di Meglios and the Madarises were proud families and neither Lee nor Angelo would engage in illegal activities that would bring shame to their family names.

"So are the two of you in?" Gause asked.

Instead of answering, Lee looked at Alex, who hadn't said a single word during the entire meeting. "What do you think, Alex?"

He valued Alex's opinion. And it wasn't because Alex

was a family member. Alex had a brilliant mind when it came to solving crime.

"I honestly don't think the two of you have a choice but to work with the bureau. However, keep in mind that if you do work with them you're taking a big chance. Everything has to look as if you're going along with the program. If the mob suspects you're not on the up-and-up, you will be placing your life in danger. And I say your life, Lee, mainly because *you,* and not Angelo, are the one running the hotel here."

The room got quiet. Eventually Gause said, "Because of the nature of the operation and the ruthlessness of the people we're dealing with, neither of you can tell anyone what's going on. Doing so will place their lives in danger as well. It's imperative that you tell no one. If word gets out in any way, it could compromise the operation."

Lee didn't say anything for a moment, knowing Angelo was leaving the decision to him. He refused to let any organized-crime group think they could muscle their way into his profits. If his hotel had been targeted, like Alex said, he didn't have much choice.

"Okay," Lee finally said. "Let's do what we need to do to take them down."

Carly turned off the stove. She had prepared a feast fit for a king. She leaned against the counter thinking in a way she *had* prepared it for a king. *Her king.*

What she'd told Heather was true. Things were going so well between her and Lee that at times she wanted to pinch herself to make sure she wasn't dreaming. How could there be so much goodness in one man? He'd shown her things that Nathaniel had not—and in ways that took her breath away.

Lee hadn't asked her about his proposal lately. She figured he was giving her a chance to make a sound decision. His offer wasn't one with a time limit. Lee was looking at forever. But could she marry a man who didn't love her and probably never would?

Maybe this was her destiny. Maybe things were meant to be this way for her. She had to admit that Lee was a good catch.

Just a few days ago, one of the cooks had ridden an elevator with Lee. Most of that evening, all the woman had talked about was how good he looked, how nice he smelled and how she would do just about anything to jump his bones.

Instead of feeling any degree of jealousy, Carly had hidden her smile. She of all people knew how good he looked, how nice he smelled and she *had* jumped his bones. More than a few times. Adrenaline hummed through her bloodstream at the thought that she would be jumping them again tonight. He was offering her an entire lifetime of doing so.

So why hadn't she made a decision yet?

Most women would say they wanted more than sex. In her case, it was all about sex…or passion, as Lee liked to call it…but it was all she had and all she would ever get.

She would go for it.

That quick, that sudden, she had decided. And she wouldn't turn back. She would tell him tonight over dinner and let him make all the plans.

There would be only one condition. She wanted to keep the marriage secret for a while. At least until they went to his home for the holidays. That would give her a chance to keep her coworkers out of her business. Most didn't think she was seriously dating anyone and a couple had even discussed fixing her up on a blind date. If she were to pop up married to the man who owned the hotel, she could just imagine the gossip.

Carly hoped he went along with that condition. Once the property Lee was giving to her as part of their agreement was hers, she would make plans to build her own café. Then she would turn in her resignation at the hotel before going with him to Texas. After the holidays she would start advertising and promotion while the café was being built.

The ringing of her phone startled her. She picked it up off the table and answered it even though she didn't recognize the number. "Hello?"

"Did Shundra call you?" a frantic voice asked.

Carly frowned, not recognizing the voice. "Who is this?"

There was a pause. "This is Gail."

Surprise made Carly's brow rise. *Gail?* That was truly sad when a person couldn't recognize her own mother's voice. Her thoughts drifted back to what her mother had asked. Shundra was the sister who wasn't supposed to know Carly was her sister. "Why would Shundra call me?"

"Because she heard Sid and I arguing. He threw you in my face. About me having you out of wedlock. We thought she was away at college and hadn't known she'd come home unexpectedly. Shundra heard everything and said some mean and hateful things to me and her father. Then she got into her car and sped off. She didn't come home last night, and Sid is out now, trying to find her. It's awful that she's found out about you."

Carly had to fight to keep from gritting her teeth. Her own mother thought it was awful that one of her children had found out about the other one?

"Well, she hasn't called. She wouldn't anyway. I haven't seen her or talked to her in years. She's nineteen now, right? I believe she was five the last time I saw her, if you recall. You and Mr. Thrasher made sure I was not a part of your children's lives."

"You are so selfish," Gail snapped. "My child is missing and all you can think about is yourself?"

Those words were worse than any slap, but Carly rebounded quickly. "Yes, Gail, I guess I am. I'm sure your daughter will find her way home. And when she does, tell her to chill because finding out about me isn't that big a deal. Goodbye."

She then hung up the phone.

Lee had kept his cool during the meeting, but as he entered his suite anger and frustration exploded within him. None of what the two agents had said seemed real, but he knew that it was. And he and Angelo were duty bound not to tell anyone about the sting operation.

But Alex wasn't duty bound to anyone. Lee knew if push came to shove, Alex wouldn't hesitate to inform anyone he felt needed to know. But still…

Lee was bothered by the thought that he would have to pretend he was intimidated by a group of thugs. His performance had to be convincing. He couldn't seem too anxious or they might get suspicious.

Once he had agreed to go along with the sting operation, Gause and Woodman had outlined how things would go down. Once he was contacted by someone from the East Coast Connection, he now knew how he was to act, what he was to say, as well as the special equipment that would be installed on his phone and in various conference rooms.

It was Lee's hope that the agent's informant had been wrong, that he wouldn't be contacted, that this was all a big mistake. But just in case it wasn't a mistake, he had to cover all his bases, especially with people he cared about. He wanted to make sure they were kept out of harm's way.

He immediately thought of Carly. Should he withdraw his marriage proposal? The thought of doing so had his stomach in knots. That wasn't what he wanted, but—

His thoughts were interrupted by a knock on his door. He knew it was Angelo, but he still checked the security video camera to be certain. Hell, already he was getting paranoid. He opened the door and Angelo walked past him and went directly to his bar.

"I need a drink."

Lee closed the door. "Pour me one while you're at it."

He sat down on the sofa. He could feel Angelo's Italian anger radiating from him all the way across the room. Angelo didn't like the fix they were in any better than Lee did.

"Here," Angelo said, crossing the floor to hand him his drink before plopping down in the chair across from Lee. Angelo took a sip and then said, "I don't like the thought of you or I having to pretend we're selling our souls to the devil."

Lee grunted before taking a sip of his own drink. "If the feds are on it like they say they are, then it shouldn't take long to wrap things up."

"Yeah. It sounds like they want these guys pretty bad. One of their own is missing for close to six months now and is presumed dead. That alone has them driven to bring these guys in."

Neither said anything for a long moment. Finally Lee spoke up. "I thought about withdrawing my marriage proposal until all this is over. But I know what Carly's going to think, especially when I can't tell her the real reason for doing so."

"What is she going to think?"

"That I'm just another person who doesn't want her."

Angelo didn't say anything for a moment as he stared at Lee. "And do you want her, Lee? *That* bad?" he asked.

Lee, who was staring down at his drink, lifted his gaze to Angelo's. "Yes, I want her. *That* bad."

He didn't care what Angelo might be reading into his words.

"Then take it from someone who's *been* there and *felt* that," Angelo said in a thoughtful tone. "Don't let anyone or anything stand in your way of having her. Do whatever you have to do to make it work while keeping her safe. Personally, I think that as long as you're doing what those thugs think you should be doing, she's of no significance to them."

Lee thought on Angelo's words. "You do have a point there."

"Besides, how many people know the two of you are involved? I sure as hell didn't."

Lee couldn't help but smile. "So far, only you. Since she works here she's not comfortable with everyone knowing our business."

Angelo chuckled. "I'm sure it will make some of her coworkers uncomfortable to know she's having an affair with the boss. No doubt there would be gossip." He took another sip of his drink. "So if the two of you are keeping the affair a secret, how were you going to explain the sudden marriage?"

"We weren't."

"Then there would be even more gossip. When people don't know details, they have a tendency to make up stuff." Angelo stood. "Well, good luck on whatever decision you make. If you need me to change my schedule to be here more than in Dubai, just say the word. Then those thugs will have the two of us to deal with."

Lee shook his head. "No, we do things as they've always been done. You take care of the operations in Dubai, and Vegas is mine to handle. Gause and Woodman claim they're going to have things under control at all times and I'm holding them to it."

* * *

Upon hearing a car outside, Carly glanced out her living room window and saw Lee get out of his car. She stared at his masculine profile—the powerful set of his shoulders and his beautifully proportioned body—and her heart swelled with…

Love.

She closed her eyes, trying to shut out the emotion, but it was no use. Her heart was already there. She had fallen in love with a man who didn't love her. A man who only wanted passion out of a marriage.

Opening her eyes, she headed for the door at the sound of the doorbell. She paused to pull herself together, and when she opened the door, he stood there. She tried to ignore the flutters in her stomach.

"I missed you," he said throatily.

Carly had to draw in a deep breath when the truth of his words was reflected in the warmth of his smile.

"You saw me this morning," she reminded him as she led him toward the living room. She had spent the night at his place but had left right after they'd shared breakfast.

"Doesn't matter," he said. "I still missed you."

"Did you?"

"Yes." He came to stand in front of her. "And do you know what it means when I miss you that much?"

She tilted her head to stare up at him. "No. Tell me."

"Let me show you," he said, reaching out to bring her body closer to his. "I want you this much."

She felt the hard length of him pressed against her. "That much, huh?"

"Yes. That much and more." Then he lowered his mouth and kissed her.

The moment his tongue slid between her lips, Carly knew this was what she needed. She loved the way he kissed, the way he made her feel—as if he wanted no one but her. Lee Madaris was a real man in the true sense of the word.

And she loved the taste of him.

He broke away to rain kisses down her throat and neck. "Mmm, you taste good," he murmured.

"Funny, I was thinking the same thing about you."

He lifted his head to gaze deep into her eyes. She knew the very moment he detected something was wrong. He frowned. "What's the matter?"

She swallowed. "What makes you think something is wrong?"

"Your eyes look sad."

Her brows drew together. *Do they?* "I don't know why they would."

But he continued to stare at her, as if he were looking deep within her soul. "What happened to make you sad, Carly? And please don't tell me it was nothing. You're dealing with a man who is so into you that I would know if your heart missed a beat."

That, Carly thought, *was deep.* Could any man be that much into a woman?

"Tell me."

She nibbled her bottom lip. "Gail called."

"And?"

"And Shundra, Gail's daughter, is missing. Gail thought that maybe she called me."

He took that in. "Do you and Shundra keep in touch?"

"No. In fact, I haven't seen her or talked to her since she was five. She's nineteen now."

He nodded. "Then why would Gail think Shundra would call you?"

Carly drew in a deep breath. "I'll tell you everything over dinner."

* * *

"Your mother actually said that to you?"

"Yes."

So Carly wouldn't see the anger in his gaze, Lee looked down at the food on his plate. He couldn't imagine any mother saying such a thing to her child. She had clearly let Carly know she preferred one child over the other.

"Sorry I told you. Now I've ruined your dinner."

He glanced up. "No, you haven't ruined my dinner, but you do have me wanting to leave here and let Kevin fuel the plane for Minnesota to pay the Thrashers a visit. It wouldn't be a nice one either."

She touched his hand. "It doesn't matter."

He heard her words but knew they were untrue. He had seen the sadness in her eyes. He never wanted to see such a look in her eyes again.

"Just to be on the safe side, I called Aunt Ruthie to see if Shundra had perhaps contacted her and she hadn't. I hope she goes back home. Like I told Gail, Shundra finding out about me isn't that serious."

Lee didn't say anything as he continued eating, anger building inside of him. It should be serious, he thought.

"So how did your day go?" she asked, breaking into his thoughts.

He knew she was trying to change the subject. Switch it to something pleasant. If only she knew.

"Okay. The usual," he said, when his day had been far from it. "Dinner is delicious, by the way."

"Thanks. I tried a new recipe with the chicken."

"Did you?"

"Yes."

"How did you prepare it?" He just wanted to hear her voice. He loved the sound of it.

"Now, you know I'm not going to give you my secret," she said, smiling.

He smiled back at her. "Just what do you do with all these secret recipes?"

"I have them filed in my computer, and just in case it crashes I make hard copies as well."

"And you keep them where?"

She pointed her fork at him, grinning. "You're smooth, but not *that* smooth. I'm not telling."

"I have ways to make you talk." He watched her expression change. Her eyes darkened and her lips parted. "You look beautiful when you get aroused," he said in an achingly raw tone.

She lifted a brow. "You think I'm aroused?"

"Baby, I know you are."

She broke eye contact with him, and when her gaze returned to his, there was another expression on her face—this one he couldn't read. "Lee?"

For some reason he felt the need to touch her. Reaching across the table, he captured her hand in his. "Yes, Carly? What is it?"

"I've made my decision about your proposal. Yes, I will marry you."

Chapter 13

Lee stared at her for a long moment, unable to breathe. He hadn't expected her decision today. In all honesty, he had stopped wondering when she would give it.

Now the one answer he had wanted to hear had his stomach in knots. For the next few months, at least until the federal government cracked their case on the East Coast Connection, his life would be at risk. Marrying him could place her in danger as well.

On the drive over he had thought about what Angelo had said. As long as the Connection assumed Lee was walking the Connection's path, they would have no reason to retaliate or seek revenge. But what if something went wrong? What if—

"However, there is one stipulation," Carly said, breaking into his thoughts.

Taking a deep, unsteady breath, he asked, "And what is the stipulation?"

"That our marriage remains a secret for a while."

He lifted a brow. "Why?"

She hesitated, and he knew she was nervous. "I thought about it, and I'm not ready for all the speculation and gossip. No one is even aware that we're seeing each other, so a marriage between us will come as a surprise. I figure, we'll know the reason we married and we'll be fine with it, but I don't want to explain things to anyone else."

He thought about what she'd said. Keeping their marriage a secret might be best all around. If no one knew they were married then the risk to her would be less. And it would still give him the one thing he wanted. *Her.*

As his wife, secret or otherwise, she would never be alone again. As long as he lived he would always be there for her. And if, heaven forbid, anything ever happened to him, she would have his family.

"I know secrecy isn't how you wanted things, Lee," she said. "But I figure I can give Chef Blanchard my notice around Thanksgiving and start concentrating on building my own place. I want to work on my menu. I have plenty of those secret recipes to pull out. Some I haven't cooked in a while. I might need to change an ingredient here or there."

"Doing that will keep you pretty busy."

She nodded and then said quickly, "Yes, but I'll always have time for you."

"There's no doubt in my mind that you will," he said, tightening his hold on her hand, thinking how good it felt in his. "What I was alluding to was that I agree—you'll be too busy to continue working at the hotel." He paused. "Keeping our marriage a secret might not be a bad idea. That way we can have the element of surprise on our side when I go home."

"You're sure you don't have a problem with us keeping our marriage a secret until then?"

"No. I don't have a problem with it. So how soon can we get married?"

She began nibbling her lip again. "How about next month?"

"How about this weekend?"

Her lashes flew up. "That soon?"

"Yes."

"But I'm scheduled to work this weekend."

"Then ask for the weekend off. Better yet, take a week off. Or two. I want to take you to the Grand MD in Dubai. You're going to love it there."

Another idea popped into his head. Maybe it wouldn't be such a bad idea to keep her sequestered in Dubai, where Angelo could keep an eye on her until the sting was over. If the operation lasted past Christmas, he'd deal with that when it came.

"Um, how would you like to move to Dubai for a while?" he asked her.

"Dubai?"

"Yes, I have a penthouse in the hotel there as well."

"What on earth would I do in Dubai?"

"The same thing you would have done here. Update all those recipes. You'll have access to your own private kitchen and willing volunteers to try the dishes. Besides, having you in Dubai instead of here might solve my problem."

"What problem?"

Lee met her gaze. He couldn't tell her the real reason he wanted her out of Vegas, so he would give her another that was just as truthful. "Knowing you are my wife will make me want to be with you that much more. Hell, I can barely concentrate on work as it is. Having you in Dubai will help me keep our secret a secret. And I can fly over there to see you as often as I want."

She didn't say anything for a long moment. "Can I think about Dubai? I enjoyed living in Paris but never fancied myself living out of the country again."

"No problem. Think about it and let me know."

He stood up. "In the meantime," he said, gently pulling her up from her chair, "we have a Vegas wedding to plan."

It was way past midnight. Carly tried to stretch and discovered she couldn't do so. Lee, sleeping beside her, had her clutched tightly in his embrace and one of his legs was thrown over hers.

Smiling, she cuddled close, loving the feel of being securely wrapped in his strong arms. She even liked the feel of his heated breath on her neck as he slept. He didn't snore. His breathing was calm and relaxed, a man at peace.

They had not gotten around to planning their Vegas wedding. All it had taken was one kiss. He'd swept her off her feet and into his arms and carried her upstairs to the bedroom, where they made love. Again and again. Her body felt pleasured in ways that only he could pleasure her.

She thought about their discussion over dinner. She was glad he wasn't against the idea of keeping the marriage a secret, and she understood his suggestion that she stay in Dubai for a while. Their secret could only remain a secret as long as neither of them gave anything away. And she knew that would be hard to do with her still working in the hotel. All he had to do was look at her and she wanted him. Sooner or later one of them would let the cat out of the bag.

He shifted and came awake. "It's not morning," he said, his voice a rumble in his throat.

"No, but we left the kitchen in a mess. We didn't even clear the table."

"Oh. I know how you are about having a tidy kitchen. Are you going to make me get up and wash the dishes at this hour?" he asked her, rubbing the tip of his nose against her neck.

That was the rule that he'd come up with. Whoever cooked, the other person did the dishes. "No, if I recall, you helped with dishes the last time, so I owe you one."

"You don't owe me," Lee said, tightening his arms around her. "And we never did make the plans for our Vegas wedding."

"I was thinking the same thing," she said.

He eased up in bed and pulled her up with him. "Okay, since we're both awake…are we in agreement that it will be this weekend? And afterwards we'll fly to Dubai for a week?"

"I'll have to check with Chef Blanchard to make sure I can get the time off, Lee. I just started working for the hotel a few months ago and haven't built up any vacation time."

"Well, if it makes you feel any better, Chef Blanchard's boss says you can have the time off."

She shook her head. "No, that doesn't make me feel better because that's not how it's supposed to work. I'd hate for anyone to think I'm getting preferential treatment."

"Any preferential treatment you get, you deserve."

He eased his legs over the side of the bed. "You go back to sleep while I do the kitchen. If I didn't say it before, dinner was fantastic."

"Thanks. You did say it before. We never made it through dessert. I prepared this mouth-watering peach cobbler that we were going to eat with ice cream."

"We still can. It's not too late."

"Lee, it's after midnight."

"That doesn't matter." He leaned down and brushed a kiss across her lips. "Stay in bed. I'll be back later."

She watched as he slid into his pants and left the room. No matter what he'd said, there was no way she would let him clean up the kitchen by himself. Easing out of bed, she belted a robe around her waist and walked downstairs. When she rounded the corner to the kitchen, he was clearing the table.

He glanced over at her. "I thought I told you to stay in bed."

"I don't follow orders well."

"I plan on changing that."

"You can certainly try."

Smiling, he gathered the dishes and headed to the kitchen; she followed after collecting the place mats and glasses. He was at the sink, making dishwater. Like her, he preferred washing dishes by hand instead of using the dishwasher. Although she would be the first to call him out on being a little heavy-handed with the dish detergent, she loved seeing him standing at her sink, shirtless, with his pants unsnapped and his feet bare. She busied herself with wiping off the place mats so she wouldn't get caught staring.

Her mind drifted to Shundra and she wondered if her sister had made it back home. She certainly hoped so. Gail was wrong about her not caring. She did care.

"Will you tell your aunt when we marry?"

She glanced back over at him. "I'm thinking that I won't. Usually I can hold her to a secret, but she'll be so happy that she'll be tempted to tell her friends. So maybe it will be best if I keep quiet. But I'll tell Heather."

He nodded as he placed dishes in the sudsy water. "I'm glad you have a friend like Heather. Sounds like the two of you share a special friendship."

"We do. Sometimes I believe people are placed in your life for a reason." She believed he was one of those people. What were the odds that she would meet someone on her birthday—a birthday she was sharing alone—and that he'd become the man she fell in love with?

"What about your cousins? The ones you're super close with. Will you tell them?"

He shrugged. "Not sure yet. I've never been worried about any of them keeping a secret before, but a couple of them are married now. They might feel compelled to confide in their wives. Like the situation with your aunt, I don't want to do that to them."

He washed dishes and she dried, and while they cleaned up the kitchen, they talked. He told her more about the hotel he wanted to build in Paris and how that project would consume his time for a while. She told him about several new recipes she'd come up with, and no matter how he tried to get the goods on the ingredients, she kept them to herself. And she told him how concerned she was about Shundra.

A short while later, he took her hand in his. "We're finished in here. Let's go to bed and get some sleep."

They walked hand in hand up the stairs to the bedroom, and she was certain when they got there, they wouldn't be getting any sleep.

"So what have you found out, Weber?" Bracey asked.

Weber sat down in a chair and studied Bracey. Even a fool would know the man had an agenda. He wanted to be the big man's second-in-command and probably would succeed. He had been sent in last year by those at the top to make sure the big man did what he was supposed to do. Weber knew Bracey and Nash didn't get along. Nash didn't trust him, and Bracey was sharp, where Nash was beginning to get sloppy. Weber intended to be on the side of the winner and he had his money on Bracey.

"Nash has been asking around," Weber said. "He's thinking the tipster might have called from the restaurant next to the alley."

Bracey nodded. "And Harrison's body? Did you find out what Nash did with it?"

"Not yet, but I will soon. I think Nash's man Grassley knows something. He and I have been hanging out. It won't be long before I get him to talk."

Bracey nodded. Grassley was Nash's right-hand man. "See that you do. Nash thinks he has a cushy position in the cartel and I want to prove him wrong."

Chapter 14

"Are you sure you didn't pull any strings with Chef Blanchard?"

Lee smiled at Carly's question. He leaned back in his desk chair as he talked to her on his cell phone. "No. Why would you think that?"

"Because he gave me the time off without any hassles."

"I did not contact the chef. So, since you got the time off that means we're good for this weekend and the week in Dubai."

"Unless you've changed your mind."

"Not hardly." And he meant it. Never had the thought of marrying anyone filled him with such anticipation. It had been hard to leave her bed this morning. He'd been tempted to wake her up, but she had been sleeping so peacefully, he had dressed and left.

"Have you heard any more about your sister?"

"No, not a word. I talked to Aunt Ruthie and she hasn't

heard anything either. I think I'm going to give in and call Gail later."

"Do what you think you must for your peace of mind."

There was a pause. "Thanks."

Lee lifted a brow. "For what?"

"For caring about my peace of mind. Considering the circumstances and what Gail said to me, some people would have told me to not give a damn."

"But not caring wouldn't be you. Just because she acted that way doesn't mean you have to act the same. I can't stop her or her husband from hurting you, Carly. But I won't let them, or anyone else, take advantage of you. I will do everything in my power to keep you from harm."

"Harm?"

A slipup. He wasn't talking about her mother or her stepfather. His thoughts had shifted to the East Coast Connection. "I was talking in general."

"Oh. I know you have to get back to work. I'll see you later."

"All right."

As soon as he clicked off the phone there was a knock on his door. "Come in."

Angelo walked in with a folder in his hand. "Here are the documents you wanted me to prepare," he said, placing the folder on Lee's desk.

"That was quick."

Angelo sat down in the visitor's chair. "I fly out later today to join Peyton in Oklahoma." He paused. "So, are you going to go through with it? Marry the chef and keep it a secret?"

"Yes. Think you can make it back this weekend to act as a witness?"

"That won't be a problem."

Lee nodded. "Good. And bring Peyton with you. She

met Carly briefly as a chef, but I want Peyton to meet her as my wife, and I know she'll keep this secret for us."

Angelo smiled. "Peyton is going to be surprised."

"A number of people will be, but none more than my great-grandmother. I can't wait to go home for Christmas."

"Sounds like you have a plan."

"I do."

A short while later, after Lee had attended several meetings and was back in his office, his cell phone rang. He inwardly cringed, immediately recognizing the gospel ringtone.

"Yes, Mama Laverne?"

"Just checking on you. How have you been?"

Lee leaned back in his chair. "Busy. How have *you* been?"

"As well as can be expected. Life is good. You haven't been home in a while."

"Been busy."

"I was worried you were hiding out in Vegas."

Lee couldn't help but smile. "Hiding out?"

"Yes, trying to avoid the inevitable. It won't help you, you know."

"I'm not hiding out. Just have my hands full running a busy hotel. Besides, I don't have time for a woman."

"That's what they all used to say, but you see all your cousins are happily married." She paused. "You are coming home for Christmas, right?"

"Yes, ma'am. I'll be home for Christmas. In fact, I'm thinking of arriving a few weeks early."

"Good. I'm going to have a surprise for you."

No, sweetheart, I'm going to have a surprise for you, he thought, widening his smile. "I hope it's going to be some of your signature bread pudding."

"It's going to be better. Can't wait to see you."

"Same here."

He couldn't help but chuckle when she clicked off the phone.

Carly had just come in from her garden when her doorbell sounded. Wiping her hands off on a towel, she moved toward the front door, stopping to look through the peephole.

Her heart almost skipped a beat. She removed the chain off the door and snatched it open. "Shundra? What are you doing here?"

It had been a long time since she'd seen her sister, but she still recognized her. The young woman standing on her doorstep appeared nervous, and it was quite obvious from the rings under her eyes that she'd missed sleep. "I need to talk to you. May I come in?"

"Sure," Carly said, stepping aside and closing the door behind her. "Come in and have a seat. Can I get you something to eat or drink?"

"No, I'm fine."

She certainly didn't look fine, Carly thought. She looked exhausted. "Does Gail or your father know you're here?"

"No," she said quickly as she sat down on the sofa. "And I don't want them to know."

Carly shook her head as she sat down in the wingback chair across from the sofa. "I can't do that to them, Shundra. They are probably worried sick about you. I wouldn't be surprised if they've filed a missing-person report with the authorities."

Shundra lifted her chin. "I don't care. They said some awful things to each other."

"Well, I do care. They shouldn't have to worry about you needlessly."

"Why do you care about them when they don't care about you? I didn't even know you were my sister, for crying out loud. No one knew Mom had a child out of wedlock. How could you let them treat you so shabbily all these years? They told us that you were a cousin and your mother had died when you were born. How could my parents be such big liars?"

Carly certainly didn't know how to answer that. It was obvious Shundra was upset, but Carly had to make her see that she couldn't just run away. She had to handle this family problem in the right way.

"I care because I'm a caring person regardless of the ups and downs life tosses me. Sometimes, if you're strong enough, struggles can make you a better person. You learn not to give in to hurt. You move on and appreciate every day as you move forward."

Carly stood. "Now, I'm going to call your parents and let them know where you are and that you're okay."

"I won't go back and they can't make me…especially now."

Carly lifted her brow. "Why especially now?"

Shundra didn't say anything for a minute. "Their argument was nasty. I've never heard my parents argue before. If they had disagreements, we didn't know about it."

"All couples argue, Shundra, and nobody, not even parents, are perfect."

"But I heard everything that day. I'm convinced Dad would not have married Mom if he'd known about you, then he was stuck because she's an asset to him. She's the perfect hostess for his business. People like her more than they like him."

Carly really didn't want to be privy to Gail's family business. "Well, first let me call them and let them know you're safe and then I'll prepare you something to eat."

Shundra jumped up. "I meant what I said, Carly. I won't go back, especially now."

Carly drew in a deep breath. "You said that before and

I asked what you meant. Will you tell me what you mean by *especially now?* If it's about me, then I can understand you being upset, but it's not earth-shattering."

Carly thought Shundra was going to break down into tears. "You don't understand. Now I know how he feels."

"How who feels?"

"Dad. Mom had you before they married, and I think deep down he never forgave her. He still thinks she's nothing more than a slut."

"I understand how you'd be upset about what he said, Shundra, but it was your parents' argument. It wasn't about you."

Shundra shook her head. "In a way it was. Because I'm pregnant, Carly, and if Dad feels that way about Mom, I don't want to think about how he'll feel when he finds out about me."

Cary stared at Shundra. "You're pregnant?"

Shundra took on a defensive stance. "Yes, and I'm not getting rid of it."

"Is that what you think your parents would want?"

"Yes. And I won't do it."

Carly didn't say anything for a minute. She glanced at the clock. She was supposed to be at work in an hour but there was no way she could go in until she decided what to do about Shundra.

"Come on. We'll talk some more over food."

"There's a call for you, Mr. Madaris, from a Colin Driskell."

Lee went still. This was the call agents Gause and Woodman had advised him would be coming. He hadn't expected it this soon. "Did he say what this call was about, Phyllis?"

"No, sir. He wouldn't say. He asked to speak with you directly."

"All right, give me a minute and then put him through."

"Yes, sir."

Switching to another line, Lee immediately punched in the three numbers he'd been instructed to use when initial contact was made. This would alert the FBI that everything was now a go. First, they would record the call. He heard the click when the connection was made. Seconds later, he heard another click when Phyllis put the call through. "This is Lee Madaris. How can I help you?"

"It's not how you can help me, Mr. Madaris, but how *I* can help *you*."

"I'm pretty busy right now, Mr. Driskell, so please state your business. Be forewarned that if you're selling anything, I have department executives that you need to speak with."

"I'm not selling anything to the hotel per se, but I need to discuss something I think will be of vital importance to you."

"Which is?"

"How to maximize your profits."

Lee didn't say anything for a moment. "And how can you do that?"

"I can't say over the phone. I suggest we meet privately."

"Fine. I'll put you back on the line with my secretary and you can make an appointment."

"No."

"Excuse me?" Lee said.

"If you're interested, we meet privately. I name the place and—"

"Excuse me again. *You're* calling *me*. If you want us to meet then we do it here. I won't know if I'm interested until you present whatever it is that you're offering. I don't conduct business with anyone I don't know outside of the Grand MD."

There was a pause. "Fine. I'll meet with you next week."

"Sorry, I'll be out of the country next week. I suggest you call back when I return. Goodbye, Mr. Driskell."

Lee released a deep breath after he hung up the phone. Less than a minute later his phone rang on a newly installed private line. "Lee Madaris."

"You did great," Agent Gause said. "You didn't appear eager to talk with him and you put him off. He didn't like it, but he won't make a move to retaliate. He'll wait you out until you return from your trip abroad. Do you really have a trip out of the country next week?"

"Yes. I'm going to Dubai to check on my hotel there." He had no intention of telling Gause that he would be on his honeymoon.

Gause paused. "If you weren't planning to go out of the country, I would have suggested that you go anyway. He's going to check it out. If you're seen in the office next week he would wonder why you lied. That would have made it hard for him to trust you in the future."

"Well, we won't have to worry about that since I will be in Dubai for a week," Lee said.

"There's no doubt in my mind that he'll be contacting you when you return. I also suspect he'll be placing some of his own people at the hotel. He probably has a few already there."

Great! That's just what I don't need to hear. "In what capacity?"

"No telling. At this point you can't trust anyone. Our people are already in place and we'll find out who his people are. We have someone in your human-resources department reviewing all your new hires, especially those working in the casino."

Lee rubbed a frustrated hand down his face. "What about that comment Driskell made about wanting to maximize my profit?"

"No crime there. He could be an insurance agent or an

investor. He knew the right things to say to stay above the law. We probably won't get anything on him until the two of you meet. We'll have to be careful. Chances are he'll bring his men with him. They'll make sure that wherever you meet, whether it's in your office or some other location, it's not bugged."

Lee frowned. "Then how are you going to record what's said?"

"We have our ways. Don't worry about it."

That was easy for him to say. "Fine. Goodbye, Agent Gause."

He then hung up the phone.

Carly served chicken-salad sandwiches, leftover vegetable soup and glasses of iced tea. And because she believed any meal eaten after noon should include a dessert, she had a tray of peanut-butter cookies. She could tell from the way Shundra's eyes lit up when she placed the tray in front of her that the girl hadn't eaten in a while. That wasn't good for an expectant mother.

They ate in silence before Carly realized Shundra was staring at her.

"Is anything wrong?" she asked.

Shundra smiled. It was the first time Carly had seen her smile since opening the door to find Shundra standing on her doorstep.

"I favor you. I actually favor you."

Carly couldn't help but return Shundra's smile. That was one of the first things she'd noticed once Shundra had stepped inside her home and she'd taken a good look at her. Shundra was a little taller and a little on the thin side. But their facial features were definitely comparable. They had the same forehead, the same almond-shaped dark brown eyes, the same nose and lips. Although to Carly's way of thinking, Shundra's lips were a little fuller. But in all, looking at Shundra was like seeing a younger version of herself.

"Yes, you're right. We do favor."

Shundra's smile widened as if she was glad to hear Carly admit it. "You're pretty. Really pretty."

Carly chuckled. "So are you."

Shundra's smile faded and she absently pulled on a lock of her hair before pushing it back from her face. "I don't feel pretty."

"But you are."

The kitchen got quiet again as they ate in silence. Shundra broke the silence when she said, "This is good. You're a good cook. No wonder you do it for a living."

"Thanks."

"I remember when you were on a cooking show that time."

"Do you?" Carly asked.

"Yes. You won."

"Yes, I won."

They finished the meal and were cleaning off the table when Carly thought to ask, "How did you find me?"

"That was easy. I looked you up on the internet."

Carly looked at her in surprise. "I'm not on the internet."

"Sure you are. Everyone is these days."

"And it gave you my address?"

Shundra smiled. "Brought me right to your door. I used the money in my bank account for the plane ticket."

Carly washed the few dishes they'd used and handed Shundra a towel so she could dry.

"Why aren't you asking me anything about the father of my baby?"

Carly shrugged. "It's really not any of my business."

"No, it's not anyone's business, but Mom and Dad are going to make it theirs."

Carly studied her nineteen-year-old sister. "Shundra,

even you have to admit it's understandable for them to want to know."

"Yes, but…the reason I went home unexpectedly in the first place was to tell them. I parked in the garage, and when I saw they weren't there, I got in bed and took a nap. Their screaming woke me up and that's when I heard everything." Looking as if she wanted to change the subject, Shundra took stock of the kitchen. "You have a nice place. You live alone?"

"Yes, I live alone."

"You don't have a boyfriend?"

Her question made Carly smile. "Yes, I'm seeing someone."

"Is it serious?"

"Pretty much." *So serious that I'm getting married this weekend,* Carly thought to herself. Deciding Shundra had asked her enough questions for now, she said, "Okay, we've finished in here. Now I think it's time, don't you?"

Shundra began nibbling at her bottom lip, something Carly did often enough to know the girl was nervous. "Time for what?"

"Time to call your parents and tell them where you are."

After attending a number of meetings, Lee was on his way back to his office when he found himself on the elevator with Chef Blanchard.

"Mr. Madaris, you haven't graced us with your presence in Peyton's Place lately."

Lee smiled. "No, and I need to do that. The last time I was there I had the Key Lime Appacula with a cup of coffee. It was simply delicious."

"Yes, Chef Briggs receives a lot of requests for that. But if you're thinking about dropping by later, don't bother. She's out tonight."

Lee went still. When he had talked to Carly earlier,

she hadn't mentioned anything about taking the night off from work. In fact, she'd planned to take a short nap before going in.

"Well, this is my floor," Chef Blanchard said. "Have a good evening."

"You do the same."

As soon as the elevator doors swooshed shut, Lee pulled out his cell phone to call Carly. When he didn't get an answer, his heart pounded in his chest. He clicked off the phone. What if she'd been forced to make that call to Chef Blanchard? Gause claimed Driskell wouldn't retaliate just because of the way Lee had brushed him off. What if the agent was wrong?

Lee punched in another number. "Fred, this is Mr. Madaris. Please have my car out front immediately."

Carly tried to busy herself while Shundra spoke to her parents on the phone. From the sound of the conversation, it wasn't going well. Shundra's phone battery had died, so Carly had let Shundra use hers. She had decided, considering the circumstances, there was no way she could go in to work tonight, so she'd called Chef Blanchard. He'd been very understanding about the extra time off. When she got the chance, she would call Lee. It was her usual routine to go to his suite when she got off work, and she wouldn't be coming by tonight.

"Don't come, Daddy! Don't! I need time to think. I need—"

Shundra took the phone from her ear and looked at Carly. "He hung up on me. That means he's on his way. He's probably having Shelton get the jet ready. Now that's a laugh."

Carly figured Shelton was the pilot. She'd heard from Aunt Ruthie that Mr. Thrasher had his own jet like Lee did. "Why is it a laugh?"

"Because Shelton is Dad's pilot and will be the one flying him here. Shelton is also the father of my baby."

"Oh. Does Shelton know?"

Shundra broke eye contact with her. "No."

"Any reason you didn't tell him?"

Shundra didn't respond at first, then she said, "If he loses his job, it would be my fault. He was instructed to fly me home from college one weekend, and we couldn't leave the runway because of the weather. So while we waited, I tempted him." A mischievous smile touched her lips. "I've had a crush on him for a while and decided on that particular day that I was going to make sure he knew it. That's how things started between us, and we've been messing around secretly for almost a year. I'm in love with him but he's never said he loves me."

After a moment Carly said, "But still, don't you think he has a right to know about the baby?"

Shundra shrugged. "It won't do any good since he can't marry me."

"Why? Is he married already?" Carly asked.

"No. He's single, but he's almost eleven years older. Dad would castrate him."

Carly had seen Mr. Thrasher's bad side twice in her lifetime and could certainly see Shundra thinking that way. He definitely would not appreciate his nineteen-year-old daughter having an affair with a thirty-year-old man. "Well, since you're convinced your father is on his way, you might as well make yourself at home until he arrives."

"Thank you, but no matter what he says, he won't force me to do anything I don't want to do. I'll be twenty in a month and that should stand for something."

Carly was about to say that when it came to domineering parents, age didn't stand for anything, but she couldn't get the words out for the loud pounding on her front door.

She frowned. Mr. Thrasher might be desperate to collect his daughter but he wasn't *that* fast.

Moving to the door, she looked out and saw Lee. She opened the door immediately. "Lee? What are you doing here?"

He entered and looked her up and down as if to make sure she was okay. "I got in the elevator with Chef Blanchard and he said you had called in and wouldn't be working tonight. I was worried."

"Why were you worried?"

Instead of answering her, he pulled her into his arms and kissed her. Instinctively, Carly kissed him back, completely forgetting they had an audience until Shundra cleared her throat.

Lee broke off the kiss and looked beyond Carly to where Shundra was standing. He looked at her closely then turned back to Carly. "Your missing sister?"

"Yes," she said. "She showed up here a few hours ago, so I called in."

He nodded. "I understand." And then he called out to Shundra, "Hello."

"Hello." Shundra smiled while looking Lee up and down. Her gaze clearly reflected her appreciation for what she saw. "This is your boyfriend?"

Before Carly could answer Lee responded, "Yes, I'm her boyfriend. Why?"

Shundra's smile widened. "Because you are one handsome dude."

Chapter 15

Lee tried not to smile. What Shundra had said reminded him of something his cousin Victoria would say. She was probably a few years older than Shundra. He and his cousins were used to Victoria's girlfriends giving them flirtatious compliments.

"Thank you," he said.

"No problem," Shundra said, still smiling.

Carly made introductions. "Shundra, this is Lee. Lee, this is Shundra." She then looked at Lee. "I insisted that she call her parents to let them know where she was. Mr. Thrasher is on his way."

Lee nodded. He heard the tension in her voice. It was obvious she wasn't looking forward to the visit. And it was also obvious there might be more to the story of why Shundra was here. Now that he knew Carly was all right, he could leave and let her deal with her family's issues. But he had no intention of doing that. They would be getting married this weekend, and as far as he was concerned, her issues were now his issues.

"Then we'll wait for Mr. Thrasher's arrival," he said, holding her gaze.

Was that relief he saw in her eyes? He had done his research on Sidney Thrasher. The man was an astute businessman who'd made his fortune in the glass industry. He was one of those wealthy individuals who looked down on those less fortunate and enjoyed intimidating those he considered weak.

Another thing Lee found rather interesting was that Thrasher's company, Vontage Glass, was one of his suppliers. Both Grand MD hotels were two of the company's biggest clients, and several resorts that Angelo owned also used Vontage Glass.

"I have a few business calls to make," he said to Carly. "May I use your office?"

"Sure."

He smiled back over at Shundra. "Nice meeting you, Shundra."

She smiled back. "Likewise."

He then headed toward the room Carly used as an office. As soon as the door closed behind him, he punched in a number for Alex.

"This is Alex."

"Hey, this is Lee. Not sure if you've spoken with Agent Gause yet, but Driskell called today."

"What did he say?"

Lee sat down behind Carly's desk. He tried to ignore how the room held her luscious scent. "He wanted to discuss maximizing my profits. As instructed, I put him off."

"Good. You don't want to appear too eager. If you had, that would have been a red flag. You have to keep your cool."

"I know, but it was hard today, considering what I know about Driskell and his group."

"I know. I know. But we have a lot at stake. Helping to expose these guys will help others."

After his conversation with Alex ended, Lee happened to glance at a writing pad on Carly's desk. She'd been practicing writing her name. *Carly Andrea Madaris.* He smiled. He liked her middle name, but he liked what would become her last name even more. It fit.

He leaned back in the chair and picked up the phone to call his parents. He had a lot of time to kill while waiting for Carly's stepfather.

Alex rubbed his chin as he studied the people in his office. He had worked with them before, when a serial killer had been on the loose in Houston a few years ago—Trevor Grant, Drake Warren and Ashton Sinclair. The older man, who looked more like a rancher than a billionaire, was his wife's uncle, Jake Madaris.

His gaze then moved to the only female in the room. Tori, mother of three, former marine and CIA agent. Her husband, Drake, often called Sir Drake, was also a former marine and CIA agent. Sir Drake had tried keeping Tori out of the action last time. Evidently he had learned his lesson.

Alex had seen Tori in action before, when she'd brought down a villain twice her size and ruptured the man's jewels in a way that meant he would never be the same. Sometimes he thought that she and Sir Drake lived for danger. Hell, their nanny was even a former CIA agent.

"I noticed when you talked to Lee a few minutes ago that you didn't mention anything about this meeting you've called," Jake said, sitting in a chair with his long legs stretched out in front of him.

Alex nodded. "I saw no reason to. Lee knows that although he's bound to keep the sting operation under wraps, I'm not. Considering the risks involved, I'm sure he figured that I would inform all of you of what's going on at some point. I have all the confidence in the world in the FBI, but there are times when things don't go as planned."

Trevor Grant leaned forward in his chair, resting his arms on his thighs. "Only problem is the three of us," he said, indicating himself, Sir Drake and Ashton, "are headed to Afghanistan. We might be out of the picture for a while. Clark will run things at TDA until we return."

Alex nodded. Clark Lovell, aka Brent Dawkins, was a former FBI agent, one of the bureau's best before an assassin put a hit on his wife and daughter, sending him into early retirement. Now he had remarried a woman with a little girl and just last year he'd become father to twins—a son and a daughter. TDA was the name of the tactical operations center the three men…and one woman…had opened a couple of years ago.

"I won't be going to Afghanistan, so I'll be available if needed," Tori said, refusing to look at her husband, who was glaring at her.

"I'm hoping backup isn't needed," Alex said quickly when he saw Tori had pushed one of Sir Drake's buttons. Tori knew just how far she could go with her husband.

"If you need backup, you got it," Ashton reiterated. "We have several trained men at TDA who won't be going with us either. Hopefully we'll be back before anything goes down."

Alex nodded. "I'll keep everyone informed. Lee's already been contacted by one of the heavyweights in the East Coast Connection, but he's put them off for a while."

Jake stood. "Make sure I'm kept in the loop. If anything happens to his grandson, my brother Lee will never forgive me for it."

Alex nodded, thinking if anything were to happen to Lee, he wouldn't be able to forgive himself.

Carly figured one way to stay busy would be to prepare dinner. She had suggested Shundra take a shower and relax while Carly washed and dried her clothes and got them ready for her to put back on. Carly couldn't help but smile each time her sister glanced across the living room to the closed office door. Evidently Shundra was anticipating Lee's return. No one had to tell Carly that Lee was eye candy, especially to a nineteen-year-old who had a thing for older men.

"He evidently had a lot of business to take care of," Shundra said with a twinge of disappointment in her voice.

Carly didn't look up from flouring the chicken to be fried. "Probably."

"What kind of business is he in?"

"The hotel industry."

"Oh, which one?"

"The Grand MD."

"I've heard nothing but wonderful things about that hotel since it opened its doors. Is he a manager of something?"

"No, not exactly." No need to tell her Lee owned the hotel. Deciding to change the subject, she glanced up at Shundra and said, "You look better."

Shundra smiled. "I feel better. I must have looked a sight when I showed up."

"No, you just looked tired, like you hadn't got much sleep and hadn't eaten in a while. You need to remember you're doing it for two now."

"I know."

"So where did you go after overhearing your parents' argument?"

Shundra nervously nibbled her bottom lip. "I figured

they would talk with all my friends, those both away at college and those still at home, so I checked into a hotel. The next day I figured, knowing Dad, he probably had the entire police force in the state of Minnesota looking for me, so after looking you up on the internet, I left the car at the hotel and caught a cab to the airport. And here I am."

Yes, here she was. "So have you made any plans for the future?"

She could tell by the expression that suddenly appeared on Shundra's face that she hadn't. "Not yet."

"Well, maybe that's something you need to think about, with a baby on the way and all. Motherhood has a way of making you grow up."

Unfortunately things didn't quite work out that way with Gail, Carly thought.

"I do have a lot to think about, don't I?"

"Yes, you do. Just make sure any decisions you make are your decisions and ones you can live with for the rest of your life."

"All right. The one thing I am sure about is that I won't do to my child what Mom did to you, giving birth to a baby and then conveniently forgetting she had a child."

As Carly fried the chicken, she came close to telling Shundra that her mother didn't conveniently forget; she chose not to remember. There wasn't much of a difference, but there was one.

"Hmm, something smells awfully good in here."

Shundra, who was sitting on a swivel barstool, twirled around so fast Carly was afraid she was going to fall off. "Carly's cooking fried chicken. And it does smell good, doesn't it?"

Lee came into the kitchen and placed his arm around Carly's waist. "Need my help?"

She smiled up at him. "No, I'm almost finished."

"Then I'll set the table," Lee said, rolling up his sleeves and going to the sink to wash his hands.

"I'll help you!" Shundra said, jumping to her feet.

Lee had placed the dishes on the counter and had opened the drawer to pull out the utensils when there was a loud pounding on Carly's front door. He leaned over and whispered to Carly, "It seems Mr. Thrasher has arrived."

Carly drew in a deep breath as she headed for the door. Just knowing Lee was with her meant everything, although she wished she didn't have to expose him to the ugly side of her family's issues.

She checked through the peephole and her heart pounded when she saw Mr. Thrasher wasn't alone. Gail was with him.

"You okay?"

Without her realizing it, Lee had come to stand beside her. He was probably wondering why she was hesitating about opening the door.

She forced a smile. "Yes, I'm fine." Bracing herself, she opened the door.

Sidney Thrasher walked in without waiting for an invitation, as if he owned the place, and Carly's mother followed behind him. He turned blazing eyes on Carly when she closed the door behind them. Ignoring Lee, the man asked in a voice loud enough to shake the rafters, "Where is my daughter?"

Shundra moved forward from the breakfast bar. "I'm here, Dad. I told you not to come."

Sidney Thrasher's expression changed when he saw his daughter. Carly swore she saw the man's features soften. "Sweetheart, your mother and I are here to take you home. It's all been a mistake."

Shundra came closer. "What's been a mistake, Dad? All the mean things you said to Mom?" Looking at her mother she said, "There's Carly, Mom. You haven't even spared her a glance. Is she or is she not your daughter?"

Gail nervously tightened her hand on the shoulder strap of her designer purse.

When she looked at her husband, Shundra quickly said, "No, I don't want him to answer for you. I want to hear you speak up for yourself, Mom."

When Sidney spoke up, Shundra turned her razor-sharp gaze on her father. "No, Dad. Let Mom tell me."

Gail lifted her chin. "I gave birth to Carly, but I don't consider her my daughter. She was adopted by my aunt years ago."

Shundra crossed her arms over her chest. "And why was that, Mom? Couldn't you and Dad afford to raise her? If you couldn't afford her in the beginning, why didn't you go back and get her? Why did you tell Mike and me that she was a distant cousin?"

"Her existence wasn't anything I felt needed to be discussed," Gail said tersely.

"Well, evidently you and Dad changed your minds about that since she was being discussed the day I overheard the two of you arguing."

Sidney Thrasher stiffened his shoulders. "Now listen here, young lady. I don't know what that woman has told you about us, but—"

"That's just it, Dad. She hasn't told me anything. In fact, if it wasn't for her pressing the issue, I would not have called you. She spoke decently of the two of you. If I were in her shoes, I would not have."

"And why not?" Thrasher all but yelled. "We haven't done one thing to *her*."

"Nor have you done anything *for* her. She made it on her own without the two of you, just like I plan to do."

Her father waved away her words. "Don't be silly, Shundra. You don't know the first thing about taking care of yourself. You have college to complete. Then law school and—"

"And I will do those things on my own. Later. None of it matters now."

"Sweetheart," Thrasher was saying in a softer tone. "Why are you letting one silly argument between me and your mother about *that* woman cause you so much stress and worry?"

"Mainly because of what you said, Dad. I heard enough to know you have little tolerance or respect for a woman who makes a mistake and has a child out of wedlock. So how are you going to handle knowing I'm pregnant?"

Gail gasped and Sidney Thrasher turned purple. Veins appeared in his neck.

"Pregnant!" he screamed at the top of his lungs. Carly figured even her neighbors heard him. "Who dared touch you? Who got you pregnant? I want a name."

Shundra glared at her father. "You're not going to get one from me."

Carly was certain she saw smoke coming out of Mr. Thrasher's ears. She watched him breathe in slowly, as if trying to control himself and gain power over the situation. Gail, she noticed, was quietly sobbing into a handkerchief.

"Come on home, baby," Sidney Thrasher said, his voice going soft again. "Your mother and I will make all the arrangements. No one will ever know."

"That's what you and Mom are good at, Dad, covering things up, making them disappear. Well, it won't happen in this case. I'm not getting an abortion. I am having my baby."

"Don't be a fool, Shundra. Of course you're getting an abortion. Why let one mistake ruin your whole life? Hell, if your mother had been smart enough to get an abortion twenty-eight years ago, we wouldn't even be having this conversation."

* * *

Lee had heard enough. Anger flared within him. He hadn't needed to feel Carly stiffen beside him to know how Thrasher's words had affected her. The man's words had even affected him.

Ignoring Carly's tug on his arm when he moved forward, he said in a sharp voice, "You have just crossed a damn line, Thrasher. I knew you were an ass when you walked in here uninvited, but what you just said proved you're a bigger ass than I thought."

Sidney Thrasher glanced over at Lee, as if noticing him for the first time. He stiffened his spine and tightened his shoulders. A furious look appeared on his features. "How dare you speak to me that way," he said in mounting rage. "Do you know who I am?"

Lee gave the man a hostile glare. "Yes, like I said, you're an ass. You have a lot of nerve saying such awful things about Carly."

Thrasher's nostrils flared in fury. "I don't give a damn about her. I'm just here for my daughter."

"And she doesn't appear to be going with you, so I suggest you leave," Lee ordered in a furious tone.

Thrasher looked at Carly. "You better tell your friend to back off or I'll make things hard for you. I'll make sure you never find employment anywhere ever again."

Carly moved forward to stand beside Lee and lifted her chin. "I'd like to see you try it."

It was obvious Thrasher hadn't expected Carly to talk back to him. "Fine. I checked out a few things on the flight here. I know that you work as a cook at the Grand MD Hotel. All it will take is a phone call and you'll be unemployed and out on the streets."

"Dad, no!" Shundra pleaded. "I won't let you ruin Carly because of me. I'll go with you and Mom, but I'm not getting an abortion."

"You don't have to go with them unless you want to, Shundra," Lee said angrily. He was mere seconds from knocking the hell out of Thrasher. "He's bluffing about having any influence over Carly's job. He doesn't know the owner."

Thrasher's features contorted with furious shock. "How dare you call me a liar?"

"I dare because Lee Madaris is the owner," Lee said, taking a step toward Thrasher. "And *I* am Lee Madaris." Lee ignored the shocked look on both Thrasher's and Gail's faces. "And since Carly plans to marry me, a job at the hotel is the last thing she needs to worry about. Now get out."

Gail and Sidney looked at Carly as if they actually thought she would intervene on their behalf. She lifted her chin and stared at them in disgust. "You heard Lee. Please go. You aren't welcome here." She looked past them to Shundra. "You can leave or stay. The choice is yours, not theirs."

Shundra lifted her chin as well. "I'm staying."

Sidney glared at Shundra. "You're making a mistake."

"If I am, then I learned from the best. My parents," Shundra said.

Then, without saying another word, an angry Sidney stormed out and Gail followed.

Lee closed the door behind them, smiled slightly and then said to Shundra and Carly, "Come on, ladies. Let's eat."

The three of them had finished dinner and were about to dive into dessert when there was a knock on the door. Although this knock was civil, Carly couldn't help wondering if Gail and Mr. Thrasher had returned.

She met Lee's gaze.

"You want me to get that?" he asked.

"No," she said, getting up from the table. "I will." If the Thrashers had returned she had choice words for them. She had tolerated their dislike of her for the last time.

Moving toward the door, Carly was very much aware that Lee was by her side and Shundra was on her heels. She looked through the peephole and frowned. A man she didn't recognize was standing there.

She spoke to him through the door. "Yes, may I help you?"

"Yes. I need to talk to Shundra, please."

"Shelton?" Shundra said, moving closer to the door.

"You know him?" Lee asked her.

Shundra nodded. "Yes, Shelton Chapman. He's my father's pilot and the father of my baby. It's okay to open the door."

Carly opened the door to what she had to admit was a very handsome man with a serious look on his face. He was respectful enough to give her a smile and say, "Thank you, ma'am, for allowing me to see her. I'm Shelton Chapman."

"You're welcome." Carly heard his Southern accent and wondered where he was from. She then proceeded to introduce herself in a way she had never done before. "I'm Carly Briggs, Shundra's sister."

The man's smile widened and Carly noticed the cutest dimple in his chin.

"This is my fiancé, Lee Madaris," Carly added, liking the way she could introduce Lee as well.

The man extended his hand out to Carly for a handshake and then to Lee. "Nice meeting you both."

"Shelton? Why are you here? Why aren't you piloting the plane to take my parents back home?"

"I was fired."

"Fired?" Shundra said in surprise. "Why would Dad fire you, especially when he needs to leave Vegas?"

Shelton hesitated and then said, "Is there someplace we can talk privately?"

Shundra waved off his request. "No need. You can say what you have to say in front of Carly and Lee. They know all my secrets."

"Evidently I don't," Shelton said. "Why didn't you tell me you were pregnant?"

Shundra's mouth dropped open. "How did you find out?"

"Your parents. When they returned to the jet, they were fit to be tied, madder than hell. I overheard what they were plotting to do. They were discussing how to get you out of Vegas even if they had to have you kidnapped. Your father went on to say that once he got you back to Minnesota he'd make you have an abortion, and he didn't care that you didn't want one."

Shundra gasped.

"I knew if you were pregnant the baby was mine, so I confronted your father."

"You did?" Shundra asked.

"Yes. I told him I was the father of your baby. Let's just say he wasn't happy about it, and what he said next doesn't matter. In the end, he fired me and said he had connections and would ruin me so I would never work anywhere again."

"Thrasher seems to enjoy throwing that threat around," Lee Madaris muttered, shaking his head.

"I'll find work," Shelton said. "I refuse to believe your father has connections with every single airline. But the reason I came here, even in spite of your parents' threats, is to ask you to marry me. I have some money saved, and I can make a home for you and our child, Shundra. You won't have all the luxuries you were used to, but—"

"You're only marrying me because of the baby? Out of obligation?" Shundra asked.

Carly felt that this particular part of the conversation was one she and Lee should not be privy to. "Lee, I never showed you my garden."

Lee looked at her strangely for a minute before getting her hint. “Oh, okay. I was wondering when you were going to get around to doing that.”

He and Carly then walked out the French doors.

“You have information for me?” Bracey asked when Weber entered the room.

“Yes,” Weber said, smiling. “I got Grassley drunk the other night by slipping some Coral into his vodka. He talked his ass off.”

Coral was the new drug on the market. The shit was hard to get ahold of and usually didn’t show up in the bloodstream for a while. The beauty of the drug was that although he would wake up with a slight hangover, he wouldn’t remember a thing.

“So what did he say about Harrison’s body?”

“According to Grassley, he helped Nash bury it in an empty lot in Miami Gardens.”

“It needs to resurface,” Bracey said.

“I thought you would say that,” Weber said. If the body resurfaced it would show the big man that Nash couldn’t be depended on to get a job done. “Nash is gonna be in hot water when the dead body he was supposed to get rid of shows up.”

Bracey was silent for a minute. “That’s what I want. And that’s also why I want to find that woman before he does.”

Chapter 16

"I thought they needed privacy," Carly said while she and Lee strolled through her backyard.

"I understand. Do you really have a garden?"

Carly smiled. "Yes. It's over there. Come, let me show you."

Her backyard was small and the paved patio extended across most of it. A high privacy fence enclosed the entire space.

Carly led him to several rows of plants. "These are my lantanas," she said, taking him to the first row. "And these are my Salvia greggii." They walked a few feet more. "And these here," she said, widening her arms to indicate multiple rows, "are my—"

"Birds of paradise," Lee finished for her, smiling.

"Yes. My favorite. Whenever I did something well in school my aunt would send me an arrangement."

Lee nodded. "How did you get them to grow here?"

She smiled. "A good irrigation system. You don't want to see my water bill."

Lee could tell she was proud of her garden and she should be. He could see that she'd spent a lot of her time out here.

He leaned against the side of her house. Carly's expression projected fulfillment, gratification. She was proud. Her plants were something she could call her own. Something she had that depended on her. He knew, in a way, she also depended on them. She gave to them and they gave back.

"Carly?"

"Yes?"

"Do you know your father?"

The look that suddenly appeared in her eyes showed she was surprised by his question. "My father?"

"Yes. The man who got Gail pregnant more than twenty-eight years ago."

Carly didn't say anything at first, but then, "No. I've never been around Gail long enough to ask, and Aunt Ruthie doesn't know. Gail refused to tell her. According to my aunt, Gail didn't have a boyfriend and wasn't dating at the time. She figured Gail must have been sneaking out of the house at night or something. Why do you ask?"

Lee shrugged. "I'm just curious. You are such a passionate person and your mother seems so..."

"Cold? Unfeeling? Heartless?" Carly said. "I often wondered if perhaps she was raped because she treated me with such dislike at times."

Wanting to change the subject and not talk about her parents any longer, Carly asked, "What do you think of Shelton Chapman?"

"He's older than your sister."

"Almost eleven years older," Carly said. "He seems mature though. Ready to take on his responsibility."

"He stood up to Thrasher," Lee said. "I like that. And I think he can handle Shundra. He's an ex-military man. I can tell by the way he carries himself."

"She deliberately tempted him into making love to her."

When Lee raised a brow, Carly smiled and said, "I know because she told me."

Lee shook his head. "In that case, he probably didn't have a chance. What do you think she'll do? Think she'll marry him?"

"I don't know. Aunt Ruthie claimed Mr. Thrasher sheltered his kids, but Shundra seems to have a mind of her own. She certainly had no problem standing up to them."

"Until she thought he was going to harm you. Then she was ready to cave in. I was surprised by that," Lee admitted. "It showed that although the two of you haven't spent much time together, she cares for you."

Carly had been surprised at Shundra's reaction as well. "She's young, but maybe marrying Shelton will be the best thing for her."

Lee moved toward Carly and stopped in front of her. "Speaking of marriage…is our wedding still on for this weekend?"

She seemed surprised by his question. "Why would you think otherwise?"

He caressed the side of her face. "You've had a lot of excitement. A sister you never got to know shows up on your doorstep. You might think playing catch-up with her is more important than marrying me."

He has to be kidding, Carly thought, looking into the deep darkness of the eyes holding hers hostage. Earlier, he had witnessed the craziness of her family. He had pretty much heard her own mother admit she'd never wanted

Carly as a daughter. And he hadn't run. He wanted her in a way no one else ever had. Yet he was standing here questioning whether she still wanted to marry him?

A shiver ran through Carly in response to the gorgeous person standing in front of her. There was more to Lee Madaris than just his looks. He had a way of making her feel special and desirable without even trying.

It had been a futile effort on her part to believe she would be marrying him just for passion. She loved him. There wasn't a single part of her that didn't love him.

Carly wrapped her arms around his neck. Knowing he wanted her and no one else sent her spirits soaring. "Nothing is more important to me than marrying you, Lee."

She inched closer. His body felt hard and solid against hers. "So, if you think you can get rid of me, think again. Do you honestly think I'd let all this passion go to waste?"

His gaze held steady to hers. "I hope not."

"I won't."

And then she leaned up on tiptoe and kissed him. Her intent was to deliver a slow, lingering kiss, but Lee took over and deepened the kiss, sending every inch of her body into a tailspin of desire.

Lee's arms spread across Carly's backside as he pressed her body closer to his. He needed this kiss as a way to affirm what would always be between them. He needed her to know that nothing her mother or stepfather said had any bearing on their relationship.

"Carly? Lee? Where are you guys?"

He broke off the kiss upon hearing Shundra's voice but kept his arms around Carly's waist.

"We're over here," Carly called out.

Moments later, Shelton and Shundra appeared around the corner of the house. They were smiling. "We're getting married," Shundra announced. "But there was a stipulation I made."

"Why doesn't that surprise me? Sisters who look alike and think alike," Lee whispered close to Carly's ear.

"Shundra wants to finish college, and I support her doing that," Shelton said.

"I think that's a wonderful idea," Carly said.

"If you need a job as a pilot, Shelton, I can sign you on," Lee offered. "My partner, DeAngelo Di Meglio, and I own the Grand MD in both Dubai and here in Vegas. Sometime next year, we'll begin construction of a Grand MD in Paris. That means we will be increasing our international travel. Kevin, my present pilot, has requested a backup so our expansion won't take more time away from his family. The job is yours, if you want it."

Shelton was shocked. "You're offering me a job? Just like that?"

Lee smiled. "Thrasher fired you and I'll hire you. Yes, just like that."

A huge smile spread across Shelton's face. "Yes, I would love to come work for you. Thank you."

"You're welcome."

"Have the two of you decided when you plan to marry?" Carly asked, smiling. She couldn't believe the job offer Lee had made to Shelton, and she could tell from the looks on the couple's faces that they were appreciative.

"Tonight. At a chapel here that stays open twenty-four hours. I've already called, and they are expecting us," Shelton said, smiling. "I don't want to discount Mr. Thrasher's threat to have Shundra kidnapped. Then tomorrow we'll fly to my home in Charleston so she can meet my family."

"Charleston is a beautiful city. I've been there a number of times," Lee said.

"Well, if my grandmother has her way you might be

visiting there again for our wedding. Although we'll marry here in Vegas, I'm sure my grandmother wants us to have a more traditional wedding when I get home," Shelton said, laughing.

"Your grandmother's name wouldn't happen to be Felicia Laverne, would it?" Lee asked, grinning.

"No. It's Ollie Mae. Why?"

"She sounds a lot like my great-grandmother."

"So will the two of you be witnesses at our wedding tonight?" Shundra asked.

Lee glanced down at Carly and smiled. Then he looked back at the couple. "We would love to."

A few hours later, Carly and Lee witnessed Shelton and Shundra pledge their lives to each other. Things had happened so quickly that Carly still couldn't believe it.

Her sister was getting married. Shelton had taken Shundra shopping for a wedding outfit—a beautiful blue dress—and Lee and Carly had met the couple at the designated chapel a little before midnight.

Carly wondered if the chapel where she would be getting married on Saturday was similar to this one. Lee was making all the arrangements. He said his business partner, Angelo, and Angelo's wife, Peyton, would be their witnesses. Heather and Joel would be flying in to attend too. Her best friend said there was no way she would be left out. Because the wedding was a secret, Carly couldn't tell Shundra about it, much less invite her to attend.

When Shelton and Shundra were pronounced man and wife, Shelton kissed his bride. Carly smiled at how happy her sister seemed to be. Shundra was young; it was a month before her twentieth birthday. Carly hoped things worked out for the couple. Thanks to Lee, Shelton had a job, which meant Shundra and Shelton might make Vegas their home.

Tonight, compliments of Lee, they had the honeymoon suite at the Grand MD.

"Ready to go?" Lee asked her.

Carly and Lee would celebrate with the newlyweds before the couple headed to their suite and left for Charleston the next day. Shundra promised to call Carly when she and Shelton reached his parents' home. Also compliments of Lee, the Grand MD company jet would fly them there.

Carly looked up at Lee and smiled. "Yes. I'm ready."

He took her hand and leaned over to whisper, "In four days it will be our time."

Chapter 17

"Last chance. Are you sure you want to do this?"

Carly smoothed down her dress for the hundredth time, loving the feel of silk and lace beneath her fingers. Heather and Joel had arrived on Thursday, and Heather had brought the perfect dress from Spain. Heather had asked what colors she preferred, and Carly had chosen her favorite color, yellow, and the color Lee loved seeing her wear, green. It was a beautiful combination.

Heather stood in the doorway in her slip, yet to slide into her own dress.

"I'm positive I want to do this." Carly paused before adding, "I love him, Heather."

A huge smile spread across Heather's face. "I knew it! I told Joel when we shared dinner with the two of you last night that you had fallen in love with him. I could see it all over your face."

Carly slid into her shoes…also from Spain. "What did I do to give myself away?"

"Nothing. I just know you. I could feel the vibes. There is a strong chemistry between the two of you. But I also felt love whenever you looked at him. It's obvious to me in a way that it never was when you were with Nathaniel. I take it Lee doesn't know how you feel."

"Of course he doesn't," Carly said, smoothing down her dress again. "And I don't want him to know because our marriage is not supposed to be based on love but on passion and convenience."

Nothing could have made that more clear than the documents he'd presented to her the other day. It hadn't been a prenuptial agreement as she'd assumed, but they had been papers proving he had purchased the property she had dreamed of owning the first day she'd arrived in Vegas. Not only had he bought that small piece of land for her, he had also purchased the land surrounding it for future expansion. It was more than she had envisioned ever owning. And, true to his word, the documents also specified he would provide all the money for the expenses of building her restaurant from start to finish.

And all she had to do was to marry him.

The ceremony would take place soon. He was sending a car for her, Heather and Joel. She still didn't know where the wedding would take place.

"I hope you ladies are ready because the car Lee sent has arrived," Joel called out from the living room.

Carly checked her watch. "He's early."

Heather chuckled. "Lee is anxious. I think he's really looking forward to this wedding."

Carly smiled. She hoped so.

"Keep it up and you're going to wear out the floor, Lee," Angelo said, leaning back against a wall as he watched Lee pace. "I'm already beginning to question things."

Lee stopped his pacing. "Question things like what?"

"Why you're getting married."

Lee rolled his eyes. "You know why I'm marrying. You're the only one besides Peyton who knows...since I'm sure you told her. Where is she, by the way?"

"Out by the pool talking to your wedding planner. Peyton found out the woman used to live on Chicago's South Side, and they happen to know some of the same people. Small world, huh?"

"Whatever." Lee began pacing again. All morning he'd kept asking himself if he was doing the right thing. Then all he had to do was close his eyes and see Carly's face and he knew he was. He wanted her. Damn, he wanted her.

"You know what I think, Lee?"

"No, what?" Lee asked.

"That you've fallen in love with Carly."

Not only did Lee miss a step, he almost tripped over himself. He glared at Angelo. "What the hell are you talking about?"

Angelo smiled. "I'm talking about the way you're acting. I remember another man acting just the way you are on his wedding day."

"Who?"

"Me." Angelo smiled. "You do know that when I was first attracted to Peyton it was only a sexual thing."

Lee waved off his words. "I know. You told me. You wanted her bad."

"Yeah, I did. Just the way you want Carly."

Lee stopped walking and turned to Angelo. "And how do you know how much I want Carly?"

"You told me. And when you did it made me remember that I wanted Peyton the same way."

Lee doubted it. Carly had done more than just get under his skin. She was so embedded inside of him that it wasn't funny. Before he could reply to Angelo, he heard a car pull up outside. Then an excited Peyton stuck her head in the room's door. "She's here!"

Lee's stomach tightened and he drew in a deep breath. Anticipation consumed him.

"Last chance to make a clean break if that's what you want to do."

Lee shook his head with a smile. "It's not what I want to do."

Angelo pushed away from the wall. "Then I guess it's time to go claim your future wife."

Joel helped Carly out of the stretch limo. The limo had driven through a security gate before stopping at a clubhouse with a pool. She saw a huge mansion on the hill and didn't know what to think. Then Lee walked out of the clubhouse. She smiled when she saw him.

Lee shook hands with Heather and Joel and then turned his full attention to Carly.

He leaned over and kissed her lips. "You look sensational."

She returned his smile. "So do you." The house was humongous, stately looking, with an immaculate lawn and beautiful flowering trees. "Where are we?" she asked.

"This place is owned by a family friend, Sterling Hamilton, and he gave me the—"

"Sterling Hamilton?" Carly asked, knowing Heather was staring hard at Lee as well. "*The* Sterling Hamilton? The movie star turned director and producer?"

Lee's smile widened. "Yes. One and the same."

"And he's a friend of your family?" Heather asked in shock.

"Yes."

"And he loaned you the pool area for us to marry?" Carly inquired, making sure she understood clearly.

Lee shook his head. "No, Sterling gave me the use of this entire estate, but I decided this particular area was best for our small group. I decided against a chapel on the Strip because I didn't want us to be married by some Elvis impersonator."

He took her hand. "Come on. Angelo and Peyton are waiting for us inside, as well as the lady I hired to plan all this."

Moments later, when Carly stepped into the clubhouse, she let out a surprised gasp at the same time Heather did. The place was immaculate. It was beautifully decorated with her favorite flowers—birds of paradise. There was an inside fountain that spouted water beneath an enchantingly decorated arch.

"Although we'll have another wedding in Houston at Christmas, I wanted this one to be special."

She drew in a deep breath, so full of love for Lee that she felt she would burst. "Thank you."

His hands tightened around hers. "The Di Meglios met you that night you came out of the kitchen as a chef, but I want to reintroduce you to them as the woman I'm marrying. And I want to introduce Heather and Joel to them as well. The minister who will be officiating the ceremony and the wedding planner are also here."

Introductions were made. Carly liked Angelo and Peyton immediately. If they knew the true nature of her and Lee's marriage, they didn't let on.

"We're ready to get things started, Mr. Madaris," Joan Crowley, the wedding planner, said, smiling.

Carly figured that Lee had arranged for a meal to be served directly after the ceremony when she saw a caterer set up a beautifully decorated food table in an adjoining room. He led her over to the beautiful arch. She stood beside him, with Heather and Angelo to either side of them. Joel and Peyton watched.

"You two can join hands," the minister said, grinning. It was meant to be a joke since it wasn't lost on the minister, or anyone else, that Lee hadn't let go of Carly's hand since she had arrived.

Lee tightened his grip on Carly's hand, seemingly not bothered by the jest.

"Now," the minister said. "We can begin."

A little while into the ceremony, when Lee slid the wedding ring—a huge five-carat diamond with an overlapping wedding band—onto her finger, Carly heard Heather gasp. The ring was jaw-droppingly gorgeous and Carly could only stare down at it in amazement. When the minister got her attention back on the ceremony and not on her rings, she placed the wedding band she had purchased a few days ago onto Lee's finger.

"By the power vested in me by the state of Nevada, I now pronounce you man and wife. You may kiss your bride, Mr. Madaris."

The moment Carly looked into Lee's eyes she was carried back in time, to the night when she had met him. Her world hadn't been the same since. He cupped her face in the palms of his hands and kissed her.

Immediately, her knees weakened, and just as she felt as if she would swoon, he released her mouth and smiled down at her.

"I present to all of you Lee and Carly Madaris," the minister said.

And it was then, at that very moment, that it hit Carly that she was truly married to Lee. She couldn't help the smile that spread across her lips. Clapping brought her back around as everyone gave her words of congratulations.

"A special meal has been prepared," Lee whispered to her when a teary and happy Heather hugged her tight and wouldn't let go.

Moments later, with her hand still tucked in his, Lee led her to the adjoining room, where a table had been set for them and their friends.

Yes, they might have another wedding when they went to his home in December, but this particular ceremony that he had planned would always hold a special place in her heart.

"I just got word from Kevin that the jet is ready," Lee whispered to her after the table had been cleared. The meal had been as delicious as it had looked.

"All right." Her bags were packed for their flight to Dubai, and she was excited about visiting a place she'd never been to before.

"I'd like to make a toast." Angelo stood with his champagne glass raised. "To Lee and Carly. I wish the two of you the best. May you have a long and happy future together."

That sentiment began a series of toasts and Carly was glad no one mentioned the word *love* when it came to their marriage. When it was time to leave, and she and Lee slid into the back of the limo that would carry them to the airport, he pulled her close to his side and placed his arm across the back of the seat.

"I meant what I said earlier. You look sensational," Lee said.

"Thanks. And you look rather great yourself." He did, in his black tux.

"So you think the wedding went well?" he asked her.

"I think it was a beautiful ceremony, Lee. Thanks for putting it together."

"Joan Crowley did all the work. You know we'll be doing this again in a few months, and knowing my family it will probably be on a bigger scale."

She nodded. "You're certain your great-grandmother will want another wedding?"

"Positive. My cousin Christy had to marry Alex when her life was in danger in some forsaken country. Alex was injured during their trip back, and their wedding was legit, but that didn't stop Mama Laverne from letting them know that as soon as Alex got back on his feet, she wanted a Madaris wedding."

"I take it she got the wedding she wanted."

Lee chuckled. "Yes, she did. It seems to always work out that way. She'll get her wedding, but I got to pick my bride."

Carly didn't say anything. Whether he had intended to or not, Lee had just reminded her why they had married. Not because he loved her, but because he hadn't wanted his great-grandmother running his life.

Bracey looked at Weber. "Everything's set for the discovery of Harrison's body?"

"Yes, I've arranged for some construction workers to come across it in a couple of weeks."

A smile touched Bracey's face. "Good. It will show the big man just how incompetent Nash is when carrying out an important task."

Weber returned the smile. "And that's what you want, right?"

"Yes, that's what I want."

Chapter 18

"How long will it take for us to get to Dubai?" Carly asked as she and Lee buckled their seat belts.

"Flight time is eighteen hours. Most of it is over the Atlantic Ocean."

"Nonstop?"

"Kevin will need to make a brief stop in Algeria to refuel."

"The farthest I've flown out of the States was to Paris, and that was only seven hours. I can't imagine being in the air for eighteen hours."

Lee smiled over at her. "I promise you won't be bored."

Carly swallowed the lump in her throat as she stared at Lee. He sat across from her, strikingly handsome, with dark eyes so sexy the tips of her breasts ached.

She had no doubt the next eighteen hours would be anything but boring. She had been initiated into the Mile High Club the last time she'd been on his jet. Memories of that time still made her blush. For this flight, he had instructed his pilot that they were not to be disturbed unless there was an extreme emergency. A smiling Kevin had simply nodded.

"I hope you're not upset that your sister wasn't invited to the wedding."

She waved off his words. "I'm not upset. We both agreed to keep our marriage a secret until we go to your home in December. Besides, Shundra has her hands full with meeting Shelton's family this weekend. She was excited about that."

"I hope you have that same excitement when you meet *my* family."

"I will." She paused. "Do you regret marrying me? It's been four hours already."

"It could be forty hours or four hundred. I doubt marrying you is something I will ever regret," Lee said softly.

Carly wished she could believe that. She loved him so much and hoped that even if he didn't love her that he would always want her. To have another person, especially Lee, not want her would be devastating.

"The plane has leveled off now," Lee said, interrupting her thoughts.

He had already unbuckled his seat belt and was standing in front of her. Like her, he was still wearing the clothes they'd gotten married in.

Wordlessly, he leaned down to unbuckle her seat belt and his scent sent anticipation stirring in her stomach. Once her seat belt was free, she reached out and grabbed his tie to pull his lips down to hers.

He returned her kiss with a passion they were familiar with, but this time there was more. More heat. A deeper craving. More than an extreme case of lust. She felt all three emotions and she was determined to make sure he felt them as well.

So when he slid his tongue between her lips, she captured it, mating with it greedily. There was nothing elegant about her response. Every part of her body trembled with a need only he could satisfy. A need that pushed her to act in ways she'd never acted before.

"Carly."

He pulled back from the kiss to whisper her name on a breathless sigh. Then he swept her out of the seat and into his arms.

"You can't carry me up the staircase."

"I know."

Instead of attempting the narrow staircase, he moved toward the counter that served as a bar for the kitchenette. Lee pressed a button. The counter retracted and a padded bench extended. He began removing his jacket.

She began removing her clothes as well, first kicking off her shoes, then sliding out of her dress. She was down to her bra and panties when a totally naked Lee said, "Let me finish."

Her agreement was absorbed by the urgency of his mouth taking hers. The invasion of his tongue shook her to the core, sending sensations roaring within her as his tongue made circular motions and caused her to moan. The featherlike licks inside her mouth were driving her mad with desire.

As if he knew she was hot and ready, he eased down on the bench and pulled her into his lap. He nudged her thighs apart so she could straddle him.

She felt it, his hard erection pulsing at the entrance to her womanly core, causing her inner muscles to tighten in anticipation. Her nipples ached with an urgency she felt throughout her entire body.

"Tell me what you want," he whispered, using the tip of his tongue to swipe across her lips. "Tell me, Carly. I'll give you anything you want."

She wanted to scream that the one thing she wanted was something she could never have. His love.

But instead she said, "You. I want you, Lee."

And he gave himself to her. She sucked in a deep breath at the feel of his hard thrust going all the way to the hilt. He held tight to her hips as he established the rhythm, grinding against her each time she brought her body down to him. They stared into each other's eyes, and Carly felt intense love for Lee—the man who was looking at her as if she was all he wanted.

The strength of his thrusts left no doubt about his desire for her. In response, she took each and every sensual onslaught as elation soared through her. If he was hungry for her, then she was starving for him. She let him know it each and every time she came down on his erection.

Suddenly he grabbed her buttocks, locking them to him, as he threw his head back and growled like one hell of a satisfied man. The sound stirred something within her, causing her body to detonate right along with his.

Caught in the throes of what seemed like an endless orgasm, she screamed his name as his release jetted full force inside of her. Aftershocks of pleasure ripped through her until she finally collapsed against him and he gripped her tight, holding her right there.

She felt him throbbing inside of her and knew he would be ready for another round in a little while. So would she. If passion was what would hold their marriage together, then let it rip. They would share enough passion to last a lifetime.

Fighting for strength, she lifted her face from his shoulder to look at him. The dark eyes staring back at her started a stirring in her belly. And then he kissed her again, hungrily.

At some point they would make it to the bedroom; she was sure of it. But for now, this place was perfect.

"I need you to go to Vegas with me, Nash," Driskell said, leaning back in his chair.

"You anticipate trouble with this Madaris guy?"

"Not sure, so bring your men in case. He put me off, claiming he had a business trip out of the country. It checked out. However, I need to make sure he understands that turning me down isn't an option. Our investors want his casinos, and what they want, they get. They've already established their people on the inside of the hotel and are depending on us to make sure they stay put."

"No problem. My men will be ready to leave when you are."

"They probably won't be needed. I got word from one of my informants that Madaris recently got married, and I'm sure he wouldn't want anything to happen to his wife. But still, I like covering all my bases."

A half hour later, when Nash was on his way to his car, one of his men, by the name of Grassley, approached. "I got a match for that woman's voice."

Nash lifted a brow. "How?"

"I talked to a waitress who works at that restaurant in Miami. Convinced her I was an undercover cop. Let her listen to the tape and she recognized the voice. She said the woman was working as a chef in the kitchen, even verified she was working the same night you took Harrison out."

Nash frowned. "*Was* working?"

"Yeah, she quit a few months back and moved to Vegas."

"Vegas? I'm sure it's just a coincidence but we're leaving for Vegas in a few days with the big man. You got the woman's name, right?"

"Yes, I have her name."

"Good. While we're in Vegas I intend to take care of her. We can't have any loose ends."

He opened his car door and got in. Before starting his car, Nash rolled down the window. "And Grassley?"

"Yes?"

"That waitress who identified the woman's voice on the tape? Make sure we take care of her as well."

Grassley smiled. "She's already been taken care of."

Nash nodded, rolled up the window and drove off. He wasn't surprised. Grassley loved to kill…especially women.

Chapter 19

"Welcome back, Mr. Madaris."

"Thanks, Phyllis," Lee said, strolling through the hotel lobby headed for his office. He wouldn't lie and say he was glad to be back, because he wasn't. He had totally enjoyed his week in Dubai with Carly and could have extended their stay for another week or two with very little effort. But there was work to do and a sting operation to begin. The latter of which he wished he had no part in.

He looked down at his hand. Already he missed the wedding band Carly had placed there on their wedding day. In just a week, it had become a part of him. It had done something to him when he'd taken it off. He wondered if she would feel the same way about removing the ring he'd given her. He couldn't wait until they could make their marriage known to everyone, especially to his family.

They had arrived back in Vegas yesterday and he'd spent most of the day at her place. He'd even spent the night, leaving before daybreak. He tried talking her into taking a couple more days off to just rest and relax but she was determined to go in to work this evening. He glanced at his watch. It was time to start his day.

A couple of hours later, after several meetings with his department heads and junior executives, he was going over various reports when the buzzer on his desk sounded. "Yes, Phyllis?"

"Mr. Driskell is on line two, sir."

Lee inhaled deeply. "Thanks. Put him on in a few. I need to finish up something."

After disconnecting the call with Phyllis, Lee entered the designated code so the call could be recorded by the FBI. He drew in another breath when Phyllis connected the call. More than anything, he wished Carly was still in Dubai, but she had returned with him and hadn't yet decided if she would go back.

"This is Lee Madaris."

"Mr. Madaris, this is Colin Driskell. I spoke with you a couple of weeks ago, before your trip to Dubai. I hope you enjoyed yourself."

Lee frowned. He was certain he hadn't mentioned where he'd been going, which meant the man had checked out his story about leaving the country. "What can I do for you, Driskell?"

"It's what *I* can do for *you,* Mr. Madaris. I mentioned having a way to maximize your profits."

"So I recall. Maximizing my profits in what way?"

"As I explained the last time we talked, we need to hold a private conversation for me to share any details. You indicated you would have some free time when you returned."

"Well, I was mistaken about that. I'm swamped with paper work. Maybe some other time," Lee said. The FBI had suggested that Lee continue to push Driskell, to see if he would get annoyed enough to say something to incriminate himself.

"Mr. Madaris, you are trying my patience."

Lee leaned back in his chair. "And who the hell are you supposed to be?"

"Someone you wouldn't want to toy with," Driskell warned. Then he paused. "I understand congratulations are in order."

The hairs on the back of Lee's neck stood up at the same time a cold knot formed in his stomach. "Are they? I wasn't aware."

"Sorry, I must be mistaken."

"Undoubtedly, you are" was Lee's comeback.

"If you determine that I'm not mistaken after all, you know how to reach me."

Lee drew in a deep breath. As far as he was concerned, he had played this cat-and-mouse game long enough. Driskell was hinting about his marriage; Lee was sure of it. Was this the man's way of letting Lee know he knew about Carly and would use her as leverage to get what he wanted? Lee would not risk anything happening to his wife.

"Wait, Driskell. I'll work you into my schedule this week. What about Friday?"

"We meet *today,* Madaris. At your hotel, in a public place. I'll decide where when I get there. I'm already in Vegas, so I'll see you in a few hours." Driskell then clicked off the phone.

Lee hung up. He was so mad he actually felt the muscles of his forearms harden into stone beneath his sleeves. He recognized the three short rings and picked up the phone immediately. "Yeah, Gause?"

"What the hell was that about?"

Lee's chest actually felt as if it would burst. "I got married last weekend. It was a private affair that was supposed to be a secret. Evidently Driskell found out about it."

"And he wanted to let you know he knew. That means he plans to use your wife's safety as leverage to make sure you do what he wants you to. Since you have every intention of working with him, she shouldn't be in any danger."

Lee stood and moved away from his desk. "I'm not taking any chances. I'm sending her away until this is over."

"To where?"

"Back to Dubai." *Or to Uncle Jake,* he thought, rubbing the top of his head in frustration. His uncle's ranch, Whispering Pines, was like a fortress. No one got in without Jake or his men knowing about it. And the men working for Jake were loyal to a fault.

"Let us know what you plan to do. In the meantime, Driskell wants to meet you in a public place at the hotel. And it seems he's not giving the location until the last minute. He's playing it safe just in case you're not on the up-and-up. He doesn't feel he can fully trust you yet. He's not giving you time to notify anyone so the place can be bugged."

"Will I be wired?"

"Yes. One of my men will arrive in a few to take care of that. You're being watched, so we need to be cautious."

"What about the men he's working for? Those businessmen and politicians? How are you going to expose them?" Lee asked.

He recalled the investigative work his cousin Christy had done a few years ago regarding international human trafficking of teenagers. The whole organization had been orchestrated by CEOs of prominent companies and a United States senator.

"We've had people working on the inside for a while, so we can already identify some of them. Most will be represented by sleazy attorneys, and we want to make the charges stick. So far there hasn't been an eyewitness to any of the crimes."

Gause paused before continuing, "Driskell has a diary of names and accounts. That's why he's untouchable. No one messes with him for fear they will be exposed, and he uses that as leverage. Over the years he's increased his power. Our goal is to find the information Driskell is hiding."

Moments later, Lee hung up the phone. This sting had only just begun, and he was already wishing it was over.

"So, where did you go last week?" Jodie asked. She and Carly were putting icing on a cake they would serve later that night in honor of a couple's fiftieth wedding anniversary.

Carly glanced over at Jodie. "What makes you think I went somewhere?"

Jodie smiled as she shrugged. "I figured you did. You were gone for a week."

Carly smiled as she wiped her hands on a towel. She wished she could share with Jodie where she had been. Telling Heather hadn't been enough. She wanted to share her newlywed joy with everyone. She would never forget the day when Lee had taken her up to the sky tower of the Grand MD Dubai to see the sun rise over Palm Island.

The island was justly named because its shape was that of a palm tree. According to Lee, the island was considered one of the wonders of the world. Man-made, the island stretched out across the Persian Gulf and contained a number of private villas belonging to the rich and famous. It had marinas that were home to some of the biggest yachts she'd ever seen and a number of luxury seven-star hotels, of which the Grand MD was one.

On their first day in Dubai, Lee had taken her on a tour of the hotel. She'd thought the hotel in Las Vegas was simply gorgeous but the one in Dubai really stood out. One of the hotel's biggest draws was the below-sea-level hotel rooms that were enclosed in glass. From anywhere in the room, it appeared as if one were beneath the water of the Persian Gulf.

They had stayed in one of those rooms their first night, and making love seemingly underwater with all kinds of sea animals floating around was totally a unique experience.

"Carly?"

She blinked upon realizing Jodie had been trying to get her attention. "Yes?"

Jodie looked around and then leaned in closer to Carly to whisper, "I missed having you around last week because I wanted to share my good news."

Carly tilted her head. "And what good news is that?"

Jodie's face broke into a wide smile. "Jerome asked me to marry him."

Carly's mouth curved in its own smile. "Oh, Jodie, that's wonderful. Have the two of you set a date?"

The smile on Jodie's face diminished somewhat. "No. He needs to break the news to his parents. We don't know how they're going to take it, but frankly we don't care. We're getting married and that's that."

"Good for you." Carly went to the sink to wash her cooking utensils while Jodie put the finishing decorations on the cake. She tried not to think about how much she wanted to share her own excitement. Having to take off her rings and tuck them in a drawer certainly didn't make her feel like a new bride.

She had talked to Shundra that morning and her sister was doing fine. Shelton's family had welcomed her with open arms, and she felt she had not only married a good man but had gained a wonderful family. Carly knew she would feel the same way after meeting the Madarises.

Her phone vibrated in her jacket and a warm glow flowed through her. Was Lee trying to reach her? Did he want her to meet him in his suite for a quickie? The thought sent passionate shivers all through her. In Dubai they'd practically made quickies an art form.

"I'm going to take my lunch break now, Jodie. I'll be back shortly," she said, heading out of the kitchen.

"Okay."

Carly rounded the corner and quickly pulled the phone out of her jacket and saw the missed call had been from Heather and not Lee. A twinge of disappointment went through her. She hadn't been able to reach Lee earlier to thank him for the flowers he had sent to her today—a beautiful arrangement of birds of paradise.

He hadn't answered his cell phone when she called, and because that was so unlike him, she figured he was in a lot of meetings. This was his first day back to work and he probably had a lot of important matters to catch up on.

She lifted a brow when a text came in from Heather.

Call me ASAP.

Curious as to what could be so important, she punched in Heather's number and her best friend answered on the first ring. "Heather, what's up?"

"Are you someplace where you can talk privately?"

She was standing right outside the door to the kitchen, close to the service elevators. The restaurant was open for business, and the waiters and waitresses would be dashing back and forth taking orders to the kitchen. But she could hear the anxiousness in Heather's voice.

"No, wait a minute. There's a room not far away that's not being used tonight," Carly said, walking in its direction. She went inside and closed the door behind her. "Okay, what's going on?"

"You were right, Carly."

Carly raised a brow. "Right about what?"

"About what you thought you heard that night behind the restaurant, in Miami."

Carly gasped as a shiver of panic rushed through her. "How do you know?"

"Like you, I had stopped checking the internet and wasn't reading the *Miami Herald,* but today I was chatting with Rhonda. You remember her. She works as a news reporter at WKZP in Miami. She happened to mention something about a news break."

Carly swallowed. "What kind of news break?"

"A man's body was discovered by workers at a construction site earlier today. It's believed to be the body of a missing federal agent. He'd been shot in the head. Although they haven't gotten a coroner's report yet, they're speculating that it happened six months ago, and that his body was buried at that site so it would never be found. Everyone thinks it's the work of the mob since he was working undercover to expose them."

Stark fear swept through Carly. "The mob?"

"Yes, the mob."

"So, we finally meet, Mr. Madaris."

Lee stared at the man who'd introduced himself as Colin Driskell and the two men who'd accompanied him whose names were given as Nash and Bracey. Although Driskell was smiling from ear to ear, both Nash and Bracey had the looks of men whose stony expressions were permanent fixtures.

He shook hands with all three men. "Yes, we finally

meet, Driskell. I've made arrangements for us to meet in the—"

"No, Mr. Madaris," Driskell cut in. "We'll select the meeting place. You have a number of restaurants here in the hotel, and it has been suggested that we dine in Peyton's Place. I hear the food is excellent, and it has a number of private rooms."

"All right," Lee said, leading the group to the elevator. Gause was right. Driskell was not taking any chances on a possible setup.

But Lee knew Carly was back at work tonight. Did Driskell know where she worked? Was he deliberately meeting at her restaurant? Was the man throwing out another hint that if things didn't go to his liking tonight, he could find Lee's wife?

Lee forced the questions from his mind, hoping he was just being paranoid now that the sting operation had begun. He wanted to believe that Driskell's desire to dine at Peyton's Place was just a coincidence. He didn't have to worry about any of them seeing Carly since she had no reason to come out of the kitchen unless she was summoned.

The ride up to the restaurant was silent. Lee studied the three men, wondering what could have propelled them to choose this line of work, a life of crime. The street gangs they funded were taking innocent lives with drive-by shootings and robberies. Did they not see any injustice in that? And the one named Bracey had a scar across his cheek that looked like the result of a knife slash.

The elevator door opened and Lee stepped out. The restaurant's manager saw him and smiled brightly. "Mr. Madaris, welcome. I wasn't aware you had reservations this evening."

"I don't, Richard. I'm hoping my guests and I can use

one of the smaller private dining rooms to discuss business."

Richard smiled. "That won't be a problem. We have several. Please follow me this way."

The man named Nash touched the upper part of Richard's arm. "No need to lead us. Just tell us where the private rooms are and we'll pick one."

It was obvious from Richard's expression that he found the man's statement odd, but he said, "Certainly. The bank of rooms is to your right."

Lee, who knew where the rooms were, led the way while the three men followed.

Carly paced.

"I knew I hadn't dreamed that night, but when a body didn't turn up… I can still hear the voice of the mean man, the one who pulled the trigger. It's one of those voices you can never forget."

"Well, it seemed that although you weren't an eyewitness, you were an earwitness. You heard everything."

The thought of that frightened Carly. "I called the tip line that night. You don't think they can trace it back to me, do you?"

"No. How could they?"

Carly wasn't sure, but she had watched enough cop shows on television to know anything was possible. Another thing she knew was that you didn't mess with organized crime. Not only were they cold-blooded killers but she heard their network was growing by leaps and bounds as they pulled unscrupulous people into their grid.

"I'm worried, Heather. What if they find out my identity and come looking for me?"

"They wouldn't be able to find you that easily," Heather said, trying to calm her.

"Shundra did. She found out where I lived on the internet. Can you believe that?"

"If you're worried, Carly, tell Lee about it. He'll know what to do."

"I can't do that. Then it would involve him."

"Then leave the country. You said Lee offered you a chance to live in Dubai for a while. No one would go looking for you there. Hopefully after a few weeks the police will have rounded up all those responsible for that agent's death and made arrests."

"You think so?"

"Yes. Cops and federal agents take a personal interest in bringing someone to justice when the culprit was responsible for the death of one of their own."

"I hope you are..." Carly stopped talking when she heard conversations flowing in from the hallway. She didn't have to peep out of the door to know one of those voices belonged to Lee. No one in the kitchen had mentioned anything about him having a business meeting in Peyton's Place this evening. She had assumed this room wouldn't be used today. It wasn't even set up to be serviced.

"I've got to go, Heather," Carly whispered into her phone. "I'll call you later tonight when I get home."

Carly clicked off the phone. The voices were coming closer, and if she exited the room now she would run smack into Lee and his guests. That was the last thing she wanted. Lee was astute when it came to reading her. All he had to do was take one look at her to know something was wrong.

She figured she would wait until they passed by the room and then hightail it back to the kitchen. Suddenly, the voices were closer, right outside the door. The doorknob began to turn, which meant they were about to enter the room where she was hiding.

Moving quickly, she raced across the room to the freestanding wooden cabinet where additional table linen, silverware, china and mats were kept and squeezed inside. Then she closed the door behind her.

She prayed she wouldn't be detected. And she hoped their meeting didn't last long.

Upon entering the room, Lee imagined inhaling Carly's scent. He knew it was his mind playing tricks on him. He'd thought about her a lot during the day.

Turning his attention back to the matter at hand, he waited until he and the three men had entered the room before closing the door behind them and turning to Driskell.

"Let me get something straight, Driskell. I agreed to this meeting but at no time do you give my employees orders. I own this hotel—you don't. I only agreed to this meeting—"

"Because you are curious about what I can do for you," Driskell interrupted, seemingly not put off by Lee's anger.

"Partly," Lee said angrily. "But the Grand MD is doing well on its own. The next time you try giving anyone here orders, I'll call security and have you thrown out on your ass."

Nash took a step toward Lee, and Driskell touched Nash's arm to detain him. Lee's stance showed he was ready for him, if need be. Mob or no mob, Lee had no intention of letting anyone intimidate him or his staff.

Driskell rubbed his chin and stared hard at Lee. Then a smile touched his lips. "I like you, Madaris. You've got spunk. We'll do well working together."

"I haven't agreed to work with you. Cut the bullshit. Tell me what you're about, then I'll decide."

"Fine," Driskell said, taking a seat at the table. "Let's sit and talk. But first my men need to check you over to make sure you're clean."

Lee lifted his chin. "And why wouldn't I be?"

Driskell shrugged. "In my line of work, I don't like taking chances. And you're not stupid, Madaris. You know why I'm here."

"Fine," Lee said. "Have your men search me. I have nothing to hide."

"Let us determine that," the man named Bracey said, moving forward to give Lee a pat down.

Lee held up his arms and let the man proceed. The federal agent Gause had sent over had installed the recording device in the heel of Lee's shoe. It was so small that it could barely be seen with the naked eye; nor could it be picked up by any scanner. However, this entire conversation was being listened to by the FBI, who had set up in a remote location.

"Take off your shoes," Bracey ordered.

Not appreciating the man's tone, Lee glared at him before stepping out of his shoes. Bracey picked them up and checked the insides before giving them back to him.

Lee tried to maintain his cool but he was nervous. "Is all this necessary?" he asked as if extremely annoyed.

"In my line of business it is," Driskell said.

Bracey took a step back and said, "He's clean."

Lee noticed Nash's and Bracey's eyes were glued to him as he pulled the chair from the table and sat across from Driskell. "Okay, I don't have all evening. State your business, Driskell."

Carly forced herself to breathe, not understanding why Lee had even agreed to meet with these men. Clearly he knew they were not typical businessmen. And she refused to believe Lee would allow himself to be a part of anything illegal. But Driskell was talking now, outlining how he and his people could triple Lee's profit in the casino.

They were discussing cuts, what his would be and what theirs would be.

And Lee was actually listening. Even asking pointed and specific questions about what the man was saying. This didn't make sense. The Lee Madaris she knew would not be engaging with these men. He would…

What if he wasn't the Lee Madaris she knew but the man she only *thought* she knew? What if he was a different sort of person beneath the surface, like Nathaniel had been? What if the man she had married was as phony as a three-dollar bill?

Her confidence in Lee began to erode.

The more she listened to the conversation, the more her doubts about him increased. She actually began to feel sick to her stomach. How could she have allowed herself to be duped by a man for a second time?

She drew in a deep breath, feeling an anxiety attack coming on. She tried forcing herself to stay calm and be as quiet as a mouse. The last thing she needed was for anyone to detect her presence.

Then suddenly she heard another voice and hairs on the back of her neck stood up. It had played over and over in her nightmares. It was the same voice she had heard that night in the alley; she was sure of it. That meant…

Fear gripped her within its clutches. Had they found her? Was Lee involved? Did he know? She clenched her mouth tight or else she knew she would scream.

Lee hoped they'd gotten enough on the recording to at least bring warrants against these three. He was pretending his interest, had even rattled them when he suggested getting a bigger cut. One time, when Lee had called Driskell a fool for one of his offers, the man called Nash had approached Lee as if he intended to do him bodily harm.

This was playing out just like Gause wanted. The mob needed the Grand MD Hotel bad and it was showing. Driskell was getting angry, and Lee knew he could only push the man so far. "Your offer sounds good, Driskell, but I'll need to think about it."

"What's there to think about?" Driskell asked, his impatience and annoyance showing.

"For one," Lee said, leaning back in his chair, "I don't have a criminal record, and I intend to keep things that way. You haven't given me any reason to believe my business will be protected, or that I'll get preferential treatment compared to any of the other hotels on the Strip."

Driskell opened his mouth to speak when his cell phone went off. He frowned when he saw the caller ID and said, "I need to take this."

Getting up from the table, he moved toward the other side of the room, leaving Nash and Bracey standing like statues beside the table where Lee sat.

Suddenly Driskell's loud expletive echoed across the room, and then he said in a loud voice, "I said I would handle it and I will."

Lee couldn't help wondering what was going on when Driskell came back to the table and said, "An emergency just came up and I need to leave. I'll get back with you on this, Mr. Madaris, and when I do I want an answer."

"And if I don't have one?" Lee said, standing up.

"It will be in your best interest to have one" was Driskell's reply.

Lee frowned. "Is that a threat?"

"Take it whatever way you like," Driskell said, buttoning his jacket. "We'll be in touch."

He then walked out of the room with Nash and Bracey trailing behind.

* * *

"What's wrong?" Bracey asked in a confused voice as they stepped on the elevator. "It's not like you to leave any business unfinished."

"That call came from Callahan," Driskell said in an angry voice. He turned to Nash when the elevator door shut behind them. "You told me you took care of everything with Harrison."

Nash frowned. "I did take care of it."

"Then you didn't do a good enough job. According to Callahan, one of his informers called and told him that Harrison's body was discovered by construction workers. The news is going to break on all media circuits tonight."

Nash looked shocked. "That's not possible."

"If it's really Harrison's body, and the police seem to think it is, it means you screwed up big-time, Nash."

When they stepped off the elevator, Driskell walked quickly toward the exit. "We'll talk more about it after we get in the car and I return Callahan's call."

Lee stood in the doorway of the private room and ran a frustrated hand down his face as he watched the elevator door close behind the three men. He hoped like hell he'd been able to pull enough information out of Driskell to help the FBI's case. But the role he'd played had made him feel dirty.

The heel of his shoe vibrated for a moment, his cue that the recording had ended. Lee felt the need to talk to Carly. Not later but now. Before he talked to Gause, Woodman or even Alex, he had to hear her voice and be reminded of the good in the world among so much evil.

He pulled out his phone and saw he had missed a couple of her calls today. He quickly pressed the redial button and jerked around when the phone rang in the room he was in. His gaze focused on the freestanding cabinet across the room.

The phone continued ringing as he slowly walked across the room, his mind whirling in confusion with each step he took. Why would Carly's phone be ringing in the cabinet? Had she been in the room earlier and left it there?

When he reached the cabinet he heard a noise and his heart almost stopped beating. *It can't be.* But a part of him knew, even then, that it was.

He snatched the cabinet door open and his body stiffened in shock.

"Carly! What are you doing in here?"

She had a look of shocked fear on her face that made his insides twist in knots. Putting her hands out in front of her as a protective shield, she tried backing away from him. "If you come near me, Lee, I'm going to scream."

Ignoring her threat, Lee reached out for her. Instead of screaming she passed out, right into his arms.

Chapter 20

Carly opened her eyes to the sound of voices and slowly looked around the room. She was in Lee's suite. His bedroom. His bed. How?

She closed her eyes again. When her memory was less clouded, she recalled being in that room, closed tight inside that cabinet, an unknown party to his meeting. She snatched her eyes back open and pulled up into a sitting position.

She had to get out of here. She had to get away.

She was about to ease out of bed and make her escape when a deep male voice stopped her. "And just where do you think you're going?"

She closed her eyes again, willing the nightmare away. Knowing Lee was not the man she thought him to be had pain weighing her down like steel.

"The doctor just left. He said you should lie down for a while," Lee said.

She could feel his body heat when he came to stand by the bed. But she refused to open her eyes. She couldn't look at him, knowing what she knew.

"The doctor?" she asked him.

"Yes. The doctor we have on staff here at the hotel. You passed out."

"How did I get here? In your suite?"

"I carried you."

She couldn't help but snatch her eyes open at that. "Carried me?"

"Yes."

She could just imagine all the commotion that had caused. As if he'd read her thoughts, he said, "I used the service elevator. Only a couple of people saw me. I told them you'd passed out and I was taking you down to the doctor. Instead, I brought you here and called for the doctor."

He sat on the side of the bed. "Chef Blanchard called. He wanted to convince me that you hadn't been overworked. I told him I wasn't worried about that."

Tilting his head, he stared at her for a moment and then asked, "So, how do you feel?"

Instead of answering his question, she said, "I want to go home."

"Your home is wherever I am, Carly."

She closed her eyes again, fighting back her tears. Had he said that yesterday, or even this morning, the words would have meant everything to her. But now…

She reopened her eyes and stared at him. "I heard everything. You aren't the person I thought you were."

You're not the person I fell in love with.

A frown settled on his features. "You are wrong. Nothing about me has changed."

She broke eye contact with him and focused on an abstract picture on his wall. "Then I really didn't know you."

He touched her chin, asking her to look at him. "You know me."

Lee slipped out of his shoes and slid into bed beside her. She stiffened beside him. Instead of gathering her into his arms, he lay on his side facing her.

"Why were you hiding out in that cabinet, Carly? I'm tormented every time I think of what could have happened if those men had discovered you there. And according to the doctor, one of the reasons you passed out is because you were robbed of oxygen while confined for so long in such a tight space. Why were you there?"

She swallowed, feeling the tightness in her throat. "Heather called and I needed to talk with her privately, so I went into the room. I heard voices. I recognized yours and knew you were with someone. I thought the room was not being used since it wasn't set up. When I saw you and your group entering, I panicked and went into the cabinet."

"But why? When we walked in, why didn't you merely excuse yourself and leave?"

She drew in a deep breath. "Because I was upset about something and I knew you would take one look at me and know. And I didn't want you to give our relationship away in front of your business associates. I thought I could wait it out. I figured it would be a short meeting."

Lee didn't say anything. He knew she'd heard everything and had formed her own conclusions. "What were you upset about that would have caused me concern?"

She looked away again. "It doesn't matter."

"You will always matter."

Lee knew at that moment just how much he meant those words. When he'd opened that cabinet and had seen her stuffed inside, and when he'd thought about the type of men he'd met with and what they were capable of, stark fear had raced through him. If anything had happened to her, he would not have been able to handle it.

He had fallen in love with her. Madly. Irrevocably. Deeply.

"And as far as what you thought you heard, Carly..."

"I know what I heard, Lee."

He nodded. A moment passed and then he said, "I didn't want you to know. I'd hoped you would agree to go back to Dubai and stay awhile until it was over. I even thought of sending you to my uncle Jake. All I could think about was making certain you were safe."

She frowned. "What are you talking about?"

"What you heard, Carly, was all part of a setup. I'm assisting the FBI in a sting operation against the mob."

Driskell slammed down the phone and turned angry eyes on Nash. "The body has been positively ID'd as Harrison's, and the authorities are frantically trying to put things together. They know he was working undercover trying to infiltrate our organization. I thought you took care of this."

The force of Driskell's rage had Nash uneasy. He'd seen Driskell angry before but never this angry. "I don't know what happened. No construction was scheduled to take place on that site."

"Evidently there was a change in someone's plans. Damn." Then as if he suddenly remembered, Driskell asked, "What about that woman who called the tip line? You were supposed to take care of her as well. Did you?"

Nash swallowed hard. "Not yet. But I know who she is. She moved from Miami and is right here in Vegas. I had planned to take care of her while I was here."

Driskell nodded. "She needs to be taken care of now more than ever. The feds are going to put two and two together and ask the caller to come forward. Then everything I've worked so hard to build will come crumbling down."

"No, it won't," Nash said, trying to redeem himself. "I'll handle it. Grassley found out where she lives. She'll be taken care of. Tonight."

Driskell's eyes filled with fury. "Make sure that she is."

Nash left and Driskell let out an explosive curse.

"Maybe I need to make sure Nash follows through this time," Bracey said.

Driskell looked across the room at Bracey. "I agree. Make sure he takes care of her, and then afterwards, I want you to take care of him. I won't tolerate those who make costly mistakes."

Bracey nodded and then followed Nash out the door.

"Sting operation?" Carly asked, her eyes widening.

"Yes. Federal agents approached me weeks ago and told me those men would be contacting me, to try and bring me into their organization."

"How did the agents know?" she asked.

"From one of their informers. He overheard the plans and gave the agents a heads-up. I'm supposed to go along with the mob and expose them."

"That's dangerous."

"Yes, but if it will bring them to justice, I'll take the chance. But I won't take the chance of you being placed in danger. Somehow they found out I got married, and I won't let them get to you to keep me in line. I need you to go home and pack. I wanted you to go back to Dubai, but I'd feel a lot better if I sent you to Texas to my uncle Jake. His ranch is like a fortress and you'll be safe there."

Carly hesitated before she said, "One of those men you met with today is a killer, Lee."

He drew in a deep breath. "They're all killers."

"Yes, but he's a real killer. Before I moved here I witnessed a murder…at least I heard a murder take place."

He frowned. "I don't understand."

Carly told Lee what had happened that night in Miami. "So, for the longest time, I thought I imagined the whole thing, especially when there was nobody reported missing. Now there is."

He lifted a brow. "There is?"

"Yes. That's why Heather was calling. It's going to be broadcast on tonight's news. The body of a federal agent was discovered by construction workers on a piece of vacant property. I believe he's the one I heard being shot that night."

She closed her eyes. "I'll never forget him pleading for his life. And I'll never forget the sound of the man's voice that ended it. He was cold, uncaring and ruthless. I knew if I ever heard it again, I would recognize it."

Her hand began trembling. "I heard it today, Lee. He was one of the men you met with. The one you called Nash."

Lee didn't say anything for a minute, and then he eased up off the bed and pulled his cell phone from his pocket. He punched in a few numbers and then said, "Agent Gause. This is Lee Madaris. I need you to come to my suite immediately."

He clicked off his cell phone and slid it back into his pocket. "That was the federal agent in charge of the sting operation. When he arrives I want you to tell him everything that you just told me." He sat back down on the bed and took her hand into his. "Why didn't you tell me about what you thought you heard that night, Carly?"

"Why didn't you tell me about the sting operation?"

He paused. "Besides giving the agents my word that I wouldn't tell anyone, I wanted to protect you."

She nodded. "As far as me not telling you, I wasn't sure what I heard. Like I said, when there was no body I thought maybe I had dreamed the entire thing. And to be honest, Lee, I'm not sure if I ever would have told you. After Heather called, I panicked, knowing it was the mob and I had called the tip line. I'm not sure how safe and secure that line is. And I knew how easy it was for Shundra to find me, so it would be a piece of cake for anyone else."

She paused again. "I decided to tell you that I wanted to go to Dubai, and I was going to use that trip to hide out for a while. I didn't want you to know the truth. You married me knowing about all my other garbage and I didn't want to add any more to it."

He released her hand and reached up to caress her cheek. "Not garbage, Carly, but challenges. All of us have them, and it would not have mattered to me. I'm your husband like you're my wife. For better or for worse." Lee stopped and then said, "For passion and for love."

She lifted a brow. "Love?"

He nodded. "Yes. Love. I know it wasn't part of our plan or what we agreed on, but I've fallen in love with you. The moment I figured out you were in that cabinet, and it hit me what could have happened had you been discovered in there, I realized what I felt for you was more than just passion. The thought of losing you twisted my heart and chilled every bone in my body. Only love could put that much fear into a person. Into me, Carly."

When he saw tears glistening in her eyes, he said softly, "I didn't tell you I loved you to make you cry. If it's because you feel bad for not loving me back, that's okay. I'm going to love you anyway with the hope and belief that one day you will love me back."

She swiped at her tears. "That's not why I'm crying."

"Then why are you crying?"

"I'm crying because I love you too, and I didn't think you would ever love me back."

Lee pulled her into his arms and gently rubbed her back. "Baby, I love you back and then some. So much."

Carly shivered at the degree of love she heard in Lee's voice. And she loved him just as much. From the first, he had let her know he wanted her and he hadn't backed down. He had broken her defenses and made her fall in love with him. And the thought that he loved her too was overwhelming.

"Carly?"

She lifted her head from his chest and looked at him, actually feeling the love. And when he lowered his mouth toward hers, she met him for a long, hard kiss that had her melting. No telling how long the kiss would have lasted if there hadn't been a knock on the door.

Lee slowly pulled his mouth from hers. "I guess I better let Agent Gause in."

Carly smiled. "Yes, I guess you better. Give me a second to freshen up and I'll be out."

"Okay."

She drew in a deep breath as she watched Lee leave the room. Now that they had revealed their feelings for each other, she should be filled with joy, but that emotion was overshadowed by anxiety. She didn't want to be involved in anything that had to do with the mob, and she wished Lee wasn't involved either.

But they were both involved and she could only hope the ordeal ended quickly.

Agent Gause removed his glasses to pinch the bridge of his nose. It wasn't that he'd found Carly's story strange because he thought it was false. He knew everything she'd said to be true. Her facts matched up with the ones his agency had already gathered, and now Agent Harrison's body had turned up.

What he found strange was the coincidence that, through no effort of their own, hers and Lee Madaris's lives had connected. What were the odds that a woman who could be a key witness to the murder of an FBI agent was now married to the man the agency was using in a sting operation to bring down the murderers of said agent?

He didn't want to think about what would happen if the mob found out about her. They wouldn't think it was a coincidence, but see it as a setup, deception of the worst kind, and they wouldn't hesitate to take out both Lee and Carly. He had to make sure that didn't happen.

"So what do you think, Agent Gause?"

He wasn't sure Lee Madaris wanted to hear what he thought. But the man had been willing to put his life on the line by participating in the sting operation, so he owed him the truth.

"I agree that we need to keep your wife safe. So far, we have no reason to believe a connection has been made between the two of you, and that's a good thing. If we play our cards right we'll bring the person who murdered Agent Harrison to justice, as well as bring down the entire East Coast Connection."

"Does that mean they don't know about me?" Carly asked nervously. She was sitting beside Lee on the sofa.

"The agency knew about the tip you called in but tried to take every precaution that you could never be identified. We even deleted the call. But someone at the police department was able to get a copy of the recording. Although the call couldn't be traced, your voice could be identified, and we believe that it was."

"How?"

"The mob figured, from what you said on the recording,

that you heard rather than saw anything, which meant you were either passing by that alley at the time or you were in a building close by. We have reason to believe that one of Driskell's men approached a waitress at the restaurant where you used to work, pretended to be a detective, played the recording to her and you were identified."

"The waitress reported this?" Lee asked.

Gause shook his head. "No. The next day she disappeared."

"Disappeared?"

"Yes. And we can only assume she was killed so she wouldn't talk."

"Who was she?" Carly asked.

"A young woman named Rebecca Toomey. Her boyfriend reported her missing."

Carly gasped. She remembered Rebecca. She was friendly and loved the beach. She worked part-time while attending the University of Miami.

"And you suspect foul play in Ms. Toomey's disappearance?" Lee asked.

"Yes. She told someone she was helping a police detective solve a case. That might have been what she assumed, but we know that wasn't true."

"And you think she identified Carly's voice?" Lee asked, his tone filled with profound anger.

"Yes, that's what we understand. However, we can only assume they haven't made a connection yet between you two. At least they hadn't when Driskell met with you earlier today. Otherwise, you would be dead, Mr. Madaris.

"One thing about this particular group—they don't like being played. They don't appreciate traitors. That's why Agent Harrison met his fate. He was identified as a traitor." Gause felt there was no need to tell them that the agency believed the person who had fingered Agent Harrison was one of their own agents whom they suspected of feeding the mob information. The fact that they had a mole turned his stomach.

Lee stood. "There's no way I'm going to wait around to see if they figure out the connection. I'm putting Carly on a plane tonight for Texas."

Carly stood as well. "I won't get on that plane unless you come with me, Lee. You're in as much danger as I am."

"Carly..."

"Lee..."

Gause could clearly see the two were at a stalemate. He thought it best to intervene. "At the moment, I don't think separating you two is the best thing. If Driskell doesn't know that the woman you married is the same woman who might be a witness to the crime his men committed, that will be for the best."

Lee glared at the man. "Best for who? Your sting operation? Do you think I care about that if my wife's life is in danger?"

"No, I honestly don't," Gause said truthfully.

He knew he had to contact Alex Maxwell and apprise him of the situation. As long as they still had a mole within the agency, he refused to play it any other way than safe.

"You're sure you don't want me to handle it?" Grassley asked, leaning back in the driver's seat of the car. He could tell Nash was pissed. He had heard the news report about Harrison's body right before Nash called asking to meet him here. They needed to strategize the best way to handle this turn of events.

"No, I'm going to handle it myself. But what bothers me is how the body was discovered," Nash said, rolling down the car window to release the smoke from his cigarette. He hadn't smoked in two years, but tonight he had started back up again.

"I heard the news report," Grassley said. "The body was found by two construction workers preparing for work on that land."

Nash shook his head angrily. "That can't be true because someone would have to dig hard to discover it, but that land is owned by me."

"You?" Grassley said.

"Yes. It belonged to someone I once knew who left it to me. Therefore, if construction workers found anything that meant they were planted. I didn't give permission for anything to be built on that property."

An uneasy feeling settled in the pit of Grassley's stomach. "Planted?"

"Yes. Someone knew the body was there, and no one was supposed to know but you and me."

It was then that Grassley saw the bulge in Nash's jacket. He knew it was a gun pointing right at him. "Wait a minute, Nash. Surely you don't think that I talked."

Anger clouded Nash's face, shone in his eyes. "What else is there for me to think?"

Fear raced up Grassley's spine. "We must have been followed that night. That had to be it, because I didn't talk."

"We weren't followed, but if we were, you should have known. I depend on you for backup and you let me down."

A shot rang out. Then a second. Grassley slumped forward against the steering wheel, his eyes open as if in shock.

"You talked," Nash said, looking at the man he'd once trusted. "You had to have talked. And before it's all over, I'm going to find out who you told."

Nash got out of the car. He had been smart to have Grassley meet him in this isolated location. Putting his gun away, Nash went to the trunk and removed a rag soaked in kerosene. Using his cigarette lighter, he lit the rag and tossed it through the open window of the car containing Grassley's body.

He then went to the rental car he'd hidden in this location. By the time he had pulled off, the other car was up in flames.

Alex Maxwell glanced up as three men entered his office. He couldn't help but smile. "I'm glad you're back."

"We're glad to be back," Sir Drake said, dropping down in a nearby chair. "It was one bitch of an operation but we got through it."

As if there was any doubt that they would, Alex thought. "Well, you got back just in the nick of time."

"Why? What's happening? Is something going on with that situation with Lee?" Ashton Sinclair asked.

Concern was reflected in his features. Half black and half Cherokee Indian, Ashton's heritage included fierce tribal medicine men with mystical powers, as well as a great-great-grandfather who'd been a Cherokee shaman. It was rumored that Ashton had the gift of visions. Since Alex had seen Ashton's visions at work on more than one occasion, he knew firsthand that it wasn't a rumor but the real thing.

"Yes, something is going on," Alex replied. He then told them about the call he had received earlier that day from Agent Gause.

"Lee's married?" Trevor asked in a shocked voice.

"I didn't hear it from Lee, so I can only assume the agent is going by what Lee told him. Lee claims he married in Vegas a couple of weeks ago but wanted to keep it a secret until he went home for the holidays. I spoke with Jake. Although I advised him it would be best if he didn't go to Vegas, he is getting his jet ready to fly me there. Thanks to the recording between Lee and Driskell today, the agent feels they are close to cracking the case."

Trevor Grant nodded. "Count me in on that flight. I'm going with you."

"So am I," Ashton said.

Sir Drake smiled. "What the hell, I haven't been to Vegas in a while. I might as well go too." And then he added, "And I might as well tell Tori and bring her along."

Alex chuckled, remembering the last time Sir Drake's wife felt she'd been left out. "That's probably a good idea."

Chapter 21

Something brought Carly awake. She pulled up in bed and saw that the spot beside her was empty. Lee stood naked, his back to her, as he looked out the window. He liked sleeping in the nude, and whenever she slept with him, she had a tendency to sleep that way as well.

The bright lights from the Strip flashed into the room, illuminating his body. She couldn't help but appreciate his manly physique. A feeling of deep love and pride washed over her. She loved him so much, and the thought that he loved her back, that he wanted her, made her love him even more.

He must have heard her sigh. He turned around and asked, "Why are you awake?"

"Why are *you?*" she countered.

"I couldn't sleep."

She nodded in understanding. "I couldn't at first either, but you took care of that." And he had done so in the most profound way. After giving her triple orgasms, she couldn't do anything else but fall asleep from exhaustion.

After Agent Gause left, they had talked, and when he couldn't convince her to go to his uncle in Texas for safekeeping, he had ended up making nonstop love to her instead.

He smiled. "I did take care of it, didn't I?"

"Let's not get cocky," she said, getting out of bed to join him at the window. He wrapped her in his arms in an exuberant hug and held her tight. She loved the feel of it.

"I can just imagine what they're thinking in the kitchen."

"What they're thinking in the kitchen is the least of my worries. I really wish you'd let me send you—"

"No. I'm staying here unless you come with me."

He released her. "I can't do that. I have work to do here."

It hit Carly then that he'd been away for a week for their honeymoon and he probably did have a lot of work to do. He still had a job to do here at the hotel, but while she was here and the sting operation was going on, he would not let her out of his sight. That wouldn't be good, if he put all his concentration on her. She'd already been planning to give her resignation to Chef Blanchard before their trip to Texas. She'd just do that sooner than she'd thought.

"Okay, I'll go to your uncle in Texas."

He looked down at her. "Why did you change your mind?"

She shrugged. "Like you said, you have work to do. As long as I'm here I'll be a distraction. You'll worry whenever I'm out of your sight."

He let out a sigh of relief as if a great weight had been lifted off his shoulders. "I'll call Uncle Jake in the morning and make the arrangements."

* * *

Driving through the night, Nash punched in a phone number and waited for the other party to answer. "Why are you calling me? I told you to lose my number. Now that Harrison's body has been found—"

"I want information, Ackerman," he said, interrupting the federal agent.

"I can't tell you anything. I told you that the last time. Gause knows there's a mole in the operation and he's suspicious of everyone."

"That's your problem, not mine." Stan Ackerman, an agent with the FBI, had been Nash's link to inside information for more than four years. The two had met in college, and although Nash had known Ackerman was working for the law, he'd also known his college friend liked to gamble. When it came to money, it was hard for Ackerman to turn down any offer.

Ackerman had been paid well by the mob and his Swiss account had a tidy sum sitting in it. He was the one who'd told Nash that Harrison was an undercover agent. And because the bureau had figured out that the information had come from within, Ackerman had told Nash not to call him again.

"I'm hanging up on you, Nash. The shit is about to hit the fan. You and your boys have too many loose ends. You've gotten sloppy."

"You talking about that woman who thought she heard something? I'm in Vegas and will be taking care of her before I leave," Nash said.

"If you're smart, you'll leave Vegas and go out of the country. Change your name and start spending all that money you've got stashed away," Ackerman said. "The bureau is onto you and your group, and I don't want to be connected in any way. That woman you're thinking about getting rid of has a husband. Can you guess who he is?"

"Who?"

"The owner of the Grand MD. The same man you and Driskell are trying to shake down."

Anger raced through all parts of Nash. "Madaris? It was a setup and you didn't warn us?" he roared.

"I couldn't. Like I said, Gause is watching everyone like a hawk. Besides, I thought you and your people were too smart to get conned."

Furious, Nash clicked off the phone, deciding to call Driskell. There was no way the man could have known their talk with Madaris had been part of a sting operation.

A sudden thought came into Nash's mind, and before he punched in Driskell's number he disconnected the call. Driskell was already pissed. He would only see the setup with Madaris as another screw-up on Nash's part. Nash was supposed to be on top of things, and Driskell would wonder why Nash hadn't known that the woman who'd tipped off the police was now married to the owner of the hotel they wanted to add to their ring.

Nash rubbed his hand down his face. Come to think of it, Madaris had asked questions, as if he were considering the idea, but he had wanted specific information about the operations. And in his eagerness to get the Grand MD, Driskell had let his guard down and said more than he needed to. If that meeting had been recorded they were in a world of trouble.

Maybe he needed to do what Ackerman had suggested and set up a new identity, leave the country, but he couldn't do that yet. Nobody made a fool of him and got away with it. Now he had more than one person to get rid of. Not only would he get rid of the woman, but he would get rid of Madaris as well.

He pulled up the contact list on his phone. It contained several names of those in their network who could assist him in carrying out his plan. Names of people already in place working at the hotel.

Lee couldn't wait until morning. As soon as he was certain Carly had gone back to sleep, he slipped from the bed. Closing the bedroom door behind him, he went into the kitchen and called Jake.

"Hello?"

"Uncle Jake, this is Lee. Sorry to call so late but I need your help."

"You got it. Are you okay, Lee?"

He heard the concern in his uncle's tone and knew Alex had kept Jake informed.

"Yes, I'm fine. But I do have a favor to ask."

"What?"

"I want to send my wife to you. I need you to keep her safe until I come for her."

"So it's true? You did get married? Alex mentioned you had."

"Yes, a couple of weeks ago, here in Vegas. I wanted to keep it a secret from everyone until I brought her home for Christmas. She was going to be my holiday surprise, but now the only thing I want is to make sure she's protected."

"Send her to Whispering Pines and Diamond and I will take care of her. Don't worry about a thing. Just take care of yourself."

"I will. Knowing she's with you and Diamond will take a load off my mind."

"And just so you know, my jet is on its way there."

Lee lifted a brow. "It is?"

"Yes. Alex felt he needed to be there, and Trevor, Ashton, Sir Drake and Tori decided to tag along."

With Carly safely out of harm's way and Alex and the gang on their way, he felt better about the situation.

"What's your wife's name?" Jake asked, interrupting Lee's thoughts.

"Carly."

"Well, you can send Carly back on my jet. I'll be there to meet it when it arrives at the airport."

"Thanks, Uncle Jake."

A short while later, when Lee slid back into bed beside Carly, she automatically shifted to snuggle closer to him. He wrapped his arms around her and then closed his eyes to join her in sleep.

"Nash knocked off Grassley," Weber reported back to Bracey.

Bracey wasn't surprised. He adjusted his cell phone to his ear. "Where is Nash now?"

"I lost him in traffic. I think he knows he's being followed."

Bracey nodded. "Okay, just keep your eye out for the woman. You have her address, right?"

"Yes. I'm there now, but it doesn't appear that she came home last night."

"She has to come home eventually, so you just stay put. I'll take care of Nash."

After clicking off the phone with Weber, Bracey left his hotel room.

"But, Lee, I need to go home and pack. I can't go to Texas with just the clothes on my back." Carly had used his laundry room to wash and dry the clothes she had worn yesterday. However, she wanted to go home and get her things before leaving for the airport.

"I put in a call to Gause and he wants you to stay put

until he sends one of his men to escort us to your place," Lee said.

"Us?"

"Yes, us."

"Don't you have work to do today?" she asked, reaching up and wrapping her arms around his neck.

"Not until after I have put you on Uncle Jake's jet to Texas."

At that moment his hotel room phone went off. "Yes, what is it, Phyllis?" he asked, placing the call on speaker.

"Mr. Madaris, just a reminder that you have a conference call scheduled this morning with sheiks Valdemon and Yasir and Mr. Garwood."

Lee rubbed a hand down his face. He had completely forgotten about that call. "I'm going to have to cancel that conference call, Phyllis."

Carly reached over to press the mute button on the phone. "Don't you dare cancel, Lee. You mentioned the conference call last week in Dubai and how important it was to talk to your new investors. Keep your conference call. I'll be fine here until you get back."

"No."

"Yes," she countered. "I promise not to answer the door for anyone. Besides, I need to call Heather, so I'll probably be talking to her the entire time you're gone."

"Mr. Madaris? Mr. Madaris? Are you still there?"

He took Phyllis off mute. "Yes, I'm here." He saw the stubborn look on Carly's face. "Okay, Phyllis. Set everything up. I'm on my way."

He hung up the phone. "Okay, I'll do the conference call, but I don't care who comes to the door. Don't open it for anyone."

"All right. All right. And what about the elevator?"

"You don't have to worry about it. No one can get in

here without a key card and there's only two. You have one, and I have the other."

She nodded. "Before you leave do I get a kiss?"

"Most certainly." He pulled her into his arms and set her aflame.

Nash walked up to the woman at the hotel's front desk.

"Yes, sir? May I help you?"

He looked at the name on the pin she wore on her jacket. "Yes, you can help me, Helen." Then in a low voice, he said, "I believe you received a call earlier with instructions about what I would need."

She nodded and then pulled an envelope out of a drawer. After she handed it to him, she said, "Have a nice day. I hope you enjoy your stay at the Grand MD."

He held her gaze, gave her a nod and said, "I'm sure I will."

He crossed the lobby floor. After rounding a corner, he paused and tore open the envelope to pull out the elevator key card for the penthouse suites. Specifically the one owned by Lee Madaris. He smiled as he headed to the elevator bank.

"Are you sure that you're okay?"

Carly smiled. "Yes, Heather, I'm fine. For Lee's peace of mind I've agreed to go to his uncle's place in Texas for a while."

"And this is the uncle who's married to Diamond Swain, right?"

Carly chuckled. "Yes, that's him."

"You lucky person."

They talked for several more moments when she heard the ding from the elevator. "I hear the elevator, so Lee's conference call must have ended early."

"Okay. Call me when you get to Texas and let me know all about the Whispering Pines Ranch. I read it's a fabulous place."

"All right. I will. 'Bye."

"'Bye."

Carly placed her phone on the table and left the kitchen. The moment she rounded the corner to the dining room she stopped. The man stepping off the elevator was not Lee.

He smiled and said, "So you're the woman who wants to cause trouble."

Icy fear twisted a knot in Carly's chest. She recognized the sound of the man's voice. She remembered the first time she'd heard it.

Backing up, she glanced around to see where she could run. He had her cornered. The only room she could escape to was the kitchen but there was no door. But she had left her phone on the kitchen table. Maybe she could at least get to it to call 911.

"I wouldn't try it if I were you," he threatened, as if he'd read her thoughts. And then she saw the gun he had pointed at her.

"I have no problem killing you right here and now, but I want to make your husband sweat a little before I kill you both," he said in that voice she remembered so well. Heartless. Cold-blooded. Merciless.

She stopped backing up when she felt the breakfast bar at the curve of her spine. "I don't know who you are," she lied. "I think you might be in the wrong room, and—"

"Shut up!" he snapped. "I don't want to hear your lies. Now come here. You're going with me, and if you try any funny business, I won't hesitate to kill you or anyone else who tries to help you. Just remember that. Let's go."

Lee hung up the phone. The conference call had gone well. The investors were all lined up. Now all he had to do was get things started with the property in Paris. He stood, stretched and moved quickly toward the door, missing Carly already. How would he handle it when she was in Texas? How long would she have to be there?

He left his office and walked into the lobby, where Phyllis was sitting at her desk. "Mr. Maxwell called as well as Mr. Gause. Both said they went up to your suite and didn't get an answer. I believe they were under the impression someone would be there."

Lee nodded. He'd told Carly not to open the door and she hadn't. She didn't know Alex, since she'd never met him, but she had met Gause. For her not to let him in meant she wasn't trusting anyone.

"I'll contact both of them to let them know I'm on my way back to my suite and they can join me there now."

He paused in the hall to send the text messages to Alex and Gause. He then called Carly to let her know he was on his way up. He frowned when his call went to voice mail. Maybe she had gone back to bed. They had made love a good portion of the night. But still, an uneasy feeling made him increase his pace toward the bank of elevators.

"Rushing off to a fire?"

He glanced over his shoulder, then stopped walking and grinned when he saw Alex. "In a way, yes. I just sent you a text."

"I know. I got it. I understand congratulations are in order."

"Yes, they are. Come on. I want you to meet Carly," he said, smiling, as they stepped onto the elevator.

"I can't wait," Alex said when the door swooshed shut behind them. "But what I really can't wait for is when you present her to Mama Laverne. Now, that should be interesting."

"Trust me, it will be."

"Now I feel sorry for Nolan," Alex said. "With you out of the way her attention will be on him."

"Yeah, and I don't envy him one bit."

The elevator door opened into his suite and Lee immediately knew something was wrong. He could feel it. "Carly, we have company," he called out.

When he didn't get a response, he went into the bedroom. Everything looked just as he'd left it. He checked the master bathroom as fear crawled up his spine. He then checked the other two guest bedrooms as well as the inside pool and entertainment rooms.

He and Alex met back up in the living room. "I checked the kitchen and she's not here," Alex said. "But I found this on your kitchen table." He handed the cell phone to Lee. "Would she have gone somewhere? Maybe she's out in the hall."

"She would not have left this suite and definitely not without her cell phone," Lee said, but he moved toward the door to check the hall anyway. There were only two rooms on this floor. His and Angelo's. And they were separated by a huge hallway with a fireplace.

"Where could she be?" Lee asked, coming back into the room. That was when he saw it. A cigarette butt on his kitchen counter.

Rage filled Lee. He pointed at the cigarette butt. "Someone has been here, Alex, and whoever was here has taken Carly."

Alex had already pulled his phone out of his jacket. He spoke quickly. "Trevor. Round up everyone. Yes, that means you need to pull Sir Drake and Tori out of the casino. Someone has kidnapped Lee's wife."

Bracey made sure he stayed a safe distance behind Nash as he followed the man away from the Strip and toward an isolated area of town. Nash had the woman and he appeared to know just where he was going, which meant he had scoped out the place.

Bracey looked at the clock on his dash. The last thing he needed was for Driskell to get worried, so he decided to make the call. He pulled out his mobile phone and punched in Driskell's number.

"Bracey?"

"Yeah, it's me."

"I was beginning to get worried."

"Don't. I told you I was taking care of things."

"I know. But a couple of our investors are getting nervous. News about Harrison is dominating the news. The FBI has sworn to bring those responsible to justice. They don't like that."

"Then tell them to cut the damn TV off," Bracey muttered.

"What did you say? I didn't hear you?" Driskell asked.

"Nothing. When do you meet with Madaris again?"

"I'll give him a call in a few days, after this thing with Harrison blows over. Right now it's freaking people out."

"Well, don't worry about a thing. I've got it all under control."

"Good. You're a man I can depend on, Bracey, and I appreciate that."

Bracey smiled. "I'm glad that you do. I won't let you down. I promise."

Chapter 22

In less than thirty minutes, Lee's suite resembled a command center. The FBI had set up in one part of the penthouse while Alex and his team used the other.

First, the penthouse had been thoroughly checked for fingerprints, and the butt of the cigarette was analyzed. It didn't take long to conclude that Magnus Nash had been there. The DNA on the cigarette butt was a match. And there was no doubt in anyone's mind that the man had wanted Lee to know his identity, which made everyone wonder just what kind of game he intended to play.

Lee didn't care about playing games; he wanted his wife back. He couldn't help worrying about Nash's sick mind, especially when it appeared that an automobile had been set on fire. Inside, a body had burned to a crisp. Dental records were being checked for the man's identity, but already the speculation was that he was someone who had crossed Nash. The man had paid the ultimate price.

As for Driskell, the agents keeping an eye on him reported that this morning he'd eaten breakfast in the hotel's restaurant and was now lying by the pool. Everyone wondered if he even knew what was going on, although his two top men, Nash and Bracey, were both missing.

Lee could feel Alex watching him. He was probably wondering how Lee had managed to marry a woman who turned out to be a star witness in a case against the mob. All of the others in the room—Trevor, Sir Drake and Tori—must be wondering the same thing. Only Ashton, who was leaning against the wall, looked as if he had all the answers. Hell, with his supernatural foretelling ability, he probably did.

"He's going to play a game with you, Lee."

Everyone turned to Ashton. He was looking at Lee but not seeing him. It seemed as if Ashton was seeing something beyond the room. "He's evil. I can block it to a point."

Lee lifted a brow. "Block it how?"

A small smile touched Ashton's features. "Too complicated to explain."

Lee ran a frustrated hand down his face. "I feel useless, like I let Carly down. I should have stayed here with her and not taken that conference call. I should have—"

"It's a good thing you weren't here," Ashton said. "He would have killed you both."

Ashton's words, spoken as bluntly as only Ashton could speak, made Lee jerk.

"I want my wife back alive," Lee said, feeling the pain of her loss all through his body.

"And you'll have her back. Alive. I give you my word. I've seen your wedding. The one planned for Christmas. Nice, by the way. And the moment your great-grandmother meets your wife..." He lifted a corner of his lips in a smile. "Priceless."

Lee stared at Ashton. He'd heard about his powers to see the present, the past and the future. Hope flared to life inside of Lee. He had to believe. "Do you know where he's taken her?"

Ashton shook his head. "Not yet."

Lee drew in a deep breath. Believing Carly would get rescued took a load off of him. "Thanks."

Gause knocked on the door before he stuck his head inside. "We know how Nash got in."

"How?" Lee asked, moving across the bedroom toward the door.

"Helen Pullman. She works the check-in counter. She's part of the mob's network. She made a duplicate key for him."

"Where is she?" Lee asked, getting angry all over again.

"We have her in custody. She's not talking now, but eventually she will."

Just then, Lee's cell phone went off. It was a number he didn't recognize. He glanced around the room and upon Alex's nod he quickly answered the call. "Hello."

"I have your wife, Mr. Madaris."

Lee swallowed. Everyone had discreetly moved into action. Sir Drake had installed a mobile tracker to pick up where the call was coming from; Alex had set a plotter on all the phones to record incoming and outgoing conversations; Tori was listening for any background noises that could pinpoint the location; and Trevor was studying a map of Vegas, all the empty warehouses and secluded locations. Ashton was standing beside him listening attentively.

"I know you have her, and I want her back," Lee said.

"It's going to cost you."

"Name your price," Lee countered.

"I'll get back in touch with you." Nash then hung up the phone.

Lee stared at the phone. "What the hell?"

"He's playing with you," Gause said. He turned to Sir Drake. "Did you have enough time to pick up the location?"

Drake smiled. "I didn't, but he did," he said, pointing over at Ashton. "He's a born tracker and has picked up the scent."

Gause looked confused. "Scent? What scent?"

Ashton gave the man a tense smile before saying, "It's too complicated to explain." Ashton then turned to Lee. "You're going to have to trust me on this. Evil forces are trying to overpower good. Evil won't win."

"So what do we do now?"

"We wait," Ashton said, sliding down into a chair. The others did the same.

Gause frowned and stared at them. "Are you telling me you have an idea of where she is?" he asked Ashton.

"No idea. I know for certain."

"Then what the hell are we waiting for?" the man asked, even more confused.

"The right time. If we move too soon, he will kill her."

Gause just stared at Ashton. "He's going to kill her if we don't make an attempt to save her."

Ashton shook his head. "No. She will live, and he will die."

Gause looked around at everyone who seemed to have taken Ashton's words as gospel. In fact, Drake Warren had pulled out playing cards and was now shuffling the deck to deal to his wife and Trevor Grant.

Gause turned to Lee. "You're willing to take a chance on your wife's life by doing what he says?"

Lee recalled all the stories he'd heard about Ashton. Sir Drake was only alive today because of one of Ashton's visions. "Yes. I'm willing to take that chance."

"Chill, Gause," Alex said. "Ashton knows what he's talking about. If you're lucky, he might be able to tell you where Driskell keeps that log of names your men have spent all this time trying to find."

Gause glanced back over at Ashton, who had stretched

his legs out and leaned his head back as if he was about to get some sleep. He had read the reports on Colonel Ashton Sinclair. He had been one of the marines' finest, and part of the marines' elite recon's Fearless Four, along with Trevor and Drake. Their rescue efforts had been flawless until that ill-fated day when the only woman on the team, Sandy Carroll, had lost her life on a mission in Haiti. It was rumored that Ashton had the gift of visions. Could it be true? The others in the room seemed convinced. Madaris was willing to risk his wife's life on it.

"Is what Alex said true? Do you think you can find out where Driskell keeps that log?"

Ashton shrugged. "Not sure. I'm getting a good scent off Nash today. I won't know until I meet this man you call Driskell."

"Okay," Gause said, leaving the room with a sense of relief that they might be able to bring an end to the East Coast Connection and expose those funding it.

"It won't be long. Just remember good conquers evil," Ashton told Lee.

Lee went back to the window, his mind filled with memories of Carly and the time they'd shared in Dubai just last week. Their time had been almost perfect.

He wasn't sure how long he stood there remembering when Ashton finally called out to him.

"Lee?"

He glanced over at Ashton, who had stood up. "Yes?"

"It's time."

"I guess I could cut off a couple of your fingers to send to your husband as a souvenir."

Carly didn't say anything. All she could do was pray that this nightmare would soon come to an end. She had tried pleading with him on the drive to this vacant cabin.

He'd just laughed and then finally told her to keep her mouth closed. She was doing just what he'd said.

"What's wrong, lady. Can't you talk? You certainly had a lot to say on the tip line that night."

He threw his head back and laughed. The sound raked across her skin. And when he reached across the table and picked up the gun he'd placed there, she drew in a sharp breath.

"Maybe I should just kill you now and then tell your husband where he can find the body. When he goes there, I can be hiding out, waiting. It will give me great joy to blow him away too."

Carly swallowed. She'd always thought Mr. Thrasher was an evil man, but this guy took the cake. Her breath caught when he lifted the gun and aimed it at her forehead.

"All it would take is one pull of the trigger. Hmm," he said with a crazy look on his face. "I don't think that's a bad idea."

"Well, I happen to think it's a lousy one."

Nash jerked the gun away from Carly and aimed it at the man who walked through the door.

"Bracey? What the hell are you doing here?"

Who was that man? What was going on? He was tall with a mean look on his face. Carly picked up on the tension between the two. Her heart pounded painfully in her chest. She had a feeling the intense dislike she could sense between them would end here.

"Driskell sent me," Bracey said. "Plans have changed. He doesn't want the discovery of her body to happen so close to the discovery of Harrison's."

Nash glared. "Her body won't be discovered. Besides, Miami and Vegas are miles apart. No one is going to make the connection."

"Driskell doesn't want to take chances. He feels he can't

trust you when it comes to disposing of bodies. He wants me to bring her to him. He wants to kill her himself."

Nash glared, holding the gun level with the man's chest. "No," he said in a hateful voice. "I ain't stupid, nor will I take the chance. I've worked with Driskell a lot longer than you have, and I know the way he thinks. I also know the way *you* think, Bracey. You're nothing but a two-bit power grabber who plans to take over. You might have Driskell fooled, but you don't have me fooled. Driskell sent you to kill me, but that's not going to happen."

Fear coiled in Carly's stomach. It was obvious one of the men was going to kill the other. Where would that leave her? For the moment, she was forgotten. Maybe there was a way she could escape while they were engaged. Her hands were tied behind her back but her feet were not tied, which meant she could run if she had to.

And go where? She knew anywhere was better than here. No matter the outcome of the two men's little power struggle, eventually one of them would kill her.

She glanced out the window. She had no idea where she was, but she knew from the drive that the place was heavily wooded. Given the amount of time it had taken to get here, she figured they were somewhere in a cabin near the Toiyabe National Forest.

The argument between the two men had escalated, but Nash was holding the advantage with the gun. However, it seemed the man Nash had called Bracey wouldn't back down. He was determined to take her to Driskell. She tried fighting the fear rising in her throat. Lee would try to find her; she believed that. But she also knew he had no idea where she was.

Then, in a movement so swift she'd barely seen it, Bracey used some kind of karate maneuver with his leg and knocked the gun out of Nash's hand. When Nash dived to retrieve it, Bracey dived after him and the fight was on.

Carly took a deep breath against panic. Pain afflicted her skin as she tore against the rope restraining her hands. The two men were going at it, fists flying, curses swarming, both trying to be the first to reach the gun.

The weapon had landed close to her feet. Deciding she didn't want to give either man an advantage, she kicked the gun with all her might and watched it roll under the sofa.

Nash saw what she'd done and snarled, "Bitch." He was about to lay into her with his fist, but the man named Bracey saw his advantage and slammed a right hook on him that sent Nash crumbling to the floor.

And then Bracey turned to her. He came at her with a small knife in one hand. She was about to scream, certain he would slash her throat, when he reached behind her and used the knife to cut through the ropes binding her hands.

The next thing she knew, Bracey was shoved out of the way. Nash had recovered from the blow and the fight was back on again. Bracey had freed her. She wasn't sure why but figured he'd done it so he could take her with him. She didn't plan to go anywhere with either man. Ignoring the pain in her wrist where the rope had cut into her skin, she jumped out of the chair and ran toward the door. It was locked.

"The bitch is getting away," Nash roared. Then she heard the crack of bones and knew someone's jaw had been broken. She refused to look back to see whose as she frantically tried to unlock the door.

Suddenly, a hand at her waist shoved her aside as someone reached up and nearly tore the latch off the door.

"Come on!" Bracey's deep voice snapped.

She froze. She wasn't going anywhere with him.

But he didn't wait for her cooperation. He grabbed her hand and pulled her through the door with him. She jerked back, trying to fight. He gave her a hard shake when they reached the yard.

"Stop it," he hissed. "I'm not going to hurt you."

He wanted her to believe that? "Let me go," she implored in a raw voice.

"No. Nash will be passed out for only a minute, so we need to move fast. I didn't have time to retrieve the gun from under the sofa or look for the knife Nash knocked out of my hands. And I lost my car keys during the fight. That means we need to escape into those woods and hide until morning. There's no doubt he'll come after us. He'll even call for backup and give them orders to kill us on sight."

Before she could open her mouth to ask why she should go anywhere with him, he gave a gruff order. "Let's go."

She dug in her heels, refusing. However, when a shot rang out and then another, they both knew Nash had regained consciousness, retrieved the gun and was now firing at them.

The next time Bracey said, "Let's go," she took off running with him.

When it seemed they had run a full mile nonstop, she jerked her hand from Bracey's and leaned against a tree to catch her breath. She was shaken but glad to be alive. She looked into Bracey's hard face and her gut-wrenching fear returned.

Carly was tempted to run away from him but knew she wouldn't get far. He had run the mile with little sweat.

"You don't have to be afraid of me. I told you that I wouldn't hurt you."

Yes, he had said that. But why? Who was he? She was almost too afraid to know. Was he an assassin? A man who did whatever the guy named Driskell ordered him to do? Even now, she could feel the violence radiating off of him, and he wanted her to believe he wouldn't hurt her?

"Who are you?" she asked in a whisper, giving in to her curiosity.

He held her stare for a long moment before saying, "I'm Addison Bracey. Special agent for the FBI. Undercover."

Chapter 23

Gause, his men and the rest of the group arrived at a section of Toiyabe National Forest in the late afternoon. It would be getting dark soon. Lee Madaris seemed to be holding up okay and Gause appreciated that. The last thing they needed was an irrational spouse on their hands.

His phone rang and he saw the call was from Woodman. "This is Gause."

"My men and I have Driskell under surveillance. He got a phone call that has thrown him into action. He's called some of his men, and they left in a car driving away from the Strip. We managed to trace Driskell's call, and it came from Nash. But we didn't have time to decipher Nash's location."

"Doesn't matter," Gause said, glancing over at Colonel Ashton Sinclair. The man was studying the environment and actually smiling. But it wasn't a regular smile. It was the smile of a man who was in his element and about to embark upon a mission. The three others—Trevor, Drake and Tori—all looked the same way.

"What do you mean it doesn't matter?" Woodman asked.

"Because we're here already. Toiyabe National Forest. One of Maxwell's friends picked up Nash's scent."

"What scent?"

Gause drew in a deep breath. "Too complicated to explain," he said, repeating exactly what had been told to him. "How many men are with Driskell?"

"Five. His usual cutthroats that work under Nash and Bracey. My next question is where the hell is Bracey?"

Carly was speechless…but only for a few seconds. "You're an FBI agent?"

"Yes," Bracey said.

There was no doubt in his mind that Nash had gotten in touch with Driskell. The big man would be sending in backup. There was also no doubt in his mind that Weber had figured out he'd been had. The only reason he'd been ordered to watch Carly Briggs's home was to get him out of the way for a while. Weber would be mad and when Weber got mad his killer instinct kicked in.

Bracey hadn't been able to get a connection on his phone. Until he did, he and Ms. Briggs would be on their own. The quicker they could make it to the ranger's station near Mount Charleston, the better. But at no time could he lose sight of the fact that they were being tracked down like animals. Nash and Driskell would make him pay for his deception.

"How long have you been undercover with the mob?" Carly asked him.

He looked back at her. "Almost four years."

"Four years?"

"Yes, it took me that long to work up the ranks and gain everyone's trust. They are a ruthless bunch, with policemen, politicians and CEOs on their payroll. In most situations it's the latter two who are funding the gang wars."

"I don't understand. How can gang wars benefit politicians and CEOs?"

"Because it keeps the FBI busy, keeps them from paying attention to what those politicians and CEOs are doing—dealing in trafficking of illegal drugs and humans. That's a big business."

Bracey glanced around again before saying, "I can't call for backup because my phone got knocked around pretty bad in my fight with Nash. So we have to keep moving."

"You think he's coming after us?" Carly asked.

"I know he is, and he'll call for backup. I just hope my commander realizes I'm missing in action and tries to figure out where we are."

Carly nodded. "What are the chances of him doing that? Figuring out where we are?"

Bracey decided to be honest with her. "Pretty damn slim. But we can hope. Come on. Let's keep moving while we have daylight."

"How are you holding up?" Tori asked Lee.

Lee drew in a deep breath. "As well as expected under the circumstances. I do, however, feel better now that Ashton told me about his vision. I just hope nothing goes wrong."

"It won't. Ashton would have seen any trouble. That doesn't mean getting her out will be easy, but she will be all right."

"How does he do it?" Lee wanted to know. He'd watched the four gear up. Trevor, Tori and Sir Drake joked on occasion. But Ashton wore a serious expression the entire time.

"Not sure," Tori answered. "It has something to do with powers handed down to him from his forefathers on both sides—Cherokee Indian and African. Already he's detected the same powers in one of his sons. The one named Wolf. He and Ashton can read each other's minds and hold a conversation without saying a word."

Lee knew Ashton and his wife, Netherland, had triplets—all boys—who were under ten, and they had one daughter.

"What about the others? Will they inherit the special powers as well?"

Tori shrugged. "Ashton thinks so but doesn't know when."

"Time to go in," Ashton said loudly, getting everyone's attention.

"You still want my men to stay back?" Gause asked.

"Yes. The four of us will handle this. We work better together. We should be back by morning. I'll get word of what's going on to Alex."

Lee thought that morning seemed like an awful long time, but he would continue to have faith.

"Bracey has the woman?" Driskell asked Nash when he arrived at the cabin.

After he'd received the call from Nash it hadn't taken him long to figure out that Bracey had been a mole within the organization. No telling what information he'd passed on.

"Yes, he has her."

"Why didn't you tell me she was married to Madaris?"

"Just found out myself. I was about to kill her when Bracey told me you wanted her kept alive," Nash said.

Driskell wanted Bracey. The man was a traitor who deserved to die.

“I want both him and the woman found,” Driskell said with profound anger in his voice.

“You want them brought in alive?” Weber asked. Driskell could tell Weber was mad as hell at the realization that he’d been deceived by Bracey all this time.

““No,” Driskell replied. “Kill them. Then bring their bodies here so we can dispose of them in a way that will make sure they are never found.” He glanced over at Palmer. “You got the acid ready?”

Palmer nodded. “As much as I could get ahold of without anyone becoming suspicious.”

Driskell nodded. “Good. Now spread out the men and don’t come back without their bodies or it will be yours boiling in the acid.”

The men knew Driskell meant business. Along with Nash, they entered the forest.

It was dusk. They wouldn’t have many daylight hours left to make their way toward the ranger’s station. Bracey had told her that much.

However, Carly had another question for him. “You were responsible for someone finding Agent Harrison’s body, weren’t you?”

Without slowing his pace, Bracey looked over at her. “Yes.”

“Why?”

“Closure. His wife and kids needed to know he was dead and not just missing. I owed them that much.”

“You knew him?”

“No, but he was a fellow agent. If I had a family I’d want that for them.” Suddenly, Bracey stopped walking and Carly stopped as well.

She saw the fierce look on his face. “What’s wrong?”

“Nash called in backup, and they are looking for us.”

Fear closed like a fist around Carly's heart. "How do you know?"

He looked up toward the sky and she followed his gaze. "The birds had settled in for the evening and now they're flying around again, which means they were disturbed. We aren't the only ones in this part of the forest."

"Can we make this quick and easy? I have a spa appointment at the hotel at noon tomorrow and I don't want to miss it."

The three men looked at Tori and shook their heads.

"We'll do our best," Drake said to his wife.

Ashton gave instructions. "We pick them off, one by one. I told Alex to inform Gause and his men to go to the cabin where Driskell is waiting. Lee is to go there as well. We'll deliver his wife to him."

"Why do I get the feeling there's something more?" Sir Drake said.

"Because there is. Something Gause conveniently didn't mention is that Carly isn't alone. An FBI agent is with her."

"The *good* you were referring to? The good who is going against the evil?" Trevor asked.

"Yes. We don't want to kill him by mistake," Ashton said.

"I don't understand. Why wouldn't Gause tell us something as vital as that?" Tori asked.

"To protect the man. Alex did mention there was a mole within the agency. They wanted to protect the man's identity at all costs. Losing one agent taught them a lesson," Ashton replied.

"Gause probably figured since you supposedly knew so much with your superpowers and all that you would know that. Want me to kick his ass for you when we get back?" Sir Drake asked seriously.

"No," Ashton said, grinning. "Thanks for the offer, but I fight my own battles. Come on. Let's go rescue Lee's wife. And, Sir Drake, let's try bringing them in alive when we can."

Sir Drake grinned. "I'll do my best."

Lee paced the cabin. Ashton had said it would be morning before they returned, but Lee was too anxious to stay still. Apprehending Driskell had been easy. He'd sent all his men into the forest to find Carly, and when the FBI agents had reached the cabin, Driskell had opened the door unprotected, assuming it was his men returning.

Gause and his men had Driskell in another room, interrogating him. There was a lot about this situation that Lee didn't understand…like how Carly had managed to get away from Nash. He didn't like the thought of her out in the forest alone with five crazed killers looking for her.

"Lee, step outside with me for a minute," Alex said, heading for the door.

Lee followed, and when they reached the porch, Alex beckoned him down the steps into the yard. Fear inched up Lee's spine. "What's wrong, Alex? Did you get a sign from Ashton that something went wrong?"

Alex shook his head. "No. But I'm sure you have a lot of questions, especially as to how Carly got away from Nash."

Lee nodded. "Yes, that had crossed my mind. Care to enlighten me?"

"Yes. Carly is with Bracey."

"Bracey?" Fear and anger coiled inside of Lee. "Why didn't someone tell me? That man is worse than Nash. He's a killer. He's a—"

"Special undercover agent for the FBI," Alex cut in to say.

Lee's jaw dropped. When he'd somewhat recovered, he said, "You've got to be kidding me."

"No, I'm not. When Nash grabbed Carly from the hotel, Bracey followed him. Not sure exactly what happened, but somehow he got Carly away from Nash and the two of them made off into the forest."

"Why didn't Gause mention that?"

"Because of the complexity of this case, as well as the fact that there's a mole within the agency. It was best that everyone continue to assume Bracey was a bad guy to protect his life. The agency has already lost one good man and they didn't want to take any chances. The reason I'm telling you now is because Driskell knows about Bracey's duplicity, so his cover has been blown. And I know how worried you are that Carly is out there alone."

Lee released a deep breath, glad Alex had told him about Bracey. He *had* been worried about her being out there all alone. "Thanks, Alex. I won't be able to rest until I see my wife."

Driskell's men were easy pickings. Most didn't know what was going on until it was too late. Two were captured without much of a fight. Two tried to put up a fight and found out what it felt like to get their butts whipped and bones broken, Sir Drake–style. And the fifth, the man named Nash, refused to give himself up. When he took several shots at Trevor, Trevor shot back, fatally wounding the man.

Bracey, who was a short distance away, heard the shots and wondered if Driskell's men were turning on each other. He decided that he and Carly wouldn't stick around to find out. She had to be tired but the farther into the forest they went, the better their chances would be.

He didn't have a weapon, but he'd found a stick and

sharpened the edge on a rock to create a spear. At least he wasn't totally defenseless.

He and Carly had walked a half mile when suddenly bright lights shone on them, surrounding them. He shoved Carly behind him and held up his spear in a defensive stance.

Out of the darkness a voice said, "Relax, Agent Bracey. We're on your team. The rescue party has arrived."

Bracey wasn't convinced. "Who are you? Show your faces."

Ashton was the first to step out. "Colonel Ashton Sinclair, and the others are Trevor Grant, Drake Warren and Tori Warren."

When all four had stepped forward so Bracey could see their faces, Ashton added, "We're all friends of Lee Madaris. He wants his wife back safe and sound."

"Lee?" Carly whispered from behind Bracey. "Lee's here?"

"Not here with us, but he's back at the cabin waiting. Driskell has been apprehended and so have most of his men."

"Nash?" Bracey asked.

"Is dead," Ashton answered.

Bracey wasn't convinced these people were who they claimed to be. "Why are you here instead of the FBI?"

"Because we're better," Sir Drake answered cockily.

Bracey, although he didn't agree with what the man had said, couldn't help but smile. He lowered his spear. "I guess this thing is useless against four automatics if you choose to use them."

Tori moved forward toward Carly. "Are you okay? Lee has been worried."

Carly nodded, fighting back tears. It was hard to believe her ordeal was over and she'd come out of it alive.

"I'm fine." She turned to Bracey. "Thank you for getting me away from Nash."

Bracey nodded. "I couldn't save Harrison's life, but I was determined to save yours."

She then turned to the three men and one woman. "And thanks to all of you for coming after me."

"Our job isn't done until we return you to Lee," Tori said. "We'll rest up here for a while and then head back before daybreak. I brought food. I figured you would be hungry."

Carly smiled. "I am. Thanks."

Through the night, Lee had been unable to close his eyes. Gause and his men were still with him at the cabin, as well as Alex. He knew the agents had questioned Driskell intensively and the man was still maintaining his innocence.

As soon as Lee saw the sun peeking through the trees in the distance he stepped out onto the porch. The cool air brushed across his face. He knew he could probably use a shave.

He heard Alex step out on the porch behind him. "Gause finally got a confession out of Driskell only after they agreed to a plea bargain. And he also provided the name of the mole. An agent named Stan Ackerman. Gause was shocked. He thought the man was loyal. Just goes to show that not everyone can be trusted."

"Where is Ackerman?"

"He works out of the Atlanta office. He was picked up and taken in for questioning. Seems he and Nash were college friends. His days of being disloyal are over."

Lee nodded, glad of that. And then he heard the rustling of the trees and he squinted his eyes against the sun.

That was when he saw them. His feet hit the ground and he took off running the moment he saw Carly.

And she broke into a run when she saw him.

He grabbed her when she was within reach, clutching her as if he'd never let her go again. He touched her everywhere—fingers through her hair, hands under her arms, over her shoulders and up and down her back. He needed to be sure she was not a figment of his imagination.

And then he stared down into the face of the woman who meant everything to him. "I love you," he whispered against her lips. He proceeded to kiss her with his entire body, with every emotion he possessed.

When the kiss finally ended, Carly leaned in and whispered close to his ear, "And I love you, Lee Madaris."

He heard someone say his name and he glanced around.

"Gause needs to talk to her and ask her some questions," Alex was saying. "Then you can take her home."

Lee nodded and took Carly's hand in his. He looked over at Ashton, Trevor, Sir Drake and Tori and said, "Thanks for everything." He turned to Bracey. "Thank you as well."

Lee let go of Carly's hand to wrap an arm around her shoulders as they headed into the cabin. Now that he had her back, he didn't intend to let her go ever again.

Later that day, after Lee and Carly had returned to his penthouse, they showered and made love, needing the most intimate connection possible. Although they were tired, the energy that flowed between them was charged—hot and raw.

They released it. A primitive force deep inside of Lee drove him to push her over the edge time and time again. He could have lost her. The woman he loved more than life itself. The woman who could arouse him as no other woman could.

Their marriage was not based on the deep carnal attraction he'd initially assumed, but on something more solid and profound. Something he hadn't thought he needed in his life or in his marriage. She had proved him wrong. Love was and always would be the force that held them together, that kept them in bondage to each other, that intensified what they shared.

"Lee!"

When fissions of fire settled deep in her womanly core, he felt them. They sent a sexual jolt through him that rocked him to the bone, triggering his explosion inside of her. He held her tight, wanting her to feel everything.

Especially the love.

Definitely the love.

The thought warmed him to the core. He would love her until the day he drew his last breath and a time after that. As long as she lived, he would make it his top priority to let her know how much she was loved and wanted.

"Lee?"

He heard his name, barely a whisper from her lips.

"Yes, sweetheart?"

"Tell me I'm not dreaming. Tell me the nightmare is over."

His body shifted off of hers and he tucked her close to his side. Their eyes met and held. "You're not dreaming. The nightmare is over." Guiding her hand to his lips, he kissed it, feeling his love for her in every pore, nerve and pulse.

Growling low in his throat, he curved his body around hers. "What I promise you is the reality of being loved and cherished in ways so profound that you'll never again doubt how much you are wanted."

And then he sealed his promise with a kiss.

It was a promise that he intended to keep. For always.

Epilogue

Lee drove through the gates of Whispering Pines, intentionally late. He'd known the family would be gathered here today for Jake's son Granite's eighth birthday. Most importantly he knew his great-grandmother would be here. His plan was to introduce his bride to his great-grandmother today, and he couldn't wait to see her face.

He glanced over at Carly, who sat beside him running a tongue over her bottom lip. She was nervous—even more so when she saw all the cars parked in front of the ranch. When he brought their car to a stop, he took her hand in his. "They're going to love you as much as I do."

She chuckled softly. "I hope so. There are so many of them."

He threw his head back and laughed. "Yes, when the Madarises and their friends get together, we can be a rather large group."

Releasing her hand, he got out of the car and opened her door.

He was so relieved to have her here with him, safe and sound. After Ashton Sinclair met Driskell, he had been able to tell Agent Gause where the man had hidden the names of the investors and sponsors in the cartel. The evidence had listed the names of several prominent CEOs and politicians with dates, proof of deposits and other incriminating facts Driskell had saved about each individual. The media had had a field day after the names had been released.

Once several arrests had been made, Lee and Carly had flown to Dubai for a couple of weeks, just to get away. They had needed the time alone and had used every single minute to reaffirm their love and their passion.

They'd spent Thanksgiving in Vegas with Nolan and his cousins. Lee had confided in all his single cousins about what would be going down today and they couldn't wait to witness it. They all felt it was time their great-grandmother knew they would marry only when they got good and ready. They didn't need her to find brides for them. They could do that on their own, if they were so inclined. Most of them weren't.

Taking Carly's hand firmly in his, he walked up the steps to the huge porch, and before they could knock on the door, it swung open and several of his cousins stood there with wide smiles on their faces.

Lee could only shake his head and smile back at them. "Hey, guys."

"We saw you coming up the driveway," Nolan said. He smiled at Carly. "Welcome to the family, officially."

"Thanks."

"Let me introduce everyone," Lee said. She had met Corbin and Emerson over Thanksgiving. "This is Reese, Chance and my brother Kane."

Carly looked from one to the other after hugs were exchanged. "I can see the family resemblance."

Lee smiled and then asked Nolan, "Where's Mama Laverne?"

"Out back on the patio, telling Victoria and Lindsay what they need to do to snag good husbands."

"For crying out loud," Lee exclaimed, laughing. "Vickie just turned twenty-five and Lindsay just graduated from high school."

"They're never too young to know the basic facts," Corbin said, grinning. "At least she hasn't harassed us today."

Lee smiled at Carly and tightened his hold on her hand. "You ready to go meet my great-grandmother?"

She smiled up at him. "Yes, I'm ready."

Carly knew Lee was a man on a mission as he strode across the beautiful courtyard with her by his side. Their destination was the older woman sitting in a huge wicker chair. Lee held tight to her hand, only nodding and saying hello instead of stopping to make small talk when they were approached. If people wondered who she was all they had to do was look down at her hand and see the huge rock on her ring finger. That was probably the reason people were staring at them. Even the music ceased playing.

In no time, they were standing in front of his great-grandmother. There was no doubt in Lee's mind that she had seen their approach.

"Mama Laverne." Lee greeted her by leaning down and placing a kiss on her cheek.

"Lee," the older woman said in acknowledgment. She looked over at Carly and a smile touched her wrinkled cheeks. "Hello, dear."

Carly returned the smile and immediately felt relaxed.

Lee's great-grandmother's smile was full of warmth and friendliness. "Hello."

"Mama Laverne, I want to introduce you to Carly Briggs Madaris, the woman I chose as my wife. On my own."

Mama Laverne switched her gaze from Carly back to Lee. With sharp eyes and her smile still in place, she asked, "You think so?"

Carly could tell Lee was taken aback by her question. It took him a moment to respond. "Yes. Of course."

Mama Laverne merely nodded and then looked back at Carly. "That's a beautiful ring, dear."

"Thank you."

"And how is your aunt Ruth?"

Carly was sure the surprise on Lee's face was just as stark as the surprise on her own. "You know my aunt Ruth?" Carly asked, shocked.

Mama Laverne nodded. "Yes, I've known Ruth for years. She and I met when I would travel each year to my church conventions. I looked forward to seeing her. She and I got to be good friends. We even traveled to the Holy Land together some years back with our church groups."

Lee felt the hairs on his neck stand up. "How close are the two of you?"

Mama Laverne shrugged. "Really good friends. Although we don't see each other as much, we still keep in touch."

Ignoring the people who were openly listening to the exchange, Lee said, "But that means nothing. I met Carly on my own. Neither you nor her aunt had anything to do with it."

His great-grandmother's smile widened. "Trying to convince yourself of that, are you?"

Lee frowned. "No. There's no need for me to do that. I

met Carly at the Grand MD. There was no way you could have orchestrated that."

His great-grandmother nodded. "Yes, you're right. I had no way of knowing the two of you would meet on your own. But Ruth and I were responsible for making sure Carly moved from Miami to Vegas. Do you recall how you became interested in applying for a job at Lee's hotel?"

Carly nodded. "Yes. One of my instructors from my culinary school in Paris, Chef LaPierre, called me. He said there was an opening for a pastry chef at the hotel and he suggested I apply. He even said he would recommend me for the position."

Mama Laverne nodded. "Yes, and he did. But your aunt suggested the idea to him. Seems they got to know each other pretty well whenever she would call the school in Paris to talk to you."

When neither Carly nor Lee said anything, Mama Laverne continued. "You applied and got the job because we were all convinced you would make Lee's hotel an excellent pastry chef and you have."

Mama Laverne turned her attention to Lee. "Yes, you met Carly on your own and that was better than I could have expected. But I already had a plan in place. That night when all of you dined at Peyton's Place, if you recall, it was Diamond's idea."

Lee turned around and found Diamond in the crowd, standing beside Jake. Lee gave her an accusing stare. She placed a tentative smile on her face. He didn't smile back. Instead, he turned to his grandmother, not sure he appreciated how things were unfolding. "Yes, it *was* Diamond's idea."

"And if you recall it was Diamond's request that Carly, who'd made such a wonderful dessert that night, be called out of the kitchen for all of you to thank her."

Lee nodded. "Yes, that was Diamond's request as well."

"Well, that was supposed to be the first time you and Carly met. I was certain once you saw her, Lee, that you would be so taken with her that you would be smart enough to take things from there."

Lee shook his head, not liking the idea that he and Carly had been pawns in his great-grandmother's scheme. "You had no way of knowing that would happen."

Mama Laverne gave her great-grandson a smug look. "Didn't I? I keep telling my grands and great-grands that I have the ability to see things concerning all of you that you can't see for yourself. Over the years, when Ruth would tell me about Carly, I knew in my heart that she was the woman you needed. Not the woman for Nolan, Corbin or any of my other great-grandsons. But *you.* I knew in my heart that she would be the perfect Madaris bride just for you."

Lee didn't say anything as he stared his grandmother down. She had outsmarted him. Even when he'd assumed he had been the one in control of his own destiny, she had been there driving the ship.

He looked around at the faces of his family and friends. They did not look surprised that Felicia Laverne Madaris could pull off such a thing. Some of them were the recipients of her meddling and handiwork. He had shown up today, just knowing he'd beat her at her own game, but in the end he'd discovered he hadn't even been in the competition.

He found Ashton Sinclair in the crowd and met his gaze. The man was smiling. Lee then recalled the one word Ashton had used to describe how the moment would be when Mama Laverne met Carly. *Priceless.* Ashton hadn't lied.

Lee looked at Carly and she was nervously biting her bottom lip. She was probably unsure of what his reaction to his great-grandmother's revelation would be. But all he could think about at that very moment was just how much he loved her, and regardless of how they met, he believed it was their fate to meet. If his grandmother had used her connections to make it happen, then so be it.

He looked back at his grandmother and saw the way her lips softened at the corners. He knew at that moment just how much he loved her and adored her. She wanted what was best for her family, and, as far as he was concerned, because of her manipulations, he had gotten the best.

He felt the rumble in his stomach as he laughed, unable to contain himself. His great-grandmother had pulled one over on one of her great-grandsons yet again. When he laughed, her smile widened, and those standing around them followed his lead and began laughing as well.

Moments later, after his laughter subsided, a smiling Lee turned to the crowd of family and friends. "Hello, everyone. I would like you to meet my wife, Carly Briggs Madaris. We were married in Vegas in October, but we've come home for a wedding. A Christmas wedding. One that I'm sure Mama Laverne is counting on seeing."

He then pulled Carly into his arms, looked down at her and whispered, "Welcome to the family, sweetheart. I love you."

And then, in front of his family and friends, he kissed her.

Christmas Day

Carly looked at herself in the full-length mirror and smiled. Her headpiece sat like a crown on her head and a one-tier, full-length veil cascaded over her shoulders and down the back of her wedding dress. She had known it was the dress for her the moment she'd seen it.

Diamond had used Jake's pilot and plane to fly Carly to

Los Angeles to a special bridal boutique owned by a friend of Diamond's, a woman she had attended high school with, who designed gowns for a number of Hollywood celebrities.

While Carly and Diamond were away in California shopping for her bridal attire, the other Madaris women were at work planning her wedding. She and Lee would get married in his great-grandmother's church. Invitations had been sent and, to her surprise and satisfaction, Lee had hired Chef Blanchard and his staff from the hotel as the caterers, flying the group all the way from Vegas. It was so nice to see everyone again. Jodie and Jerome had gone ahead with their Vegas wedding and Jodie had to tell her all about it.

Lee had also surprised her with her aunt's arrival. Shelton, who was now officially one of Lee's pilots, had flown the jet to Alabama to get her aunt. Shundra had accompanied him, and it had been a joyous reunion for Aunt Ruthie to see Shundra again. It had been years. Too long.

According to Shundra, Gail and Sidney had called a number of times, pleading with her to come home, divorce Shelton, get an abortion and go on with her life as before. But she'd told them she was completely happy being pregnant and married.

Shundra and Shelton had purchased a home in Vegas. And she had transferred her college credits and would attend the University of Nevada in January to complete her last two years of college.

"You look beautiful, sweetie."

Carly turned at the sound of her aunt's voice. Since Aunt Ruthie's arrival last week, she had been spending a lot of time with Lee's great-grandmother. Carly could see how the two women had become friends all those years ago. Since Mama Laverne was older, she had become the confidante Aunt Ruthie had needed.

Once Carly had a chance to sit down and reflect on how Aunt Ruthie and Mama Laverne had schemed to get her and Lee together, like Lee, she couldn't be mad at them. They had done it out of love. Mama Laverne had convinced Aunt Ruthie that Carly needed someone like Lee and both women had been right. She did. He was everything she could possibly want and more.

And talking about want… Because of Lee she knew in her heart that she would never feel unwanted again.

"Thanks, Aunt Ruthie. I feel beautiful and I want to thank you for everything. For being there when I needed you the most, and for being the one person I know I can depend on. As far as Gail is concerned, not sharing a relationship with me all those years is her loss."

"Yes, it was. You don't have to thank me. Everything I did for you, I did out of love."

There was a knock on the door. "Come in," Carly called out.

Both Shundra and Heather came in, smiling from ear to ear. "We just took pictures with Sterling Hamilton," Heather said, gushing.

"And he told me I was just as pretty as my sister," Shundra said, barely getting the words out for her excitement.

"Did he?" Carly asked, smiling. She had met Sterling, his wife, Colby, and their offspring when they'd first arrived at Whispering Pines. The couple had since invited her and Lee to spend a weekend with them and their family at their beautiful cabin in North Carolina.

"You don't have much time left, child," Mama Laverne said, coming to the door on her cane. "That great-grandson of mine is anxious for everything to begin and to be over."

Carly was anxious as well. The past few weeks had been special, and although she and Lee were already married, to have a ceremony performed in front of family and friends meant everything to her.

"I almost forgot," Mama Laverne said, coming into the room to hand her an envelope. "I promised Lee I would make sure you got this before the wedding. At least he didn't try to see you himself today. He respected my rule that the groom is not to see the bride on their wedding day before the ceremony."

Carly took the envelope, deciding to read it later, in private. However, as if the others knew her thoughts, they excused themselves to give her a chance to read it.

She tore into the envelope and pulled out the sheet of paper.

Carly,

From the moment I set eyes on you, a part of me knew you were special. At the time, however, I didn't know just how much. Now I do.

It's Christmas Eve, the night before our wedding, and I'm sitting around my fireplace alone, wishing you were with me. But I agreed to honor tradition as my great-grandmother requested. So instead of being with you, I'm here thinking of you and I decided to jot my thoughts down on paper. I won't see you again until the wedding. However, I will see you at church, the moment you walk down the aisle to me.

When you do, know that you are wanted and desired. Know that you are admired, respected and appreciated.

Know that you are mine as I am yours.

And above all, know that you are loved.

We will spend the rest of our lives together and at

times the journey won't always be easy. But please know that I will always be there for you and with you. You are my heart and soul, and now you are my reason for living.
Until tomorrow,
Lee

Carly drew in a deep breath and held the letter to her heart. She fought not to cry. If she did, Heather would get all over her for messing up her makeup. She turned when she heard a knock on the door. It was her aunt.

"It's time, Carly."

She nodded. "Yes, it's time."

Lee's breath caught as he stood beside his father, who was his best man, watching Carly walk down the aisle to him. She looked absolutely beautiful. Stunning beyond belief. More gorgeous than any woman he knew.

And she is mine.

His heart beat hard in his chest with every step she took toward him; their gazes locked together. Over the past few weeks, a part of him wondered why he was torturing himself with this wedding when they were already married. Now he knew. She deserved a chance to do this. Walk down the aisle wearing her veil and her beautiful wedding dress. She deserved to have everyone stand up in her honor the moment she strolled by their pew. And she deserved the dedication and loyalty of a man who would love her forever. On this day, Christmas Day, she was making her way to him and he felt so fortunate that he had been the one chosen to receive such a perfect gift. Priceless.

After the wedding reception, they would fly to Hawaii to spend two weeks, and he couldn't wait for his honeymoon to begin. He intended to make it even more special than the last one in Dubai.

Then she was there. He reached out and took her hand, lifting it to his lips, holding her gaze as he kissed it. Then they faced the minister, ready for the service to begin. They had said their vows before and would repeat them again today, reaffirming the promises they'd made to each other.

A short while later, the minister finally said the words Lee had been waiting for. "Mr. Madaris, you may kiss your bride."

Lee gently turned Carly to him, lifted her veil and whispered, "I love you," and then he lowered his mouth to hers. This, he thought, was worth the wait.

Nolan Madaris stood with the others who watched Lee and Carly drive away from the wedding reception at Whispering Pines. When the car was no longer in sight, he turned and almost bumped into his great-grandmother. He hadn't known she was standing beside him.

"Mama Laverne."

"Nolan. You've been avoiding me today."

"Have I?"

"Yes, you have. You know what they say. You can run, but you sure can't hide."

"Thanks for telling me that."

Nolan had news for her. He had no intention of hiding. Lee had tried it, and it hadn't worked. Nolan would stay in plain sight and would gladly be the one to show her once and for all that she couldn't choose everyone's mate. Nobody would choose the woman he would marry…if there was such a creature. At the moment, he had no reason to think there was. He thoroughly enjoyed being single and didn't mind the whispers that he'd picked up where his cousins Clayton and Blade had left off.

There was that one thing, however, that had him confused. "I'm curious about something," he said.

"And what are you curious about, Nolan?"

"I heard you and that lady at bingo. The two of you were scheming—" he cleared his throat "—I mean, *planning* to marry her granddaughter off to Lee. But things didn't work out that way, so did I hear wrong?"

"Partly," his great-grandmother said, resting her hands on her cane as she stared up at him. "You heard what we wanted you to hear."

"Oh." He tried not to frown. "So she doesn't have a granddaughter."

Mama Laverne smiled. "On the contrary. She has a beautiful granddaughter. But it wasn't Lee's wedding I was planning."

He was definitely confused. "If it wasn't Lee's wedding, then whose wedding was it?"

His great-grandmother's lips curved in a smile. "Yours."

Nolan didn't say anything as he stood and stared at Mama Laverne. Then he turned and walked away.

* * * * *